THANKS FOR
YOUR SUPPORT

MW00941402

A Stranger
In My
Own Hometown

A Brendan O'Brian Legal Thriller

J. W. Kerwin

GREY SQUIRREL PRESS

ISBN: 1537295616
ISBN 13: 9781537295619

A Note from the Author

The novel you're about to read is a self-contained story that you can understand and (hopefully) enjoy without having read the first Brendan O'Brian novel, *Slow Death in the Fast Lane*. However, reading *Slow Death* before you begin this book will enhance your reading experience by providing background information about the characters. The e-book version of *Slow Death* is available from Amazon at a discounted price.

"The mosques are our barracks, the domes our helmets, the minarets our bayonets and the Muslim faithful our soldiers..."

– *Recep Tayyip Erdogan, President of Turkey*

1

"How could he make a diagnosis without seeing you?"

It's difficult having a normal conversation with the person who killed your wife, especially when that person doesn't realize you know he did it, and even more so when he's a client.

Four years ago, just before Thanksgiving in 1988, Eddie Rizzo killed my wife, presumably to protect me, after learning about her supposed contract to have me "whacked," to use his colorful term. As it turned out, Eddie's information was wrong. There was no contract on my life, but Aimee ended up dead nonetheless.

In fairness to Eddie, I should admit that I'm not one hundred percent certain he was responsible for Aimee's death. True, I did see someone leaving the scene of the crime. And that person had the distinctive white streak bisecting an otherwise jet black head of hair, the telltale tonsorial trait that had caused northern New Jersey's less-than-solid citizens to refer to Eddie Rizzo as Eddie the Skunk.

As an officer of the court and a semi-respected member of the bar, I had a duty to report the murder, which I did. And as a more-or-less upstanding citizen, I had an obligation to tell the police about the man I had seen leaving the scene of the crime, which I did.

I didn't, however, mention the white streak.

Perhaps my silence was the result of some perverse form of gratitude. After all, Eddie's act, though terribly misguided, had been well intentioned. Or maybe it was because turning in your own client is considered bad form in the legal profession, the sort of thing that causes clients to seek representation elsewhere. The law firm of Santorini, Woodson, Glickman & O'Brian, of which I'm a partner, could afford to lose Eddie as a client, but losing all the "business associates" he referred to us would put a serious dent in our bottom line.

Deep down, I suspect the real reason I wasn't more forthcoming with the police is the fact that I'm scared of Eddie, and for good reason. Having represented him for many years, I know what he's capable of doing. What I don't know is how he'd react if he knew I had seen him. And I'm not sure I want to find out.

Whatever the reason, my silence kept Eddie Rizzo from spending time behind bars, thus allowing him to arrive at my office in the suburban town of Troy Forge, New Jersey on a sunny afternoon in October, 1992 to seek legal representation yet again. Only this time, he didn't need my services to defend him. This time, he wanted to retain me to sue someone.

Dressed in his customary jeans, white polo shirt, and with a thick gold chain draped around his neck, Eddie leaned forward and told his tale of woe. "So there I am driving through Jersey City, minding my own business, when this fuckin' Arab runs a stop sign and rams my car."

"How do you know the other driver was an Arab?" I asked.

"Cause he looked like an Arab. You know, scraggly beard, beady eyes, swarthy complexion." I was tempted to point out that "swarthy" was a particularly ill-chosen adjective given

Eddie's own ancestry, but thought better of it. "And this was a brand new Caddy. I only had it a week. Wasn't even broken in."

"Was anyone injured?" I asked.

"Yeah, me."

Eddie looked unscathed. No crutches, no bruises, no neck brace, nothing that would suggest any sort of injury. "What kind of injury did you sustain?"

"I got whiplash," Eddie answered. "That's what Dr. D'Amico said."

"When did you see Dr. D'Amico?"

My question elicited an answer I didn't want to hear. "I ain't been to see him yet. But I talked to him on the phone and he said I definitely got whiplash."

I discovered somewhat later that D'Amico was indeed a licensed physician, having mastered the rigorous curriculum of a Caribbean medical school highly respected by its graduates, if not the medical community at large. I also learned that D'Amico was Eddie's third cousin on his mother's side, and always happy to provide Eddie and his business associates with whatever medical assistance they required, including whiplash diagnoses by telephone. Had I known this at the time, I wouldn't have bothered asking, "How could he make a diagnosis without seeing you?"

"Trust me, counselor," Eddie replied. "I got whiplash. And it's bad. Hurts like hell. I got headaches, can't sleep. D'Amico says I got serious permanent injury. His exact words." I suppressed a laugh. Of course D'Amico used the phrase "serious permanent injury," the statutory language that allows an injured party to sue for so-called pain and suffering in addition to medical expenses and lost wages.

Eddie's tone of voice made it clear that the good doctor's diagnosis was definitive and unalterable, and it was time for me to move on. So I did, but not before jotting down the name of

Eddie's doctor on my legal pad. Being able to diagnose patients without ever seeing them was a rare skill, one that might come in handy in other cases.

"Did you get the name of the other driver?"

"Nah, he drove away right after he hit me," Eddie said, quickly adding, "He knew he done wrong and wanted to get outta there as fast as he could." *Or perhaps he realized sticking around would have resulted in some impromptu street justice.*

"So you didn't get his name?"

"No, but I got his plate number." Eddie reached into the pocket of his jeans, fished out a scrap of paper and handed it to me. To my surprise, it contained a complete license plate number with "NJ" scribbled beneath it to indicate it was an in-state plate. "I'll have Biff get us the owner's name," I said, referring to Tony Biffano, the retired Paterson cop who handles investigative work for our firm. I realized later that Eddie never asked who Biff was. Either he didn't care or, more likely, he already knew. Eddie has a knack for knowing things you wouldn't expect him to know. Years ago he pointed out that attorneys are better off not knowing certain things about their clients, but in his business he needed to know as much as he could about everybody and everything. Of course, it was never really clear what business Eddie was in. The first and only time I asked, he simply said "investments" in a tone of voice that made it clear this was another one of those things I was better off not knowing.

"Yeah, you do that," Eddie said. "I was gonna have people I know check up on the bastard, but figured it might be better to do everything by the book. I don't want this scumbag to get away on a technicality."

Eddie had vast personal experience with getting away on a technicality, but instead of pointing that out, I said, "good idea."

"And when you find out the guy's name," Eddie instructed, "I want you to sue the fucker for wrecking my car, wrecking my neck, pain and suffering, punitive damages, infliction of emotional distress, and anything else you can think of. I want this bastard to know I mean business."

Most minor auto accident cases are settled without the injured party filing suit, but I wasn't about to explain that to Eddie, who clearly wanted to go to war, confirming his intentions by telling me, "I want you to make this guy pay for screwing with me."

After assuring Eddie that I would file suit the moment I learned the evildoer's name, I asked, "What kind of car was the other guy driving?"

"Wasn't a car," came the answer. "The bastard was driving a white Ford van." Eddie proceeded to provide a remarkably detailed description. "It had a roof rack, the tail light on the driver's side was smashed, and one of the doors on the back had rust on it." He thought for a moment before adding, "And the side of the van looked like it had some sorta company name that was painted over."

Eddie spent the next half hour answering my questions and volunteering information about the accident, much of it unhelpful. I took notes, attempted to dampen his expectations of a big payday by explaining the workings of New Jersey's no-fault law, and promised once again that I would "sue the bastard" the minute I learned his identity, if not sooner.

After Eddie left, I continued reviewing the file for *CIRR v. McCain*, the defamation suit the Council for Islamic Religious Respect had filed against Stacey McCain, my part-time girlfriend and full-time newspaper reporter. The case was actually two separate cases that the Superior Court Assignment Judge in Morristown had consolidated on the grounds that both grew out of the same series of newspaper articles Stacey had written for the *Ledger*. CIRR was the plaintiff in one case, and Bob Proctor, the mayor of Troy Forge, was the plaintiff in the other.

Combining the cases may have resulted in what judges refer to as judicial economy, but it created some interesting dynamics. Although Billboard Bob, as Proctor was known throughout Morris County, seemed to be chummy with the people at CIRR, the putative allies' lawyers were anything but.

CIRR's attorney was Tinoo Barahi, living proof that affirmative action is a bad idea, particularly when it's used for law school admission decisions. He was well known to judges and attorneys throughout northern New Jersey, and was despised by both groups. Attorneys hated him because he could never be trusted to keep the gentleman's agreements that lawyers routinely make with one another. Judges hated him because he wasted their time with frivolous motions and foolish arguments. The fact that Barahi routinely missed deadlines, and seemed to deliberately misinterpret court rules didn't win him admiration from anyone.

Proctor's attorney represented the opposite end of the legal spectrum. Emerson Lambert was an older, silver-haired member of the state's legal establishment who had set up a solo practice in Troy Forge the same year as Rick Santorini, our firm's founder. Unlike the brash, incompetent newcomer representing CIRR, Lambert was well liked and well respected by members of the bar and the judiciary. He was the scholarly patrician to Barahi's unwashed plebian. Early in the proceedings, Lambert made it quite clear that he had little regard for Barahi, a rift that I fully intended to exploit at every opportunity.

The judge assigned to the case was Duncan MacAndrew, a polite, soft-spoken gentleman with a reputation for honesty, fairness and, above all, patience. He and Lambert would get along just fine, but Barahi was another matter. An Ottawa native, MacAndrew attended college at NYU, became a U.S. citizen, went to law school at Seton Hall, and joined one of the big firms in Morristown. Fifteen years later he became a Superior

Court judge. His trials almost always take longer than those presided over by any other jurist, but he's also the only judge sitting in Morristown who has never had a decision overturned by the Appellate Division. If they ever remake that television show about a starship, and the actor who played the engineer isn't available, Judge MacAndrew would be the perfect replacement. He might not have the right accent, but he's got the right look.

The case Judge MacAndrew would preside over centered on half a dozen newspaper articles Stacey had written alleging that Mayor Proctor arranged for the so-called fairgrounds property in my hometown of Troy Forge to be illegally rezoned to allow construction of a traffic-generating mosque in the middle of a quiet, residential neighborhood. Naturally, His Highness, Proctor the Great, took exception to any suggestion he would ever do anything improper, much less illegal. CIRR was equally aggrieved at Stacey's assertions that the group was connected to terrorists. Proctor and CIRR were both suing Stacey and the newspaper she worked for, the *Ledger*, for defamation. In keeping with his reputation for off-the-wall legal reasoning, Barahi had filed a complaint on behalf of CIRR that included a second count that was novel, to say the least.

"Brendan, you have a visitor." I looked up to find Carolyn, my secretary, standing at my office door. I assumed Eddie the Skunk had returned with some piece of earth shattering information he had forgotten to mention. As it turned out, I was wrong.

2

"I owe him that."

The young man Carolyn ushered into my office was someone I had never met, so I was understandably taken aback
when he greeted me by saying, "Good to see you again, Mr.
O'Brian." He was in his twenties, well dressed, very clean-cut.
After taking a seat across from me at the desk, he introduced
himself as Billy Kane. "I'm sure you don't remember," he said,
"but we met in somewhat awkward circumstances a long time
ago. I was with Machias Phelps when you encountered us by
the reservoir."

Years ago, when Kane was perhaps thirteen or fourteen, I
had caught him *in flagrante delicto* with Phelps, a strange little
man who worked in the Troy Forge Town Hall. Phelps apparently assumed I would report his amorous activities, and when
I didn't, he became a willing purveyor of information about
the inner workings of the Proctor administration. Back in
1988, around the same time Aimee was murdered, Phelps was
involved in a mysterious auto accident. The Troy Forge authori-
ties determined that Phelps had borrowed a town-owned car
for some unknown purpose and then proceeded to drive it into
a tree in a remote part of the community. This explanation conveniently overlooked the fact that Phelps was legally blind, had
no driver's license, had never driven an automobile, and was

known to rely exclusively on an undersized bicycle for transportation. But since the Proctor administration has never been overly reliant on facts, an unfortunate auto accident became the official explanation for the death of Machias Phelps.

"I was away at college when Machias died," Kane continued. "When I read about his death in the newspaper, I realized something wasn't right. Poor Machias was as blind as a bat. There was no way he would have tried to drive. Hell, he was almost as scared of cars as he was of Mayor Proctor."

"What was the story with Phelps and Proctor?" I asked. Everyone knew that Phelps had a habit of scurrying out of sight whenever Proctor appeared, but nobody was ever able to figure out why. The leading theory was that Phelps had somehow displeased His Majesty and maintained a low profile to avoid losing his job.

"Not sure," came the answer. "All I know is Machias used to tell me that Proctor wasn't the person people thought he was."

I was trying to make sense of this when Kane continued, "After I finished college, I moved to Texas to start a job. This is my first trip back to New Jersey." He scanned my diplomas on the wall to his left before continuing. "I should have come back sooner. I owed it to Machias. He and I broke up while I was off at college, but he was always very good to me, even after we split."

"Yeah, he was a generous guy," I said. "He named me as the sole beneficiary in his will. Not sure if you knew that. I felt kind of funny taking his money, not that there was much there."

"The reason his estate was so small," Kane explained, "is because he used most of what he had to pay for my college tuition." The kid leaned back and looked at the ceiling. "Machias never spent any money on himself. He seldom left that little apartment of his, never went to the movies or out to dinner. His entire wardrobe could fit in a single suitcase. Not that he really needed a suitcase. In all the years I knew him, the only vacation he ever took was a one-week trip to Maine."

The kid was getting teary eyed and I though he was about to break down and cry. But instead, he took a deep breath, leaned forward, looked me in the eye, and said, "I want to hire you to find out who killed Machias. I owe him that."

"I'm an attorney," I said. "What you need is a private investigator."

I opened my desk drawer and retrieved one of Tony Biffano's business cards, but before I could hand it to Kane, he said, "No, I want to hire you. You're the only person Machias ever trusted. That's why he left you the key." I assumed he meant the key I had found in the envelope containing Machias' Last Will & Testament, but before I could confirm that, Kane asked, "You did get the key, didn't you?"

"I have it, but I don't know what to do with it," I answered. "Any idea what it opens?"

"Machias told me it opens a trunk in his aunt's garage."

"What's the aunt's name?" I asked, reaching for a legal pad.

"I don't know," Kane said as he slumped back in his chair. He seemed emotionally exhausted from talking about the late Machias Phelps. Or perhaps he was just feeling guilty for waiting so long to contact me. "That's all Machias told me."

"Any idea where she lives?"

Kane just shook his head no.

Now I had two people for Biff to track down.

3

"Everything has merit in MacAndrew's view."

It was the third time Rick had told the same story on the drive to Morristown, and I had long since tuned him out.

Although he seems to be doing better recently, Rick clearly has a problem. My partners and I can't decide if he's suffering from Alzheimer's or plain, old-fashioned senility. As the founder of our firm, he deserves better than being shoved aside, so we take turns having him "ride shotgun," the term we use for keeping him occupied with busy work, out of the view of clients and away from anything that could really be considered legal work. Besides, the Santorini name still carries considerable weight in Troy Forge, Rick being one the few remaining attorneys from the days when the town had more farms than strip malls.

Today's busy work consisted of Rick driving with me to the county seat to meet Tony Biffano, the retired cop turned investigator. Biff had left a message with Carolyn, my secretary, that he had learned the identity of both Machias Phelps' aunt and the driver of the vehicle that hit Eddie the Skunk in Jersey City. He could have given that information to Carolyn on the phone or sent a fax, but he insisted on meeting me in person, most likely so he could pad his bill. As it turned out, that wasn't the reason.

"Was she familiar with the case?" Out of the corner of my eye I saw that Rick had stopped talking and was looking at me, apparently waiting for a response. At some point after I had tuned him out he had ceased his storytelling and asked a question.

"Sorry," I lied, "I was lost in thought."

"Quite all right, my boy. I do that myself sometimes."

"What was the question?"

"I asked if Stacey was familiar with *Sullivan*," Rick said, obviously referring to *New York Times v. Sullivan*, the 1964 Supreme Court case that requires public figures to prove actual malice, rather than mere negligence, to win a defamation case.

"Stacey knows *Sullivan* as well as I do. What she doesn't understand is how trials work. I can't get her and her boss – particularly her boss – to understand that a case is won or lost before the trial begins. He keeps complaining that we're running up the bill with depositions, interrogatories, and motion hearings."

"He's probably been watching too many courtroom shows on television," Rick said.

I maneuvered into the right hand lane as we rounded the Green, the park that's stood in the center of Morristown since 1715. Through the years it's been the site of everything from a military base to Santa's cottage during the Christmas season. As I made the turn onto Washington Street where the courthouse is located, I said, "The thing that annoys me the most is that a lot of what we're doing is beyond our control. If CIRR's idiot attorney files a motion, we have to respond, regardless of how nonsensical his motion is. And Judge MacAndrew isn't the kind of guy who'll make CIRR pay our costs, even when the motion is completely without merit."

"Everything has merit in MacAndrew's view," Rick said. "Duncan's a patient man, perhaps too patient. That's why his trials take so long."

"We'll see how patient he is when he hears Barahi's motion for summary judgment on the second count of CIRR's complaint."

Rick laughed. "I read Barahi's motion. The man is entertaining, I'll give him that. There's no way Judge MacAndrew is going to grant that motion. Unfortunately, he probably won't grant your cross-motion to dismiss it either."

"You're probably right, but I hope not. There's no legal basis for Barahi's second count, but you never know what a jury will do. I want it gone before the trial begins."

I pulled around a car that was making a valiant effort to parallel park, turned right at the next corner and entered the parking lot across from the courthouse. As I began my search for Biff's gray Cadillac, he stepped out from between two parked cars and pointed to an empty parking spot. I pulled my Mustang into the empty space, and Rick and I got out. Tony Biffano strolled over to join us. Biff is only a few inches taller than me, but he's built like a gorilla, with long arms, wide shoulders, and massive biceps. He probably spends half the day lifting weights, but the end result is an imposing physique that's downright menacing. When Biff asks someone a question, he always gets an answer.

After exchanging pleasantries, Biff got down to business. "I have the information you wanted on both of those individuals. One was relatively easy, the other is a little strange, which is why I wanted to meet in person." Biff opened the small notebook he always carries and began to read. "Eleanor Lange, maternal aunt of the late Machias Phelps. Lives just outside Belvidere in Warren County." He ripped a page out of the notebook and handed it to me. It had the aunt's address written on it, along with a vague description of where her home was located.

"I'm guessing that was the easy one," I said as I pocketed the information.

"You guessed right." Biff reached into a different pocket of his blue blazer, this time withdrawing a folded piece of paper. "Here's the strange one," he said, handing the paper to me. It was a photocopy of a driver's license for someone named Mohammed Salameh whose photo matched Eddie's description of the driver who had collided with him in Jersey City.

"The guy's a Jordanian who came here three years ago," Biff said, "and he's a lousy driver. Been in one accident after another. Nothing serious, all fender benders."

"Nothing strange about that," I said. "New Jersey is filled with lousy drivers, particularly in places like Jersey City."

Biff laughed. Judging by the number of dents and dings in his Caddy, he had apparently met some of those drivers up close and personal. "True, but what's strange about this guy is the fact that someone else is asking questions about him. Lots of questions."

"I'm not surprised," I said. "If Salameh is as accident prone as you say, there's a good chance he's involved in other litigation."

"That's what I thought at first, but my source at DMV says the guy asking questions was sent by the Feds." As a general rule, employees of the Department of Motor Vehicles don't reveal that kind of information, but Biff's contact was the exception to the rule. He or she was either a personal friend or the recipient of a generous gratuity. I'd find out which when Biff rendered his bill at the end of the month. "My contact says the Feds are really looking hard at this Salameh character. I'm not sure what he's in to, but you better watch your back with this guy."

That was my first clue that Eddie Rizzo's lawsuit was going to be anything but the typical personal injury case.

4

"You need to show the mayor more respect."

I told Mr. Rizzo you wouldn't be able to see him until after three o'clock," Carolyn said as I passed her desk on my way to the conference room.

"How did he take the news?" I asked. After being told about the photo I had gotten from Biff, Eddie the Skunk had wanted to see it "right away," and Eddie's the type of person who expects the world to operate according to his schedule.

"I can never tell with him," Carolyn said.

When I arrived at the conference room, I found two uniformed Troy Forge police officers blocking the doorway, apparently part of Mayor Proctor's private palace guard. I said, "Excuse me," but they didn't budge.

"It's okay, let him in," commanded a high-pitched, nasal voice from behind the conference room door.

The cops stepped aside, and I entered the room. Bob Proctor was seated at the head of the table flanked by his attorney, Emerson Lambert, and the court reporter who would make a transcript of the deposition. Two plainclothes cops in their late thirties stood behind Proctor the Great. Tall, muscular and imposing, they made the diminutive mayor seem even smaller by comparison. "Damn nice of you to let me into my own conference room, Your Majesty," I said to the mayor. He smiled the big, toothy, crocodile smile that graces countless billboards throughout the town reminding his subjects of all the wonderful things he's done for them ... at taxpayer expense, of course.

One of his conference room centurions, who seems to go everywhere Proctor goes, and who I had nicknamed "Scarface" for the jagged scar on his left cheek, stepped forward, pointed at me and said, "You need to show the mayor more respect." Proctor touched the cop's forearm, and before I had a chance to explain that I was showing the mayor exactly the respect he deserved, Scarface took a step back, clasped his hands in front of him, and resumed the pose of a wary, silent sentinel.

"Counselor," I said, nodding toward Emerson Lambert. "Welcome to Santorini, Woodson, Glickman and O'Brian. Always good to see you." That ended the pleasantries, and the deposition of Bob Proctor, mayor of Troy Forge, got underway.

I began with a number of seemingly innocuous questions designed to get basic facts into the record. I established that Proctor had been born in a small town in the Pine Barrens at the southern end of the state, had served as mayor for more than a dozen years, and was intimately familiar with virtually every aspect of town administration. He used my question about his role in running Troy Forge to hold forth on all the wonderful things he had done for his loyal subjects, from road projects and parks to libraries and senior citizen housing projects. He neglected to mention that all of his wondrous achievements were accomplished with taxpayer funds, and that most of those funds were paid to his politically connected pals, who always seemed to win public works contracts even when they were the high bidder. I could have asked Proctor about the dozens of billboards the town erected trumpeting the Lord Mayor's great achievements, but decided to keep things non-confrontational, at least for the moment. My goal was to allow Proctor to remain in his comfort zone and ramble on, hoping that he would inadvertently reveal something that could prove useful.

After Proctor had finished regaling me with his great contributions to the betterment of my hometown, I asked him a series of questions about town history. Proctor knew the location of the colonial era iron forge that gave the town its name, but when I asked him where Barr's Corner was located, he answered, "Before my time."

If we had been in court, Emerson Lambert would have objected to all these questions as being irrelevant to the case. But with a few exceptions, objections are prohibited in a deposition, so Lambert sat quietly, drawing pictures of palm trees on his legal pad. I guessed he was thinking about a trip to warmer climes when snow began falling in New Jersey. The doodling abruptly stopped when I asked Proctor if he was familiar with the location of the county fair that used to be held in Troy Forge.

Before the town lost its rural charm to the developers, the fair was held every August on a twenty-eight acre parcel that had been the subject of a full-scale war between Troy Forge and Martin von Beverwicjk, one of our clients. Martin's attempt to sub-divide the so-called fairgrounds property into building lots had been thwarted by a series of ridiculous demands by the town's planning board. Shortly before his death, Machias Phelps had confirmed my suspicion that Proctor was orchestrating the delays to force a sale of the property to one of his cronies. As it turned out, a company named Andalusia Holdings appeared out of nowhere and bought the land from Martin for much more than it was really worth. We all assumed the company was connected to Proctor, and would use those connections to get the approvals that Martin was unable to secure, transforming the twenty-eight acres into yet another development of lookalike homes. But instead of filing its own subdivision application, Andalusia began construction of the town's first mosque on what was ostensibly land zoned for single-family homes. Shortly thereafter, Stacey's newspaper articles began appearing in the *Ledger*.

"That was a little before my time," Proctor said in response to my question about the fair.

I decided it was time to get to the heart of the matter. "Did you bring the items I requested under 4:18?" I asked Lambert, referring to the Civil Practice Rule that requires litigants to produce documents relevant to a case.

"Some of them."

"Why not all of them?"

Lambert hesitated before delivering what was obviously a well-rehearsed answer. "Rule 4:18 only requires us to provide you with documents that are in the possession, custody, or control of my client. The items you want belong to the Town of Troy Forge, not to Mr. Proctor. You really should be asking the town's attorney for those items since I'm representing Mr. Proctor as an individual, not in his official capacity as mayor." Lambert seemed embarrassed to have given that answer, but apparently he was following marching orders.

"Come on, Emerson," I said. "Those documents might not belong to your client, but as mayor he has control of them. Hell, Bob Proctor has control of everything in Troy Forge, as he's just spent the last half hour telling us. If I had known you were going to pull a stunt like this, I would have gone to the Town Clerk's office and picked up copies myself." That wasn't exactly true, of course. I had already tried, and failed, to get those documents from the Clerk's office. They had either been destroyed in a mysterious fire that occurred around the time of Machias Phelps' equally mysterious auto accident in November of 1988 or they had never existed in the first place.

"Calm down, Brendan," Lambert said. "We're all just doing our job here." He reached into his well-worn leather briefcase and extracted a handful of folded papers. "Here are some of the items you asked for." I unfolded the proffered peace offering and discovered three copies of the town's zoning map, all public documents paid for with my tax dollars. I handed them to the court reporter, who marked them as exhibits before returning them to me.

I gave the first map to Proctor and had him identify it as the town's official zoning map as of July 1, 1975. Next, I had him identify the location of the so-called fairgrounds property where the town's first mosque now stood.

"Now, looking at the color coded legend on this map, please tell me how that property was zoned in July of 1975."

"Look like it was in an R-3 zone," Proctor said.

"Which means the property was zoned for single family homes on one-third acre lots, correct?"

"I believe that's correct," Proctor said.

I repeated the process with the second map, which was dated July 10, 1988. Once again, Billboard Bob identified the property where the mosque now stood and testified that the property was zoned for single-family homes.

When I asked him how that property was zoned on the third map, dated January of 1989, he answered, "ERM."

"What can built on property zoned ERM?" I asked.

"Buildings for educational, religious or medical use. Things like schools, hospitals, churches."

"So between July of 1988, when that property was owned by Martin von Beverwicjk, one of my firm's clients, and January of 1989, roughly six months later, the property was re-zoned from R-3 or residential use to ERM, correct?"

"That would appear to be the case," Billboard Bob said, quickly adding, "not that I remember every piece of property in Troy Forge."

"In your experience, how long does it usually take for a parcel of this size to be re-zoned?" I asked.

"I'm afraid I don't know that," Proctor said. "You'd have to ask someone from the planning board."

"Would you agree that it ordinarily takes more than a year for a parcel this size to go through the re-zoning process?"

"I'm not sure I know the answer to that," Billboard Bob said. "I suppose every case is different."

"Walk me through the re-zoning process."

"Well, I'm no expert on zoning law," Proctor said disingenuously, "but I think the way it works is that the town council votes to change the zoning, usually on the recommendation of the planning board."

"Is that how this property was re-zoned?" I asked.

Proctor looked me right in the eye and smiled. "I assume so, counselor, but as I just said, I'm not familiar with every piece of property in town."

"And since you failed to bring the documents I asked for, documents dealing with that re-zoning, I'll just have to take your word for it that everything was done by the book." It came out a bit more sarcastic than I had intended.

Proctor shrugged his shoulders and gave me a big smile, the combined effect of which was to clearly convey, *"Fuck you."* The deposition transcript, however, would show that I said, "Then I guess we're done for today."

My secretary and Avery Glickman, one of my partners, were both waiting for me when I left the conference room. "You first," Avery said to Carolyn, who informed me that Eddie Rizzo was waiting in my office before heading back to her desk. As soon as she and the Proctor entourage were out of earshot, Avery asked, "How did it go?"

"About as I expected," I said. "Proctor claims he doesn't know a thing about the re-zoning. I was more interested in seeing how Lambert reacted."

"And?" Avery prompted.

"I still can't be certain whether he's working with Proctor or being played by him. But my gut tells me a class act like Lambert will eventually lock horns with our illustrious mayor."

"I need a favor," Avery said, revealing the real reason he was waiting for me. "Rick was supposed to ride shotgun with me tomorrow, but something's come up."

"No problem. Stacey and I are driving out to Warren County tomorrow. Rick can go with us." *So much for a romantic ride in the countryside.*

When I got back to my office, I found Eddie the Skunk stretched out on my sofa leafing through a magazine. The tranquility ended when I showed him the driver's license photo Biff had gotten from his contact at the Department of Motor Vehicles. The sight of Mohammed Salameh threw Eddie into a rage. "That's the fucking Arab that hit my Caddy. I want you to sue that bastard's ass off."

I filed suit the following morning before leaving for my two's-company-three's-a-crowd drive to Warren County. If I had known then what I know now, I would have suggested that Eddie deal with Salameh in a dark alley instead of in a courtroom.

5

"You must be the prize patrol."

The deposition of Lisa Cunningham, chair of the Troy Forge Planning Board began promptly at nine o'clock. Five minutes later it became obvious that I was wasting my time and, as Stacey's boss was sure to point out, the *Ledger's* money.

I began by asking her to identify the fairgrounds property on the zoning maps I had used during Mayor Proctor's deposition. She pointed to the land in question. I also got her to agree that the maps showed the property had been zoned for residential use in July of 1988, but on the January, 1989 map it was designated as being zoned ERM, allowing the construction of educational, religious and medical buildings.

That was the last straightforward answer I got from her that morning.

"Did the planning board recommend the town council rezone the property from R-3 to ERM?" I asked.

"I assume so," Mrs. Cunningham answered with a shrug of her shoulders, "That's what usually happens, but I don't really remember. We deal with a lot of properties each year."

"Any idea how many?" I asked.

"Oh, I really couldn't say. It varies from year to year."

I decided that line of inquiry wasn't likely to be helpful. Mrs. Cunningham was apparently suffering from the same amnesia that had afflicted Mayor Proctor. So instead of trying to establish she could reasonably be expected to remember that particular property, I asked, "Did you bring the minutes of the meeting at which re-zoning this property was discussed, as I requested?"

"I'm afraid I couldn't do that," came her answer.

"Why not?"

"All of the planning board minutes were destroyed in the town hall fire back in November of 1988."

"And is it your understanding that the minutes of the town council meeting where the property was re-zoned were also destroyed in that fire?"

"That's my understanding," she said, "but you'd have to ask the council to be sure." I had already done that and gotten nowhere. Everyone on the town council was a personal friend of Mayor Proctor, re-elected again and again thanks to generous campaign financing from local business people who, miraculously, won contracts with the town, even when they were the high bidder.

"Why is it that the zoning map survived that fire, but the minutes of both the planning board and town council meetings where the re-zoning was approved were destroyed?" I asked. The obvious answer was that Billboard Bob and his cronies needed the map to "prove" the property had been re-zoned even though it hadn't been, but I didn't really expect one of Proctor's political allies to come right out and say that.

Before Mrs. Cunningham could answer my question, Roy Harkin, the attorney for Troy Forge held up his hand signaling her to remain silent. "I don't think Mrs. Cunningham is in a position to know that. Any answer she gives would be pure speculation."

"Speculation is fine." If you can get a witness talking, you never know what might slip out.

Harkin didn't pursue the matter, so Mrs. Cunningham said, "I don't know for sure, but I'm guessing someone had removed the zoning map from the room where the planning board minutes are stored."

"Any idea who?"

"I have no idea."

She also had no idea about anything else involving the mysterious re-zoning, so after another dozen questions, I conceded defeat and ended the deposition.

Rick was waiting for me outside the conference room. We followed Roy Harkin and Mrs. Cunningham to the elevator, but instead of riding to the ground floor with them, waited for the next elevator.

"Learn anything useful?" Rick asked as the elevator door closed.

"I learned that nobody in the Proctor administration knows anything when it's convenient for them not to know."

"And at other times, they know everything about everything," Rick said as we got out of the elevator and made our way to the building's back door. We arrived at the parking lot just in time to see Harkin and Cunningham drive away in a Troy Forge police car. "Apparently our police department runs a taxi service on the side," I said.

"Helps keep taxes low," Rick replied.

We picked up Stacey at her apartment and headed west on Route 46 in search of Eleanor Lange, Machias Phelps' aunt. There was considerable westbound traffic, but it thinned out once we made it through Hackettstown. "You could have taken I-80 and avoided all the congestion," Stacey said.

"True," I replied, "but I thought this would be a nicer drive. Besides, we're in no rush."

We drove in silence, Stacey and I enjoying the sunny autumn day, and Rick dozing in the back seat. "You missed your turn," Stacey said as we passed the exit for County Route 519.

"It's such a nice day, I thought we'd take the scenic route," I replied.

Rick, who apparently hadn't really been asleep, leaned over the Mustang's front seats and asked, "Are we going to drive through Belvidere?" Without waiting for an answer, he continued, "I love Belvidere. Haven't been there in ages. I don't usually drive that far anymore."

Before I could remind Rick that he hadn't had a driver's license in years, Stacey said, "Tell me about Belvidere, Rick." I assumed she was humoring him.

"Oh, it's a cute little town," Rick said. "It's reputed to have the largest collection of Victorian Era homes in New Jersey." He stopped speaking and stared into space, and I was afraid he was about to have another one of his episodes, as everyone at the firm called them. But he was apparently just thinking. "Of course, Ocean Grove and Cape May have a lot of Victorian homes, too."

"Interesting," Stacey said. It's her all-purpose word that can mean pretty much anything she wants it to.

Rick took it as a sign of genuine interest, and launched into a history lesson about Belvidere, starting from colonial times when it was known as Greenwich on the Delaware. We heard about William Penn surveying the area, and how Robert Morris, one of the financiers of the Revolutionary War, bought land there. I usually tune out Rick's ramblings, but his historical tutorial was actually quite interesting.

Rick was talking about George Washington passing through Belvidere on his way to Morristown as I exited the highway onto County Route 620, also known as Water Street. With the Pequest River tracking the road on our left, we headed southwest into town. The Pequest continued toward its rendezvous with the Delaware River, and we turned left onto Greenwich Street. A few minutes later we were on County Route 519, the road we would have taken if I hadn't opted for the long way through Belvidere.

Biff had provided me with an address for Eleanor Lange, and told me her street was somewhere south of town off of 519. Unfortunately, that's all he told me, so the three of us began watching for road signs. We had just rounded a sharp curve when Rick said, "There it is on your left." His mind might not be as sharp as it once was, but his eyesight was still 20/20.

What started out as a paved road became gravel half a mile later. Another half mile and the gravel gave way to dirt. As we crossed a small stream, the two-lane dirt road became a one-lane dirt road, squeezed on both sides by wild blackberry bushes. The ruts and potholes, a minor nuisance at first, became a major headache at about the same time that the thorns on the blackberry bushes began scraping the paint off my carefully restored 1965 Ford Mustang. Until now, my pony car's only imperfections had been door locks that sometimes work and sometimes don't. I made a mental note to make an appointment with a local body shop run by one of my clients.

Lacking a place to turn around, and not wanting to try my luck running the sticker bush gauntlet in reverse, I kept driving.

"Looks like the road ends up ahead," Stacey said as I inched toward a particularly menacing thicket of blackberries. But as we got closer, it became apparent that the bushes that seemed at first to block our way marked a sharp bend in the road instead. I eased around the corner, not sure what I would find, and brought the car to a halt.

"Nice going, O'Brian," Stacey said, giving my shoulder a playful punch. "You made a wrong turn somewhere and we ended up in Brigadoon."

A white picket fence lined the road to our left, behind which sat six slate-roofed stone cottages, each with a neatly manicured lawn. Behind the row of cottages was a field of wildflowers, and beyond that a lake.

"I never would have expected something like this out here," Rick said from the back seat as we bounced along the last stretch of road, checking the street numbers on each mailbox we passed. The fourth one matched the number Tony Biffano had identified as the home of Eleanor Lange, Machias Phelps' aunt.

I parked the Mustang on the street in front of the house, and we got out. We were halfway up the stone path leading to the front door when Stacey said, "This can't be the right place."

Before I could ask what she meant, the front door of the cottage swung open to reveal a frail, elderly woman in a green dress. "You don't look like salespeople," she said, "so you must be the prize patrol from that magazine outfit that gives away money."

After ascertaining that she was, in fact, Eleanor Lange, I told her that we were attorneys, not the prize patrol, and that we were there about the estate of her late nephew. She invited us in, perhaps because she thought our visit meant she was about to come into money or perhaps because she was just glad to have visitors. We followed her through a living room cluttered with knickknacks of every description to the kitchen where we took seats at an oak table while our hostess poured water from a kettle on the ancient stove. She offered us tea, which we declined, so she poured herself a cup and joined us at the table.

I realized this wasn't going to be easy when she said, "So, tell me about Machias. I haven't seen him in years."

I explained, as gently as I could, that her nephew was dead.

"Oh, I'm sorry to hear that. He was an odd, little fellow, but he was a gentle soul."

Thinking a visual aide might prompt her memory, I withdrew the key from my pocket and held it up so she could see it. "We found this in the envelope containing your nephew's Last Will and Testament. We're told it opens a trunk Machias left in your garage.

"Oh, I'm afraid you must be mistaken," the woman said. "I don't have a garage."

Stacey, who was sitting on my right, put her hand on my forearm. "She's right. None of these little cottages has a garage. This can't be the right place."

I wasn't about to give up. "Perhaps I was mistaken about the garage," I told the woman. "But I'm reasonably certain the key opens a trunk Machias left with you at some point."

"No," the elderly woman said slowly, shaking her head from side to side. "I don't remember any trunk." She stared off into space, either lost in thought or entering her own private world of memories, much as Rick does from time to time.

I looked to see how Rick was reacting to the woman's state, thinking it might be making him uncomfortable. We made eye contact, and he nodded. Then, to my surprise, he leaned over, touched the elderly woman on the shoulder and asked, "Did Machias leave anything with you?"

"Just the box," she said, still staring into space.

"May we see it?" Rick asked gently.

His question seemed to snap her out of her semi-trance, and she slowly made her way to a cabinet in the corner of the kitchen, withdrew a battered cardboard box, and carried it to the table. It certainly wasn't a trunk, and it clearly hadn't been stored in a garage, but hoping Billy Kane had been mistaken about the details, I removed the lid and we all peered inside. The box contained a small bound volume, which Stacey picked up and began to leaf through, and three trading cards featuring baseball players I had never heard of: Bob Stanley, John

Cumberland, and Ron Tingley. Only later did I realize that Machias might have left those particular cards as a clue.

"This appears to be someone's personal journal," Stacey said as she turned the pages. "Judging by the subject matter, I'd say this was written by a child. For example, here's an entry about a part-time job at a place called Dempsey's Dairy Delight."

Stacey laid the book flat on the table so Eleanor Lange could see the writing. "Is this your nephew's?"

"Oh, yes, that's Machias' all right. He always kept a journal, even when he was a little boy. And after the incident in school, he always printed in large and small capital letters. He never wrote longhand."

"What incident?" Stacey asked.

"One of his teachers made fun of his terrible handwriting and made him stand in the corner. He was so embarrassed that he never wrote in longhand after that." She looked off into space and smiled, perhaps remembering a younger version of her nephew. "I've only seen him a couple of times since he moved to New Jersey." She looked right at Stacey and asked, "How is he these days?"

I saved Stacey the trouble of coming up with an appropriate answer to that awkward question. "I think it's time for us to head back," I said, getting up from the table. It was clear that we weren't going to get any usable information from the woman. Rick and Stacey followed my lead, and we walked to the cottage's front door with Eleanor Lange shuffling along behind us.

"Thanks very much for your time," Stacey said, holding the cardboard box as we exited the cottage.

Either Eleanor Lange didn't realize we were taking the box with us or didn't care because all she said was, "No trouble at all. I don't get many visitors these days."

We were halfway to my car when Rick turned back toward Ms. Lange, who was waving at us from the open door, and asked her a question so obvious I kicked myself for not having thought of it. "Does Machias have any aunts other than you?"

The elderly woman thought for a moment before replying. "Well, there's his aunt in the town Machias grew up in." When Rick asked if she knew the name of the town or where it was located, Eleanor Lange stared off into space before slowly shaking her head. "No, my memory's not as good as it used to be." She demonstrated that painfully obvious fact by adding, "Tell Machias I said hello the next time you talk to him."

6

"Odd suit for an attorney."

I had just finished reading the last case involving defamation *per se* in preparation for the upcoming motion hearing when my secretary announced that Tony Biffano, the firm's investigator, was calling on line two.

"How did it go with Proctor's deposition?" he asked, getting right to business.

"I know nothing, I see nothing," I replied, doing a poor imitation of Sgt. Shultz from the *Hogan's Heroes* television show.

Biff laughed. "Yeah, that's about what I expected. Nothing happens in Troy Forge without Proctor's approval, but to hear him tell it, he only thing he knows is what he reads in the newspaper."

I hate talking with my mouth full, but it was almost noon and I was hungry. So I unwrapped my sandwich and took a bite. Besides, it was a phone conversation, so Biff couldn't see me eating. He could apparently hear me, however. "You eat one more tuna sandwich and you're going to grow gills."

"How do you know I'm eating a tuna sandwich?"

"Because you're always eating a tuna sandwich," Biff said. "It's the only thing I've ever seen you eat."

I ignored his culinary critique and asked, "Anyone you spoke to at town hall give you anything useful?"

"Not much. Nobody knows anything. They're all either part of Proctor's inner circle or too scared to talk. And after what happened to your buddy, Phelps, can you blame them?"

"Machias wasn't my buddy, he was just an informant."

"Buddy, informant, mole, it doesn't matter what you call him, the bottom line is he's dead, and other town employees don't want to end up like him."

"I just can't understand how the fairgrounds property could be magically re-zoned overnight and nobody knows how it happened."

"Easy," Biff said. "Proctor just went ahead and did what he wanted. As far as he's concerned, Troy Forge is his town and he can transform it any way he wants. And anyone who gets in his way is dealt with."

Biff spent the next few minutes telling me about his conversations with various members of the Troy Forge police department. I was hoping that as a former cop, he would manage to get someone to talk, but that didn't happen. The legit cops like my high school buddy, Sean McDermott, weren't privy to the inner workings of the Proctor political machine. And the cops who were part of Proctor's palace guard professed to know nothing.

I had given up hope of finding anyone who could provide helpful information when Biff said, "I've got one possible lead that might pan out. When I was in town hall asking questions, one woman acted as though she might know something, but didn't want to talk in front of the others." He paused and, judging by the sound, was flipping though his notes. "Cecilia Marcus," he finally said. "Know her?"

"I recognize the name," I replied. "I think she's been there for years, but I've never had any dealings with her."

Biff concluded the call by telling me he'd try to speak with Cecilia Marcus in private, and that he'd be sending me his bill.

I had just hung up the phone when Carolyn re-appeared at my door to announce I had a visitor. I wasn't expecting anyone, so I assumed Eddie the Skunk had once again dropped by without an appointment. I was wrong.

"There's a Mr. Obduhali here to see you," Carolyn said, slowly sounding out the name one syllable at a time. "He says he represents Mohammed Salameh." She handed me a business card identifying Obduhali as an attorney from Union City.

I had filed Eddie Rizzo's complaint against Obduhali's client less than a week ago, so I wasn't expecting a response this soon. And I certainly wasn't expecting an unannounced visit from Salameh's attorney. Perhaps Obduhali was hand delivering an answer to the complaint so he could use the opportunity to size up his adversary. I considered having him leave the answer with Carolyn, but his move intrigued me, so I asked her to show him in.

The pickle that had accompanied my tuna on rye had just found its way into the trash when Carolyn returned with a tall, dark-skinned man. He was carrying what appeared to be a very expensive leather briefcase and wearing a pale blue suit that reminded me of the leisure suits popular in the 1970s. Smiling the sort of forced, artificial smile that was the trademark of Bob Proctor, he extended his right hand as he strode toward me. "I am Omar Obduhali, Esquire," he said, apparently unaware that no self-respecting attorney would ever utter the word "Esquire" when introducing himself to another attorney.

Obduhali took a seat across from me at the desk, and we exchanged a few strained pleasantries before my adversary got to the reason for his visit. "I am here to deliver an apology from my client to yours, and to see if we can quickly resolve this unfortunate matter in a way that is satisfactory to all concerned. Mr. Salameh is relatively new to your country and is afraid that he will lose his driving license if he does not quickly make amends with your client. He is a poor handyman and needs to be able to drive his van to see customers. I have tried to explain that's not how things work in your country, but he will not listen."

Obduhali had to be a U.S. citizen to be a member of the New Jersey bar, so his use of "your country" - not once but twice - was a bit peculiar. But instead of pursuing the issue, I asked, "What do you have in mind?"

"Mr. Salameh has authorized me to offer your client five thousand dollars for damage to his car. We believe that is more than enough to cover the cost of repairs."

He was right about that. Eddie Rizzo had provided me with a bill showing he had spent just under three thousand dollars for repairs. And the fact that the body shop was owned by one of Eddie's associates suggested that the actual cost was considerably less.

"I'm not sure five thousand will do the trick," I said in an effort to find out just how anxious Salameh was to settle quickly.

Obduhali's smile never wavered. "And another five thousand for your client's inconvenience."

"I don't think so."

Obduhali continued to smile. "Mr. Salameh will, of course, pay an additional five thousand dollars to cover your fee."

"My fee is between my client and me."

"Yes, yes, I understand," Obduhali said. "What I meant was that Mr. Salameh will pay your client a total of fifteen thousand dollars."

I might have considered presenting the offer to my client if my client had been anyone other than Eddie the Skunk. But Eddie had made it clear that he was out for blood. And besides, Obduhali was much too anxious to settle the case. There was something wrong here, and I had a feeling I knew what it was. "Mind giving me the name of your client's insurance company?" It was information I'd get eventually during pre-trial discovery, so there was no reason for Obduhali to withhold that information.

But instead of answering my question Obduhali calmly retrieved his briefcase from the chair to his left, placed it on my desk, and spun it around. He opened the briefcase, revealing stacks of hundred dollar bills, each bundled with a paper strip bearing "Banque Saud USA" and a very prominent "$5,000." I did some quick mental calculations and realized there had to be at least fifty thousand dollars in the briefcase. Poor New Jersey handymen were obviously well paid.

I pointed to the briefcase. "I'll interpret that to mean your client doesn't have insurance." Obduhali didn't respond, so I continued. "That presents a problem. My client has suffered serious permanent injury," I said, using the words of the no-fault law's verbal threshold that would allow Eddie to collect for pain and suffering.

That should have caused Obduhali to ask for a medical report supporting my contention. But instead, he stood up and said, "If you would excuse me for just a moment, I have to make a phone call." He disappeared through my office door without looking back, leaving the briefcase filled with cash sitting on my desk. Resisting the temptation to remove a few bundles, I leaned back in my chair and waited, wondering what sort of game my adversary was playing. Obduhali returned a few minutes later, glanced at the briefcase, and calmly took his seat across from me as though leaving a cash-filled briefcase on a stranger's desk was just business as usual. "How much does your client want for his pain and suffering?"

"How much are you offering?"

"I have brought fifty thousand dollars with me today," Obduhali said, nodding toward the briefcase. He waited, and when he didn't get a response, added, "but I can bring more if this isn't enough."

"At this point, I don't know the extent of my client's injuries," I said. "So it's impossible to know how much is enough."

"Mr. Salameh is very intent on resolving this matter quickly," Obduhali assured me, as if a briefcase filled with crisp hundred dollar bills wasn't assurance enough.

Attorneys don't walk around with fifty grand in cash to settle a case that's just been filed. Something else was going on here, and until I could determine what it was, my best course of action was to play along. "I share your client's desire to resolve this matter amicably. I'm sure my client does too. But, as I said, until I know the extent of my client's injuries, I'm not in a position to settle the case."

Obduhali reached into the inside pocket of his suit coat, and I assumed he was about to serve me with an answer to the complaint I had filed. But instead, he presented me with a wrinkled business card. "When you are ready to settle this matter, please call me." He got up, nodded politely, and headed for the door. Our meeting was obviously over.

I walked Obduhali out to the elevator without either of us saying a word, and waited to ensure he left before continuing to Rick's office. Rick was reading a book about baseball when I entered. "Sorry to interrupt," I said, moving to the window overlooking the parking lot behind the building. "Mind if I borrow your window?"

"As long as you give it back when you're finished," Rick said, laying the book down and joining me at the window.

I had originally planned to handle Eddie's case like any other fender bender: serve interrogatories, a set of questions the other side is required to answer, provide answers to the other side's interrogatories, then sit back and wait for an offer in settlement. But Obduhali's eagerness to settle the case for far more than it was worth convinced me I needed more extensive discovery. At the very least I needed to depose Salameh and demand he produce his vehicle for inspection. A deposition would cost money, but I was curious to meet the supposedly poor handyman who could come up with fifty thousand dollars on short notice.

Obduhali exited the building a moment later and made a beeline for a black Lincoln with tinted windows.

"Who's he?" Rick asked.

"Mohammed Salameh's attorney."

"Odd suit for an attorney," Rick said.

"That's not the only thing that's odd about the guy. That briefcase he's carrying contains fifty thousand dollars in crisp hundred dollar bills that he tried to use to settle Eddie Rizzo's personal injury case against his client."

"Interesting," Rick said, using one of Stacey's favorite words. "Troy Forge isn't exactly a high crime area, but who in his right mind walks around with a briefcase filled with cash?"

"You'd think he'd have some sort of security when carrying that much money."

As if in response to my comment, a man in a Troy Forge police uniform got out of the Lincoln as Obduhali approached it.

7

"I've heard enough."

It was the sort of idiotic motion for which Barahi was famous, or should I say, infamous. This morning, he was asking a Superior Court judge to enter summary judgment against Stacey and the *Ledger* on the second count of CIRR's complaint alleging that she had "slandered Islam." His moving papers, as near as I could figure, argued that as a matter of law, his client had a right to judgment because Stacey's newspaper articles constituted "defamation *per se*." Like most of Barahi's work product, this motion was just plain wrong for a whole bunch of reasons.

"Good morning, counselors," Judge MacAndrew said.

"Good morning, Your Honor," I replied.

Barahi had apparently never appeared before MacAndrew because he launched into his argument instead of providing the response the judge was expecting.

The judge held up his hand and shook his head from side to side. Embarrassed laughter filtered through the courtroom from other attorneys who knew what Barahi obviously didn't, that Judge Duncan MacAndrew was a stickler for courtroom niceties. When he said "good morning, counselors," the only acceptable response was, "good morning, Your Honor."

The judge looked right at Barahi and waited.

Barahi seemed genuinely confused, and for a split second I almost felt sorry for him. Seconds passed that felt like minutes. When Barahi finally turned toward me, I silently mouthed the words the judge was expecting to hear.

He got the hint. Sort of. "Oh, good morning, judge," Barahi said. If he had stopped there, he would have been okay, but he kept going. "Please forgive me. This is the first time I have had the privilege of appearing before Your Honor and was unaware of the proper protocol in your courtroom."

Barahi's attempt at kissing up to MacAndrew elicited a terse, "Counselors, enter your appearance."

"Tinoo Barahi appearing on behalf of CIRR, the Council for Islamic Religious Respect," my adversary said, pronouncing CIRR as "seer."

"Brendan O'Brian for the defendants," I said.

"Mr. Barahi," the judge asked, "is counsel for Mr. Proctor aware of today's motion?"

The question seemed to catch Barahi off guard. He reached for a file folder and began frantically leafing through it. "I'm reasonably certain I served Mr. Lambert with notice," Barahi said. "If the court will allow me just a moment, I think I..."

That was as far as he got before Emerson Lambert stood up in the back of the public gallery. "I'm aware of the motion, Your Honor."

"Mr. Lambert," the judge said, acknowledging the older attorney. "Always a pleasure to have you in my courtroom. Will you be participating in today's motion hearing?"

"No, Your Honor," Lambert said before abruptly sitting down. Lambert could have sat at the counsel table with Barahi since the motion, though not directly involving his client, could potentially impact his case. But he clearly wanted to distance himself from CIRR's attorney.

"Very well," the judge said. "You may proceed, Mr. Barahi."

"Your Honor," Barahi began, "the newspaper articles written by the defendant, McCain, and published by the defendant, *Ledger*, are filled with slanderous remarks that constitute defamation *per se*.

"You can leave out the word 'defendant' when referring to the parties," MacAndrew instructed. "I think we all know who everyone is."

I heard snickers from the public gallery behind me. "Yes, I am so sorry, Your Honor," Barahi said before proceeding to dig a deeper hole for himself. "For example, in the article that I have marked as exhibit number one, Miss McCain refers to Islam as a dangerous ideology inconsistent with Judeo-Christian values. She writes that Islam is not a true religion as that term is ordinarily used, but rather a political system with a religious gloss."

That's as far as Barahi got before the judge interrupted him. "Mr. Barahi, I've read the newspaper articles in question, which you appended both to your complaint as well as to your motion for summary judgment. There's no reason for you to read them to me."

"But, Your Honor," Barahi protested, "these are serious, slanderous statements that Miss McCain has made. It is necessary for the court to understand how objectionable and hurtful they are to the Muslim community. I want Your Honor to know..."

"Mr. Barahi," MacAndrew interrupted, "I've read your motion as well as the affidavits attached to it, all six of them. What I need from you now is the legal reasoning behind your motion for summary judgment."

"I believe the affidavit of the mosque's imam explains things quite clearly," Barahi said, leafing through the stack of papers he was holding. He started reading from what I assumed was the imam's affidavit. "Defendant McCain's statements about the prophet Mohammed are slanderous on their face, hold Muslims up to ridicule, and infringe on the Muslim community's right to free expression of religion."

The judge was clearly getting exasperated. "Mr. Barahi, I've already read that affidavit. You don't need to read it to me."

Before Barahi could respond, Judge MacAndrew nodded in my direction. "Mr. O'Brian," he said, signaling he wanted to hear from me.

"Your Honor, the second count of the complaint Mr. Barahi filed in this matter fails to state a claim on which relief can be granted, which is why I filed a cross-motion to dismiss it."

"Your reasoning, counselor?"

"For starters, Your Honor, the complaint accuses the defendants of slandering Islam, notwithstanding the fact that slander requires a verbal statement and the statements made in the newspaper articles are written. The second count is defective on its face and should be dismissed on that basis alone."

"That is a mere technicality," Barahi said indignantly. "Libel and slander are simply different forms of defamation. I will file an amended complaint alleging libel instead of slander."

"Very well," Judge MacAndrew said. "We'll proceed on the assumption that the complaint alleges the defendants committed libel, not slander. Continue, Mr. O'Brian."

"Even if we deem the complaint amended to charge libel instead of slander, it doesn't comport with Mr. Barahi's moving papers, which allege my clients committed defamation *per se*."

"I'm not sure that's a fatal defect," Judge MacAndrew said. "Defamation *per se* is a special form of defamation in much the same way that libel and slander constitute different ways of defaming someone."

"Yes," I said, "defaming some*one*, not some*thing*. Under New Jersey law, defamation *per se* is defined as statements falsely accusing someone of committing a criminal offense, having a loathsome disease, engaging in serious sexual misconduct, or having characteristics or conduct inconsistent with the person's business, trade or office. None of these apply in this case. The only reason Mr. Barahi is arguing defamation *per se* is because it's not necessary to prove actual damages with a defamation *per se* claim. And the reason he can't prove damages is because there aren't any. A belief system can't suffer damages, only a person can. It's possible to defame some*one*, but not some*thing*."

"That is not so," Barahi said. "Miss McCain has accused my client of committing a criminal offense by associating with terrorists. She has made numerous defamatory statements to that effect in her newspaper articles."

"But the second count of the complaint, which is what today's motion pertains to, has nothing to do with Mr. Barahi's client, Your Honor. It alleges that the defendants slandered Islam, not the Council for Islamic Religious Respect."

"Libeled Islam," Judge MacAndrew reminded me. "We're proceeding on the assumption that the complaint has been amended to use the correct terminology."

"But under New Jersey law," I replied, "defamation of Islam, or any religion for that matter, isn't a recognized tort. It doesn't matter whether the alleged defamation is written or oral, libel or slander. It's impossible to defame a belief system, whether it's Islam, Catholicism, democracy, communism, vegetarianism."

Judge MacAndrew held up his hand to signal he had heard enough. "You've made your point."

He looked in Barahi's direction for a response, but before Barahi could say anything, I continued, "More importantly, my clients have a First Amendment right to express an opinion about Islam or any other belief system. Mr. Barahi's client is simply trying to deny them that right. There simply is no actionable tort in this case, and even if there were, Mr. Barahi's client wouldn't have standing to seek redress."

"You raise an interesting point, Mr. O'Brian," the judge said. "Mr. Barahi, let me hear from you on the standing issue."

"Miss McCain's articles are filled with defamatory statements, whether they're classified as defamation *per se* or plain vanilla defamation," Barahi said.

"Per quod," I said, before Barahi could continue. "Plain vanilla defamation is known as defamation *per quod*."

Barahi was clearly embarrassed and annoyed by my little lesson, which was exactly what I intended. Judge MacAndrew wasn't embarrassed, but he was annoyed, which wasn't what I wanted. "Sorry, Your Honor. I apologize to the court and to Mr. Barahi."

That seemed to placate the judge, who turned to Barahi and said, "What I'm asking from you is an explanation of why you think your client has standing to pursue this matter when the statements in question are critical of Islam, not your client."

"Because by slandering Islam, Miss McCain's newspaper articles are slandering Muslims, and the Council for Islamic Religious Respect represents Muslims."

I couldn't help myself. "Says who? Who appointed your client representative of all Muslims?"

"Mr. O'Brian, please address your comments to the court, not to counsel," the judge said. "Continue, Mr. Barahi."

"The newspaper articles in question all pertain to the new mosque in Troy Forge, which is operated by the Council for Islamic Religious Respect. The defamatory statements in those articles ridicule Islam, and by extension, my client."

I was about to poke holes in that argument when the judge held up his hand to signal me to stop. "I've heard enough," he said, gaveling the hearing to a conclusion. "I'll take this under advisement and render a decision next week." True to his word, he rendered a decision the following week, but it wasn't the one I was expecting.

8

"It could just be a coincidence, but then again, maybe not."

I called Obduhali a few days day after his unannounced visit to my office and arranged to depose his client and to photograph the van Salameh had been driving the day of the accident. My adversary was not only cooperative, but anxious to resolve the matter as quickly as possible. We arranged for me to depose his client at an address in Jersey City that I assumed was Mohammed Salameh's place of business. Obduhali assured me that both his client and the van would be there, ending our conversation by telling me, "Perhaps we might even settle this unfortunate matter on the spot."

On the day of Salameh's deposition I met Eddie the Skunk at Palermo's Deli in Jersey City and we drove ten blocks to an especially rundown commercial area. The street we were driving on was lined with stores whose signs were all written in some language other than English. When we passed a butcher shop with a sign reading "halal" hanging in the window, Eddie said, "Halal is Arab for kosher."

"Actually, I think halal is a Muslim term."

"Muslim, Arab, same thing," Eddie said. I have several Lebanese Christian clients who would disagree, but I wasn't about to get involved in an argument with Eddie the Skunk.

We eventually came to the address that Omar Obduhali had given me over the phone. It was a concrete block building that hadn't seen a coat of paint in years. There were four overhead doors and a steel door that I assumed led to an office. As we entered, I said to Eddie, "Remember, don't say a word to Salameh or his attorney. Anything you say can be twisted around and used against you in court."

I hadn't really wanted Eddie to accompany me, but he insisted, arguing that he was the only one who could identify the van that hit him. "What if they show you some other van that don't have any damage and claim the accident was just a little fender bender?" I had to admit that he had a point, hence his presence that morning.

Once through the door we found ourselves not in an office, but a dark, cavernous space that was much bigger than I had expected. While we waited just inside the door for our eyes to adjust to the darkness, a voice boomed out, "Ah, welcome, my friends." Omar Obduhali appeared out of the gloom, with an outstretched hand and a big, plastic smile. After handshakes that were entirely too enthusiastic on Obduhali's part, I asked, "Where's your client?"

Obduhali looked shocked. "Didn't my secretary call you? Mr. Salameh was taken ill and could not be here today."

"Son of a...," Eddie muttered. I put my hand on his elbow before he could finish.

"I am very sorry," Obduhali said. "I will admonish my secretary sternly when I get back to my office."

"No problem," I replied. "Maybe she called and my secretary forgot to tell me." I knew that wasn't the case. Carolyn never fails to relay messages. But I figured working for Obduhali was no picnic, so there was no need to make trouble for his secretary.

"How about the van?" I asked.

"That is here," Obduhali said, gesturing for us to follow him into the gloom. He led us to the back corner of the building, switched on a bank of overhead fluorescent lights and pointed to a tan Chevy van.

Eddie's response was immediate. "That ain't it. That ain't the van that hit me."

I wasn't sure if Obduhali was genuinely surprised or was simply feigning surprise. "Are you sure?" he asked. "My client has several vans and this is the one he said he was driving that day."

"No, this ain't the right van," Eddie insisted. "The van that hit me was white and had..."

"This is the wrong van," I told Obduhali, cutting off Eddie's description before he could reveal any details. "Call your client and see if he can get the right vehicle over here."

"I will see what I can do," Obduhali said as he disappeared into the darkness, presumably to telephone Mohammed Salameh.

Minutes passed as Eddie and I stood in the dimly lighted, cavernous building. "This don't smell right," Eddie finally said. "The guy owns so many vans he don't remember which one he's driving when he has an accident? Gimme a fuckin' break." I silently agreed with Eddie's assessment, if not his colorful language. How many vehicles could a supposedly poor handyman own?

Obduhali eventually reappeared and announced that he was unable to reach his client on the phone. "Mr. Salameh is most likely at the doctor."

"Look," I said, "my time is valuable. I've wasted the better part of a day driving to Hudson County for a deposition that won't take place and to view what's obviously the wrong vehicle. If you and your client really want to settle this case, this isn't the way to do it."

"Mr. Salameh is very much interested in settling the matter amicably," Obduhali assured me. He turned to Eddie and bowing slightly said, "And he has instructed me to apologize to you, and to assure you that he wishes to make amends."

"Apologies are fine," I said, "but when can we see the right vehicle, and when can I depose your client?"

"I will contact Mr. Salameh this evening and call your office to arrange a convenient time," Obduhali said. "And I will bring both Mr. Salameh and the vehicle to your office so you will not have to make another trip to Jersey City."

Obduhali escorted Eddie and me back through the dimly lighted building to the door where we had entered. "I will be in touch," he said as we got back into my car.

"I don't trust that guy," Eddie said as we pulled into traffic. "This whole thing stinks. It's like his client is stalling so he can get the van repaired and then argue all we had was a little fender bender." As it turned out, Salameh was stalling, but not for the reason Eddie thought.

When I got back to the office, I found Rick sprawled out on my sofa, eyes closed and with a road atlas across his chest. I thought he was asleep until he asked, "How was your trip to beautiful downtown Jersey City?" At times Rick can be almost as sarcastic as I am.

I told him about Obduhali producing the wrong vehicle. "Cheer up," he said. "While you were looking at the wrong van I was finding the right aunt."

"How did you manage that?" I asked.

"Actually, Linda did it," Rick said, referring to the woman who was the firm's first computer operator. These days, all the secretaries have a computer, but Linda is still the only person in the office who can make her machine do things that seem almost magical. Instead of explaining what Linda had done, Rick asked,

"What do Bob Stanley, Ron Tingley, and John Cumberland have in common?"

I was still annoyed about my wasted trip to Jersey City and was in no mood to play guessing games. "I have no idea," I said, perhaps a bit too brusquely.

"Remember the baseball cards we found at Phelps' aunt's house?" Rick prompted.

"What about them?"

"Those were the three players on those cards," Rick said. "All three were born in Maine."

"That's an interesting piece of trivia, but what does that have to do with Phelps' other aunt?"

"Remember the journal entry about working at Dempsey's Dairy Delight?" Apparently assuming I remembered, Rick continued, "Dempsey's is a five store chain located in Maine."

"Just because Phelps apparently worked at a place in Maine doesn't mean the aunt lives there. And even if she does, how do we find her? Maine's a pretty big state."

"Ah, but remember Eleanor Lange told us that the other aunt lives in Machias' hometown. And one of the towns where Dempsey's has a store is called..." Rick paused, either for dramatic effect or to see if I would supply the missing name. I shrugged my shoulders, which caused Rick to finish the sentence. "Machias, a little town up near the Canadian border. It could just be a coincidence, but then again, maybe not."

I wasn't convinced Rick had found the missing aunt, but searching for her would be a good excuse for a romantic getaway with Stacey.

9

"You sure know how to show a girl a good time."

"Don't forget who figured out the aunt was in Maine," Rick said in support of his request to join Stacey and me on our trip to Machias, a town of two thousand people less than fifty miles from the Canadian border. "I may not be as sharp as I once was, but I can still pull my weight."

"I'm not denying that," I responded, "but a long, tiring drive to Maine isn't like a day trip to Warren County." To illustrate my point, I drew a red circle around Troy Forge on the map I had spread out on my desk, and another one around Machias. I suppose if I had wanted to be completely accurate, I should have drawn a circle around Boston and explained that Stacie and I were flying to Boston and then driving from there to Maine. But the prospect of a romantic getaway at a cozy, little inn in a quaint seacoast town overcame my inclination to provide Rick with an accurate description of our intended journey.

The map trick worked, and two days later Stacey and I landed at Boston's Logan Airport, rented a car and headed north to Maine. We made it all the way to the town of Ellsworth before Stacey brought up a topic I knew we'd have to deal with at some point. "You do realize that my boss is really pissed at what this new expert witness is going to cost, don't you?"

"Ezra is pissed every time I spend a dime," I replied. "But as I've told both of you over and over, cases like this are won or lost before the actual trial begins. And Judge MacAndrew's ruling on the second count of the complaint doesn't leave me much choice."

"That was a stupid ruling," Stacey said. "I'm not an attorney, and even I can tell that was just plain dumb."

"Dumb or not, that's how he ruled. And that's why I need an expert witness like Daniel Stern."

"He doesn't come cheap," Stacey said.

"No, he doesn't," I agreed. "But if you want the country's leading expert on Islam, you have to be prepared to pay top dollar. Besides, we're lucky to be able to get his services. Dr. Stern is incredibly picky about who he gets involved with. The main reason he agreed to consult on your case is because he was impressed with your observation that Islam is more like a political system than a religion." That elicited a hint of a smile from Stacey. "He was also impressed that the *Ledger* had the guts to publish your articles."

My compliment elicited an unexpected reaction. "Guts? Everything in my articles is true. Since when does it take guts for a newspaper to publish the truth?" There was a flash of anger in her bright green eyes. "You do believe what I wrote is true, don't you?"

"It doesn't matter what I think," I responded. "The only thing that matters is what a jury thinks. And with the number of Muslims moving into New Jersey, there's a good chance we'll end up with at least one on the jury. How do you think they'll react to accusations that most Muslims want to convert, subjugate or kill non-Muslims?"

"That's a basic tenant of Islam," Stacey said. "It comes right out of the Qur'an, their so-called holy book."

"It may be in the Qur'an, but I suspect only a tiny minority of Muslim feel that way. The vast majority of Muslims don't mean us any harm."

"What if you're wrong?" Stacey asked. "What if it's the other way around and the vast majority of Muslims really do want to do us harm?"

"I have a hard time believing that."

"That's probably because you've never set foot in a mosque."

"And you have?"

"As a matter of fact, I have," she said. "And what they're preaching right in your hometown of Troy Forge should scare the living daylights out of you."

"You've been in the new mosque?"

"How do you think I got the research for my articles? Or do you think I made the whole thing up?"

"I never suggested you made it all up," I protested.

"No, just most of it, huh?"

"I didn't say that."

"You didn't have to. It's obvious that's what you think."

We drove in icy silence for what seemed like hours, but which, according to the dashboard clock, was only thirty minutes. The next time Stacey spoke it was to announce, "We're lost."

I wouldn't admit that she was right, particularly after our heated discussion, but I knew she was. "I'll ask directions the next time I see someone."

"That's the problem," Stacey said. "We haven't seen a soul for almost an hour."

"More like ten minutes," I countered.

"We haven't seen a road sign, a building, or anything, for that matter," she said, surveying the countryside."

All that changed when we rounded a bend and spotted a man in overalls by the side of the road. He was retrieving mail from a dilapidated mailbox on a wooden post that looked as though it was about to tip over. I stopped the car beside him and Stacey lowered her window. The man eased over to our car, leaned down, and rested his forearms on the door. He was probably in his sixties, with leathery skin and piercing blue eyes.

"Is this the road to Machias?" Stacey asked.

"No Machias in these parts," came the answer. He shifted his gaze skyward, either giving her question more thought or perhaps simply assessing the weather. "We got a place called Machias though," he said, pronouncing the "ch" as it sounds in "chicken" rather than sounding like a "k."

"Machias," Stacey repeated, this time using his pronunciation. "That's what we're looking for."

"Keep going up the road a bit and you'll come to it eventually," he said before turning back toward a farmhouse that was almost as tilted as the mailbox.

"I'm guessing that was an example of Down East humor," I said to Stacey as we pulled away. "Never understood the whole Down East thing. On a map, south is down and Maine is up."

"When you sail east along the Maine coast, you're sailing downwind," Stacey explained. I interpreted that as a sign we were once again on speaking terms after our earlier heated discussion.

We reached Machias just before sunset and set about finding a place to stay. Our first stop was a quaint little bed and breakfast. So quaint in fact, that it had been booked solid for months. The second B&B we tried was equally quaint and equally full. The innkeeper, a garrulous retired cop from Boston named Sullivan, explained that every room in town had been booked solid for months. He did, however, provide directions to a place outside of town that he thought might have a vacancy.

After ten minutes of driving, we spotted a sign with the words "Shady Rest Inn" and a painting of a cozy country inn that could have been a Currier and Ives print. Unfortunately, the sign was the only thing about the place that could be considered quaint. The actual structure was a dilapidated concrete block motel that appeared to have been built back in the 1950s. It had a central office flanked by rooms on either side, the entire structure painted a horrendous shade of pink.

I parked the car in front of the office, and we got out. "I'll take in the ambiance," Stacey said, leaning against the car, "while you go in and find out if they have a room that hasn't been condemned yet."

When I entered the office, a woman with a cigarette dangling from the corner of her mouth looked up from the magazine she was reading. She was wearing a nametag that identified her as Shirley.

"Hi, Shirley," I said. "Do you have any rooms?"

Her eyes narrowed and she eyed me suspiciously. Perhaps I shouldn't have addressed her by name. "How many you need?"

"We only need one room."

My use of the plural pronoun caused Shirley to shift her gaze to the front window where Stacey was standing in form fitting jeans that made the most of her assets. "You two married?" she asked.

"No, why?"

"I've got two very nice rooms," she responded with a disapproving frown. Before I could explain that we only needed one room, she added, "One at each end of the second floor."

As promised, the rooms were indeed on the second floor, and they were, in fact, at opposite ends of the motel. Whether or not they were nice depends on how high or low your standards are. I was in the process of deciding on the best way to dispose of the dead flies on the bathroom counter when someone knocked on the door. I was hoping for the motel insect mortician, but it was Stacey, who was laughing so hard there were tears streaming from her bright green eyes. "This five star establishment features free in-room movies," she said when she finally calmed down enough to be understandable.

"What's so funny about that?" I asked. "Lot of places offer free in-room movies."

"Oh, not like this," Stacey said as she walked to the back of the room and opened the curtains to reveal a loudspeaker mounted on the wall. "In this classy establishment, the in-room movies aren't actually in the room." I joined her at the window and looked to where she was pointing. The room had a bird's eye view of the drive-in movie theatre behind the motel. "You sure know how to show a girl a good time."

I closed the curtains. Then I showed her a good time.

10

"End of story."

The following morning we drove back into Machias and had breakfast at an establishment that looked like the kind of place the locals would frequent. We struck up a conversation with a very young and very pretty waitress, and eventually got around to asking if she knew of Machias Phelps.

"No," she said, "but, like, I've only been in town a few years. Moved up here from Boston." Ten minutes later, having provided far more personal information than I wanted to know, including a detailed description of a romantic relationship gone terribly wrong, she called an older male colleague over to where we were sitting. "This is Thomas," she said. "He's lived here, like, forever. He knows, like, virtually everybody in Machias."

"Thank you," I said as she turned away. "You've been, like, very helpful." Stacey kicked me under the table. Thomas smiled. The waitress, apparently oblivious to my dig, just said "whatever" and moved on to refill coffee cups at the next table.

Thomas, who told us he was eighty years old, but didn't look a day over sixty, did know virtually everyone in Machias, having spent his entire life in the town. "Phelps is a pretty common name in these parts," he explained. "They were one of the early settlers. But there was only one Phelps nutty enough to name her kid after the town. That'd be Carrie Phelps. Lived out near the fort, but died years ago."

"What fort?" I asked. "Why would a little town like Machias have a fort?"

"Fort O'Brien. Guards the Machias River. Named after Jeremiah O'Brien, who commanded the ship that won the first naval battle in the Revolutionary War," Thomas said with pride in his voice. I later discovered that because of that 1775 battle, Machias claims to be the birthplace of the U.S. Navy.

"Maybe you come from a long line of war heroes," Stacey said, landing a playful punch on my shoulder.

"I doubt it," I said. "I prefer to do my fighting in a courtroom."

"You a lawyer?" Thomas asked warily. Out-of-town lawyers are apparently regarded with suspicion in Machias, as they are in many small towns.

"I am," I replied. "My firm was named as executor of the estate of Machias Phelps." Actually, Rick was named as executor, not the firm, but why get bogged down in details? "I'm looking for the aunt of the late Mr. Phelps." I thought referring to Machias as "Mr. Phelps" made it sound more professional. With any luck, old Thomas would think the aunt was about to come into money and tell me where I could find her.

It worked. "You're probably looking for Harriet Phelps," he said. "Lives out east of here." He then proceeded to provide directions that only a local could understand, replete with things like "turn right at the Johnson farm" and "go left at the intersection where the fuel oil truck skidded off the road last winter."

Despite the vague instructions, which I suspect is a type of Down East joke played on outsiders, we eventually arrived at a home with a faded "Phelps" hand lettered on the mailbox. It was the antithesis of Eleanor Lange's tidy, little stone cottage in Belvidere. There was a rusting pickup in the driveway with a missing wheel. Not just a missing tire, but a missing wheel. What used to be a lawn was a weed patch that hadn't been mowed in years. And the house had a peculiar lean that mimicked the home of the gentleman who instructed us on the proper pronunciation of Machias. "Must have strong winds in these parts," Stacey said, nodding toward the ramshackle house.

The woman who answered the door turned out to be the aunt we were searching for, but like the house she lived in, this aunt was the exact opposite of her New Jersey counterpart. Eleanor Lange had looked like a kindly, old grandmother from a children's book. Harriet Phelps, on the other hand, was more like a retired roller derby queen. She had wide shoulders, mean eyes, and a cigarette dangling from the corner of her mouth that bobbed up and down as she spoke. And instead of inviting us in for tea, this aunt greeted us with a brusque, "What do you want?"

But at least this aunt was of sound mind. No sooner had I introduced myself and explained the reason for our visit than she said in a gravelly voice, "I figured you'd show up eventually. Good thing, too, because next week I was going to clean out the garage, including the crap my odd, little nephew left."

"Tell me about Machias," I said to Harriet Phelps as she walked us back to the ramshackle garage behind the house. "Your nephew, I mean, not the town."

"What's to tell?" came her response. "My idiot brother knocked up a crazy bitch who gave birth to an odd, little bastard. My brother took off for parts unknown, the crazy bitch committed suicide, and I ended up with the little shit. End of story."

"Did Machias live with you when he was growing up?"

Harriet Phelps looked at me as though I had asked her if the sky is blue. "Didn't I just say I ended up with the little shit?" She removed the half smoked cigarette dangling from the corner of her mouth, threw it on the weed infested gravel driveway, and stomped on it with a vengeance. "End of story."

Stacey got into the act. "Do you remember Machias working at a place called Dempsey's Dairy Delight?"

The evil aunt, as I had come to regard her in my mind, glared at Stacey. "Odd, little shit worked at lots of places." She lit a cigarette to replace the one she had just discarded. "Yeah, I seem to recall he worked at Dempsey's. Never could hold a job for very long. End of story."

"When did you last see Machias?" I asked.

I thought it was an innocuous question, but apparently it wasn't. "What part of 'end of story' don't you people understand?"

We walked the last stretch of driveway in silence. When we got to the garage, Harriet Phelps reached down, grabbed the handle of the overhead door, and violently yanked it up. Emitting a screeching sound like fingernails on an old fashioned blackboard, the door opened to reveal an interior as decrepit as the rest of this Down East Shangri-La. She pointed to the back corner and said "over there" before lighting another cigarette and walking back to the house.

"She's a charmer," Stacey said when the evil aunt was out of earshot.

We picked our way around piles of boxes, half-used bags of fertilizer, stacks of newspapers, a rusted lawnmower (missing a wheel like the pickup in the driveway), and clutter of every description. We never found a trunk, but we did eventually discover a gray three-drawer file cabinet against the back wall of the garage.

"This is the only thing with a lock," I said as I moved the remains of a rusting bicycle blocking the cabinet, and fished in my pocket for the key that had accompanied Machias Phelps' Last Will and Testament. I inserted the key into the lock at the top of the filing cabinet and twisted it. The key turned, a good first step. I held my breath as I released the tension and watched the mechanism pop out, signaling the cabinet was unlocked.

I opened the top drawer and found that it contained nothing but clumps of what looked like dust. "Ayuh, we got big dust bunnies in these parts," Stacey said with what I assumed was supposed to be a Down East accent.

The second drawer yielded the same results. This time Stacey said, "Strike two. One more and you're out." My disapproving look didn't stop her from delivering the coup de grâce. "But at least we had a chance to watch movies in our fancy hotel room."

I tried to open the bottom drawer, but it wouldn't budge. I pulled harder and it slid open enough for me to see that something was catching on the filing cabinet's frame, preventing the drawer from opening all the way. I pushed down on the offending object and managed to slide the drawer open, revealing a stack of school yearbooks.

Stacey crouched down next to me. "Jackpot," she said. "A treasure trove of molding school yearbooks. Well worth the trip to Maine." Ignoring her sarcasm, I lifted the yearbooks out of the cabinet and put them on the cracked concrete floor. "But wait, there's more," Stacey said in her best imitation of a television pitchman. "With every stack of molding yearbooks from a backwater school in the middle of nowhere, we'll throw in a rare, antique manila folder."

Stacey removed the folder that had been under the yearbooks and began leafing through its contents while I studied the yearbooks. There were six of them, covering consecutive years. Each contained individual student photos, followed by group shots of clubs and sports teams. I flipped through the pages of the oldest yearbook until I came to the photo of a youthful version of the Machias Phelps who had kept me apprised of the inner workings of the Proctor administration in Troy Forge. Like the middle-aged Phelps, the one in the photograph had bulging eyes peering out from behind thick glasses, delicate features, and wispy blond hair. The caption identified him as being in seventh grade. I repeated the process with the second book, finding the eighth grade version of the odd, little man who had served as my town hall informant.

I was in the process of opening the third yearbook when Stacey said, "Well, isn't this interesting." She was gingerly holding an old, yellowed tax return with two fingers as though it might be infested with some type of deadly bacteria indigenous to decrepit Down East garages.

"What's so interesting about a tax return?" I asked. "We know Phelps worked at Dempsey's Dairy Delight when he lived here, so he probably filed a tax return to report that income."

"True," Stacey agreed, "but this isn't a copy of Phelps' tax return."

"Then whose is it?"

"Someone named Robert Proctor," Stacey replied. "And the copy of the W-2 attached to it shows that Proctor also worked at Dempsey's Dairy Delight."

"Interesting," I agreed, "but hardly surprising. There are probably thousands of people named Robert Proctor in the country."

"It could just be a coincidence," Stacey said, "but you have to admit, it's pretty weird. Why would Machias Phelps have a copy of someone else's tax return, much less someone named Robert Proctor, which just happens to be the name of our illustrious mayor?"

Stacey handed me the tax return. "Notice anything about the handwriting?"

Robert Proctor's name and address were neatly handwritten using large and small capital letters. "Interesting," I said, expropriating Stacey's favorite word. "Could just be another coincidence."

"Or it could mean Machias Phelps prepared the return for his friend, " Stacey said as she continued leafing through the manila folder.

I turned my attention back to the third yearbook in the stack in front of me. I assumed it would contain the ninth grade version of Machias Phelps, but before I had a chance to confirm that, Stacey said, "Oh, my God."

"What's that?" I asked, putting the yearbook aside and nodding toward the yellowed document she was staring at.

"Robert Proctor's birth certificate," she said, holding the document up so I could see it.

"Obviously a different Robert Proctor," I said. "That was issued by the State of Maine, and Billboard Bob was born in southern New Jersey."

"Was he? How do we know that?"

"What do you mean, how do we know that? Every time he talks to the media he rolls out his 'poor boy from the Pine Barrens who climbed the ladder of opportunity' shtick. That story's in every piece of his campaign literature since he first showed up in Troy Forge."

"But what if it's not true?" Stacey insisted. "Has anybody ever verified his claim, or has everyone just assumed he was telling the truth?"

"Careful," I said, "you're getting perilously close to sounding like one of those conspiracy nuts."

"Right, politicians never lie," she said sarcastically. "Any journalist who accepts a politician's word on anything is in the wrong business."

"But why would he lie about where he was born? No one really cares, and besides, at this point what difference does it make?"

"What difference does it make? I can't believe you said that." Our discussion was apparently about to turn into an argument.

I needed to cool things down. "Look, nobody would be happier than me to expose Billboard Bob as a fraud. But to do that, we need proof. For starters, we need to prove that birth certificate is real. And if it is, then we need to prove that the Robert Proctor named in that document is the same Robert Proctor serving as mayor of Troy Forge." I wasn't sure what impact any of this would have on Proctor's political fortunes, but it would certainly wreak havoc with his credibility in the defamation case against Stacey and the *Ledger*.

"Agreed," Stacy said, thankfully putting an end to the budding argument. "And I know how to get the proof we need. Well, part of it, at least."

11

"It's all Ted Kennedy's fault."

"Take the highway this time," Stacey said as we left Machias. "Less chance of getting lost. And if we have to stop for the night, better chance of finding a decent place to stay." So instead of taking the scenic coastal route that passes through picturesque little towns, I drove inland to Route 9, which according to my map would take us to I-95 in Bangor.

The weather was warm, but not hot, and Stacey managed to find a radio station we could both agree on. We made it all the way to Bangor before Stacey turned down the volume on the radio and asked, "Why do you think Mayor Proctor arranged for the fairgrounds property to be rezoned so CIRR could build their mosque? Do you think he's a Muslim?"

"No, I don't think Billboard Bob is a Muslim," I answered, perhaps a bit too quickly. "I think he's a corrupt politician, and CIRR probably paid him off to do it."

Stacey didn't respond at first, leading me to believe she agreed with my assessment of Proctor's motivation. But as we passed over the Penobscot River, she said, "I don't disagree that Proctor is corrupt, but there's more to it than that. He's gone out of his way to praise Islam every chance he gets, he put a Muslim in charge of the town's Office of Diversity, and he's saddled the police department with all sorts of special rules when dealing with Muslims.

"What kind of special rules?" I asked.

"Well, for example, cops have to take off their shoes before entering the mosque, even if they're in pursuit of a suspect."

"He's sucking up to the Muslim community because he wants their votes," I said. "He does the same thing with every voting bloc. Proctor may be corrupt, but he's a shrewd politician." I genuinely believed that, but I nevertheless made a mental note to get more information about the supposed special rules from Sean McDermott, my high school buddy who's now a Troy Forge cop.

"We're in agreement that Proctor is both corrupt and shrewd," Stacey said. "But I still think it's more than that. He went out of his way at the mosque groundbreaking to repeatedly tell everyone that Islam is a religion of peace."

"What's wrong with that?" I asked.

"You don't need to spend a lot of time in a mosque to realize Islam's not a peaceful religion. It's a dangerous supremacist ideology that doesn't belong in Troy Forge, or anywhere in the country for that matter."

As we left Bangor behind us, my thoughts turned to Augusta, the state capital, where with any luck we might find part of the proof needed to undermine Bob Proctor's credibility. Stacey, however, wasn't ready to move on. "It's all Ted Kennedy's fault," she said.

Her comment, seemingly unrelated to anything we had been talking about, caught me off guard. "What does Kennedy have to do with the mosque in Troy Forge?"

"He was the sponsor of the Immigration and Nationality Act of 1965. Before Kennedy changed the law, America was primarily a nation of white, English speaking people of European ancestry who adhered to a Judeo-Christian worldview. Now we're a Third World, multicultural Tower of Babel."

The last I checked, the country's immigration system couldn't be changed by one man, but I wasn't about to get into an argument with Stacey. However, I had to concede she was right about how much the country had changed in the last few decades. When I was a kid growing up in Troy Forge, we had only two minority families in town, one black and one Asian, or Oriental as we called them back then. These days, when I go to the grocery store down the street from my office, I'm frequently the only English-speaking Caucasian in the building.

I turned up the volume on the radio as the DJ announced the next of the top one hundred songs of 1992, Eric Clapton's *Tears in Heaven*. We drove in silence for the next ninety minutes, listening to music and, at least in my case, wondering why Machias Phelps had left a stack of yearbooks, an old tax return, and a birth certificate in his aunt's garage.

Clouds rolled in and the wind picked up as we got off the Interstate onto U.S. Route 202 in Augusta. We eventually came to a traffic circle, which in New England is referred to as a rotary, dodged vehicles driven by people who couldn't figure out who had the right of way, and ended up on Grove Street, which turned into Water Street after a bend to the left. We found the Vital Records office on our left, parked the car and went inside.

We waited in a line that was surprisingly short by New Jersey standards, and within just a few minutes found ourselves face to face with a middle-aged woman with a nervous tic that made her wink as she talked to me. It's nice to know the Americans with Disabilities Act protects winkers. The next time a cute young thing objects to my winking at her, I can claim to be a member of a protected class.

I put the birth certificate we had found in the evil aunt's garage on the counter and slid it toward the winking woman of Vital Records. "Can you tell us if this is a genuine birth certificate?"

"I would hope so," she replied. "I've seen more birth certificates than I can count during the thirty years I've worked here." She held the document up to the light, apparently searching for something, but not explaining what. Then she laid it on the counter and ran her index finger over it. Next, she withdrew a book from a drawer beneath the counter, flipped to a particular page, and laid the birth certificate next to the open book, comparing the document we brought with us to an illustration in the book.

"Looks legit," she finally said. "But that's not a guarantee. If you want to be certain, you'll have to pay for a certified copy of the original vault document."

"You mean all I have to do is fork over the fee and you'll give me a certified copy of someone else's birth certificate?"

She looked at me as though I had asked her if the sun rose in the east. "Why wouldn't I?"

"Because it's someone else's birth certificate," I said. "In New Jersey, where I live, you have to jump through hoops just to get a copy of your own birth certificate. Getting a copy of someone else's is darned near impossible."

"That's New Jersey," she said, "and this is Maine. We're an open records state, like Vermont, Massachusetts, Minnesota, and a few others. In an open records state, public records are just that, public. That means they're open to the public." She shrugged her shoulders and helpfully added, "And you're a member of the public, aren't you?"

I paid the fee, and ten minutes later Stacey and I were on our way back to New Jersey with a genuine, official, certified copy of a birth certificate for Robert Proctor.

12

"I will consult with my client and get back to you."

When I got back from Maine, I turned my attention to Eddie Rizzo's personal injury case, determined to find out what was really going on with Mohammed Salameh and his oddball attorney. The first thing I did was arrange for Obduhali to bring both his client and his client's van - the correct one this time - to my office. Thinking Eddie might have been right about Salameh stalling until he had the van repaired, I arranged for one of my clients who runs a nearby body shop to stand by so he could point out any recent repairs. Salameh had a right to repair the van, of course, but he and his attorney couldn't conceal the work. If they did, I'd have more bargaining leverage, and the proposed fifty thousand dollar settlement, despite being ridiculously high, could grow even higher.

Eddie arrived as I was finishing my tuna on rye. Together we walked to Rick's office, which overlooks the parking lot behind our building. It was a few minutes before twelve o'clock, and Obduhali had promised to arrive promptly at noon. During the ten minutes we waited for Obduhali and his client Eddie told me more than I wanted to know about some television show involving a sheriff named Harry Truman. "And the cops are always eating donuts," he was saying as a white van entered the parking lot and pulled into one of the empty spaces next to the building. A man dressed in an ill-fitting grey suit got out of the passenger's side of the vehicle. A moment later a shorter man got out of the driver's side.

The taller of the two men was Omar Obduhali. I had no idea who the second man was, but I assumed he was Mohammed Salameh until Eddie said, "That ain't the guy that hit me," adding, "That guy ain't even an Arab."

"Yes, I think you're right," I agreed. "He looks Indian."

Eddie seemed confused by my identification. "An Indian? Like cowboys and Indians?"

"No, Indian as in someone from India."

Eddie laughed. "That ain't no Indian. That's a Paki. Indian's got dots on their forehead, Pakis don't. Other than that, they look the same."

I didn't know whether to laugh or be appalled, so I did nothing. Not that anything I said or did would have changed Eddie the Skunk's worldview.

We made our way to the parking lot where Omar Obduhali, wearing the same fake smile he had displayed at the garage in Jersey City, greeted us with outstretched hand as Eddie and I approached. "It is a pleasure to see you again, my friend."

I was in no mood for pleasantries. "Where's your client?"

"Oh, it is such a tragedy, my friend." Obduhali said, a bit too dramatically I thought.

"What are you talking about?"

"My Salameh's brother is very sick and he had to go to Michigan to take care of him."

"How convenient," I said. "When will he be back?"

"That I do not know," Obduhali said, "but as soon as he returns, I will bring him to your office for a deposition." He turned toward the van and pointed. "But, as promised, here is the van my client was driving the day of the accident."

"That ain't the right van," Eddie said.

Obduhali seemed offended. "Oh, yes, I am assured that this is the correct vehicle."

"No, it ain't," Eddie insisted. "The van that hit me was..."

"Hold on," I said, before Eddie could supply any details. "Mr. Rizzo and I would like to take a closer look at the vehicle." Obduhali probably thought I intended to convince Eddie he was wrong, because he said, "Of course, of course. Please take your time." What I really wanted was to stop Eddie from providing our adversary with details. One of the keys to winning in court is to always know more than the other guy.

When we were on the far side of the van, out of earshot, Eddie said, "Counselor, I'm tellin' you this ain't the van that hit me."

"I believe you, but I didn't want you to say too much. The less the other attorney knows, the better."

"Got it," Eddie said. To his credit, Eddie the Skunk is one of those clients who will usually follow the advice he pays for. Usually, but not always.

We worked our way around the vehicle and came back to where Salameh's attorney was standing. "This is definitely the wrong van," I said to him. "I consented to an extension of time for you to file your answer to the complaint on the understanding that you would produce both your client for a deposition and the vehicle he was driving. This is now the second time you failed to make your client available and to produce the vehicle."

"I am very sorry," Obduhali said. "I am sure this is all just a misunderstanding. He removed a rectangular object from his briefcase that I recognized as a smaller version of the portable phone Harvey Berkowitz had let me use four years earlier during his tax fraud trial in Newark. "I will consult with my client and get to the bottom of this," Obduhali assured me as he walked far enough away that we could hear him talking, but couldn't tell what he was saying. He returned a few minutes later and said, "You are quite right, my friend. I am deeply embarrassed and offer you my most sincere apologies. Before leaving for Michigan, my client left instructions for one of his assistants to bring the vehicle to my office, but the assistant brought the wrong van." So now the supposedly poor handyman had multiple assistants, as well as multiple vans. The case just kept getting more and more curious.

"Look, counselor," I said, "you keep telling me you and your client want to resolve this case. If that's true, this is the wrong way to go about it. This is the second time you've produced the wrong vehicle. The first time might be a mistake, but the second time? And this is the second time your client was a no show."

"I assure you, my friend," Obduhali said, "that Mr. Salameh would like to resolve this matter as quickly as possible. Tell me how much you and your client believe is fair and I will see what I can do."

Eddie touched my elbow and cocked his head to indicate he wanted a private word. We moved several yards away, and when we were out of Obduhali's hearing, Eddie said, "So why don't we toss out a number and see if they go for it?"

I had an ethical obligation to tell Eddie that the other side had already offered fifty thousand dollars. I also had an obligation to tell him that fifty grand was more than fair in view of the fact that the only real injury he sustained was to his ego. But while I was trying to figure out a diplomatic way to explain that, Eddie said, "Tell him I want his scumbag client to pay me five hundred thousand."

"They've offered fifty thousand," I said.

I expected Eddie to ask why I hadn't already told him about that offer, but instead, he said, "Not enough. Not even close.

Remember, D'Amico said I got serious permanent injuries. He'll testify to that."

It was unclear whether Eddie had an unrealistic expectation of what his case was worth, a common problem with clients who watch too many lawyer shows on television, or whether he simply wanted to inflict as much financial punishment as he could on the "scumbag" he despised. Or perhaps he thought demanding half a million dollars for a minor fender bender was a good negotiating strategy. "That's kind of high," I told him. "In my experience making a demand like that more often than not ends negotiations."

"Counselor, "I got serious permanent injuries," Eddie replied, once again using the language of the no-fault law that allows an injured motorist to collect for pain and suffering. Dr. D'Amico had done an excellent job of coaching his patient. And the fact that he had apparently done it without even examining Eddie made it even more remarkable.

"How about we ask for two hundred thousand," I suggested.

"Not enough," Eddie shot back.

"Okay, then, three hundred."

Eddie was adamant. "No, five." His tone of voice made it clear that was the end of the discussion.

I was reasonably certain demanding half a million dollars for a fender bender would end any discussion of a settlement, at least for today. But maybe that was just as well. There was something troubling about this case, and although it would be nice to settle quickly and collect my percentage, I was curious to find out what was going on with Salameh and his attorney. So to buy time as well as to placate Eddie, I walked back to where Obduhali was standing and, fighting to keep a straight face, said, "I think we might be able to put this case to rest for five hundred thousand."

I assumed Obduhali would laugh off my demand, but to my surprise, he said, "I will consult with my client and get back to you." Either my adversary was the kind of attorney who felt he had an obligation to present outlandish offers to his clients or Salameh was a "poor handyman" with exceptionally deep pockets.

13

"These people don't kid around."

Igave Obduhali a week to bring me the correct vehicle, but he never did, so I filed a formal demand to produce the van under Civil Procedure Rule 4:18. Emerson Lambert had gotten away with ignoring my Rule 4:18 demand to produce zoning documents, but Obduhali wouldn't. In my cover letter, I made it clear that if he failed to produce the van and make his client available for a deposition, I would file a motion to compel his cooperation.

Five days later, Carolyn, my secretary, walked into my office waving a letter. "You got a response from Salameh's attorney to your demand to produce the van in the Rizzo case," she said, "and you're not going to believe it."

I quickly scanned the letter she handed me. It was written in the same overly friendly, stilted style Obduhali used when speaking. My adversary was very sorry that I was so upset that I considered it necessary to file a formal demand, but "perplexed" why I did it since he had "already produced the vehicle in question." It was an incredibly brazen move, even by my standards.

"He doesn't even mention his client's deposition," Carolyn pointed out.

"This case is just plain bizarre," I said.

"Having Eddie Rizzo as a plaintiff instead of a defendant is just as bizarre," she replied.

I laughed. "True, but the defendant's attorney is in a category all by himself. The guy offers to settle a fender bender for fifty thousand dollars without even asking for a medical report, and then won't produce the vehicle his client was driving."

I called Obduhali several times that day, but each time his secretary informed me, in heavily accented English, that her boss was on another line, in conference with a client, or otherwise unavailable. Each time she assured me that he would return my call, but he never did. So, after polishing off a tuna on rye for lunch, I drafted a motion to compel discovery and had just handed it to Carolyn when Eddie the Skunk called.

"Counselor," Eddie said, "I got a guy who can get the dirtbag's van for us."

"No, Eddie," I replied. "Tainted evidence won't do us any good. It's inadmissible in court."

"Hey, it won't be tainted," Eddie said. "My guy'll wear gloves."

"That's not the point. I'd still have to explain to the judge how we got the van."

"No, no," Eddie said. "You don't understand. I'm not talking about taking the van, just pictures of the van. My guy takes pictures and gets out before anyone knows he was even there."

I spent the next five minutes explaining why Eddie's plan not only wouldn't work, but could make things worse. Then I turned my attention to Stacey's defamation case. Her tightfisted boss had refused to allow me to file a counterclaim against the Council for Islamic Religious Respect, arguing that it would simply run up the *Ledger's* legal costs and, besides, he insisted the paper should easily win the defamation case. "CIRR and Proctor are both public figures, so under *Sullivan* they have to prove actual malice," he told me at every opportunity. I tried, without success, to explain that legal theories go right out the window as soon as unpredictable human jurors are factored into the equation.

Fortunately, a jury might never hear the most explosive testimony, thanks to Judge MacAndrew's somewhat unusual ruling on Barahi's motion and my cross-motion. But to prevail at the hearing the judge had scheduled, I would need the testimony of Dr. Daniel Stern, the expensive expert who was scheduled to arrive at my office within the hour.

While waiting for Dr. Stern, I reviewed Judge MacAndrew's ruling. It was much longer than the typical order in response to a motion, as scholarly as a law review article and extensively footnoted with case citations going back to the 19th century. The judge had agreed with my argument that under New Jersey law it was impossible to defame a belief system such as Islam. However, relying on a Law Division case from the 1960s, he ruled that because Stacey's articles dealt with one particular mosque built by CIRR, defaming Islam could reasonably be regarded as tantamount to defaming CIRR. He then cited a long line of cases for the well-settled proposition that truth is an absolute defense to defamation, and ordered an evidentiary hearing to determine whether Stacey's statements about Islam were truthful. If he decided they were, he would dismiss the second count of the complaint and we'd go to trial on just the first count. Stacey's boss wasn't happy about this arrangement, correctly assuming it would increase the newspaper's legal fees. He calmed down a bit, however, when I explained that if we succeeded in convincing the judge, we wouldn't have to litigate the defamation of Islam issue in front of a jury that might contain one or more Muslims.

I had just finished reading the case Judge MacAndrew had cited in footnote 52 of his order when Carolyn appeared at my door with a stocky, bearded gentlemen in a blue suit who I recognized from photos as Dr. Daniel Stern.

"A pleasure to meet you in person," I said as I came around the desk to shake hands. "Glad you could make it."

"I almost didn't," Dr. Stern said. "Had to make some changes to my itinerary in response to a new threat, and almost missed my plane."

"A new threat?"

"I get death threats from Islamic groups all the time," he said. "Most never lead to anything, but a few over the years have turned out to be serious enough to get the FBI involved." He settled into one of the chairs on the other side of my desk, leaned back and crossed his legs. "Don't be surprised if you get threats before this lawsuit you're involved in is over. The Council for Islamic Religious Respect is notorious for that sort of thing."

"Tell me about CIRR," I said.

"They're a front group for the Muslim Brotherhood, an organization devoted to seeing Islam rule every country on earth. I don't know how much you and your clients know about the Brotherhood, but Miss McCain is one of the few journalists I've come across who seems to understand what Islam is all about," Dr. Stern said.

"And what's that?" I asked.

"In a word, supremacy. The ultimate goal of Islam is to bring the entire world under Muslim rule and impose sharia or Islamic law. I jotted "sharia" on my legal pad as a reminder to do additional research. Sharia law wasn't covered in any law school course that I could remember, even the ones I actually attended.

"Imposing Islam on the entire world sounds like a pretty tall order," I said.

"True, which is why most people dismiss it as pure nonsense. Unfortunately, politicians and military men think in terms of wars fought with guns. And while Islam had been spread through armed conquest in the past, these days it's being spread through *al-hijra*, or the Islamic doctrine of immigration. There's a passage in sura four of the Qur'an that says Muslims who leave their home to spread Islam will find abundance, and if they die, they'll be rewarded in the afterlife."

"What's a sura?" I asked.

"It means chapter," Dr. Stern replied. When we quote the Bible, we refer to chapter and verse. When we quote the Qur'an, we refer to sura and verse.

"We've always had immigrants," I pointed out. "The country was built on immigration."

"True, but past immigrants assimilated. They learned English, learned our history and our customs, and made an effort to become Americans. Muslim immigrants don't assimilate. They stay to themselves and form their own country within a country. The process is just getting started here in the U.S., but it's well underway in Europe. Once their numbers reach a critical mass, they play the victim card and start demanding equal rights, which are really special rights."

His comments reminded me of the discussion Stacey and I had on our trip to Maine. I made a mental note to talk to Sean McDermott, my buddy on the Troy Forge police force about the special rules Mayor Proctor had supposedly put in place for dealing with Muslims at the new mosque.

Dr. Stern's comments about Islam were interesting, but I decided it was time to discuss what I needed from him in the way of testimony. However, before I could steer the conversation in that direction, he said, "Of course, for purposes of your trial, we need to focus on CIRR and its tactics, not on individual Muslims, who range from the extremely devout to the ones who are Muslim simply because their parents were Muslim. We don't want to paint with a broad brush and end up alienating any Muslim jurors."

"Actually, that won't be a problem," I said. "We'll be arguing this in front of a judge at a hearing rather than at a jury trial. And the judge is pretty fair-minded. He'll make a decision based on the testimony presented rather than his own pre-conceived notions."

"That makes things easier," Dr. Stern said, reaching into his briefcase and withdrawing a copy of the complaint CIRR had filed. "Allow me to make a suggestion, if I may. I don't want to tell you how to handle your case, but based on my experience with CIRR, I think the first thing you need to do is make them cite specific things your client published that they contend are defamatory. That way I can refute each specific allegation instead of getting involved in an open-ended discussion about Islam. I've seen these guys operate, and, believe me, they've mastered the art of obfuscation. If you don't nail them down, they'll use a trial or a hearing to glorify Islam and vilify your client in the process. One of their favorite tactics is to tell juries that the word Islam means peace, and that people who oppose Islam are against peace. In reality, of course, Islam means submission, not peace."

"Already done," I said. "I included a demand for specifics in my first set of interrogatories, which will be served on CIRR within the week."

"And then you'll wait for a response," Dr. Stern said. "And wait and wait and wait."

"Then I'll file a motion to compel discovery," I said.

"Yes, which will cost your clients money and delay things even more. Then CIRR will provide answers that don't really answer your questions, forcing you to file another motion. I've seen how these groups operate. They engage in what some people refer to as lawfare, using the law to wage war against anyone who stands up to them. They hope you'll eventually decide it's cheaper to settle the case than continue to fight them in court."

"Not going to happen," I assured him.

"No, I'm sure it won't because of your relationship with Miss McCain. That's one of the reasons I agreed to consult with you on this case. Unfortunately, most defendants end up settling for what seems like a reasonable amount of money. But every time that happens, it sets a precedent that slowly whittles away our right to free speech."

For the next hour Dr. Stern provided me with a surprisingly comprehensive - and disturbing - overview of Islam and its legal system. I was impressed by the fact that his understanding of Islam came from reading, in the original Arabic, the books that Muslims themselves consider authoritative. He had just finished explaining why Christians and Jews are referred to as *dhimmis* under Islamic law when he looked at his watch and said, "I'm afraid we'll have to wrap things up. I have a flight to catch." As he was re-filling his briefcase he said, "I hope you took me seriously when I told you to expect threats. These people don't kid around."

14

"This stuff ain't stolen, just borrowed."

I had a sense of being followed shortly after turning onto the main boulevard in Mountain Springs that leads to Route 46, the highway that would take me east to my office in Troy Forge. I didn't actually see anything suspicious. There was no mysterious black sedan following at a discrete distance, occasionally changing lanes in an attempt to remain inconspicuous. It was just that feeling I sometimes get that something isn't quite right. Or perhaps I was just thinking too much about Stern's warning to watch my back.

Despite that creepy feeling, my drive to the office was uneventful, though much slower than usual because of the weather. We had received a light dusting of snow the previous evening, the first sign that winter would soon enshroud northern New Jersey in grey skies and frigid temperatures. I hate winter. Everything bad that's happened in my life has taken place in the chill of winter. Aimee, my late wife, was murdered the day before Thanksgiving. My grandfather keeled over while putting up Christmas decorations, and my parents were killed in an auto accident on their way to a ski resort. Some day I'll make good on my threat to move someplace where winter skies are blue instead of a somber, forbidding grey.

I'm not the only one who's adversely affected by winter. Though he seems to be doing much better this year, Rick's "episodes" as we call them at the firm seem to become more frequent and to last longer during the short, dark days of winter.

So I wasn't overly surprised when I got to the office and found Rick seated on the sofa in the waiting room with the school yearbooks we had brought back from Maine spread out on the table in front of him. He was going through each book, pointing to the children in a class photo and reciting in singsong fashion, "Fat girl, skinny boy with glasses, tall girl, cute little blond, Phelps, athletic kid, future beauty queen, science fair winner..." There must have been at least a dozen different descriptions. I was impressed by Rick's ability to repeat the list verbatim as he went through one yearbook after another, but dismayed that this behavior might be a sign that his recent improvement was only temporary.

Instead of asking Rick what he was doing, I sat quietly, observing his behavior and allowing things to play out, just in case there was some method to his madness. He eventually stopped his imitation of an old Armour hotdog jingle, stabbed the last yearbook in the stack with his finger and said, "The athletic kid is missing. He's in all the photos right up through ninth grade, usually standing next to Machias Phelps, but he's gone after that." Though I was relieved that my partner and mentor was apparently thinking clearly, I wasn't sure why a kid missing from a tenth grade class photo mattered until Rick explained. "The athletic kid is Bob Proctor."

"Then I guess that confirms that the Bob Proctor who worked at Dempsey's Dairy Delight with Machias Phelps in Maine is a different Bob Proctor, not our imperial mayor. Billboard Bob is anything but athletic."

"Maybe," Rick said. "It could all just be a coincidence, two different people with the same name. But why would Phelps have an old tax return for Bob Proctor? And why would he stash it away with a bunch of old yearbooks, and leave you the key to retrieve everything? If it's all just a coincidence, he went to an awful lot of trouble, perhaps even getting himself killed."

"Believe me, I'd like nothing better than to find out Billboard Bob was born in Maine, not the Pine Barrens of southern Jersey as he claims. That would destroy his credibility and make my defense of Stacey and the *Ledger* easier. Not to mention what it would do to his political career. But I need proof, not speculation."

"So, how do we get the proof?" Rick asked. "Get Tony Biffano to poke around the Pine Barrens?

"No, I think I've got a better way. Stacey's boss probably won't like it, but I think it's the way to go."

Before I could explain what I planned to do, Elaine, the firm's receptionist, walked through the glass entry doors of our suite. "You two are in early," she said, making a beeline for the coffee maker in the corner of the waiting room. "Remember to take your meds," she said to Rick, touching his arm as she passed us. He waved an acknowledgment, but didn't say anything. I not only wondered what medication Elaine was referring to, but how she knew about it. Elaine was Rick's secretary when he first opened his law office. Years later, after her arthritis made it difficult to type, she became the receptionist for what by that time had become a four attorney firm. Perhaps there was more to their relationship than I realized.

I didn't bother asking Rick what medication Elaine was referring to. It wasn't really any of my business and he probably wouldn't answer my question anyway. Instead, I said, "Would you call Stacey and tell her what you found in the photos?"

"Always happy to speak with the lovely Miss McCain," Rick said with a twinkle in his eye as he joined Elaine at the coffee maker.

I retreated to my office and began drafting a Rule 4:18 request for a copy of Bob Proctor's tax returns for the past two years. Emerson Lambert, Proctor's attorney, would most likely object, forcing me to file a motion to compel compliance, much to the annoyance of Stacey's budget-minded boss. But I had a good reason for wanting those documents.

I had just finished drafting the request when Carolyn, my secretary, entered my office. "Sorry to start your day on a sour note, but Eddie Rizzo is in the waiting room and he says he needs to see you right away. He says it's urgent."

"Everything is urgent with him," I said. I asked Carolyn to send Eddie in and to get me a cup of coffee, not necessarily in that order.

Eddie arrived before the coffee. He was carrying a cardboard filing box, which was apparently full, judging by the way he was holding it. "I got stuff we might be able to use against the fuckin' Arab that hit my car," Eddie said as he placed the box on my desk.

"What kind of stuff?" I wanted to know.

"Papers, records, stuff like that," Eddie replied. "I figure we might find something that tells us where he's hiding the van he was driving when he rammed me and wrecked my neck." We had apparently gone from "hit" to "rammed" in the blink of an eye and thrown in a "wrecked" neck for good measure.

"Where did you get this stuff?" I asked.

"From the dirtbag's apartment," Eddie replied, quickly adding, "I didn't get it, someone who owes me a favor had a friend of his get it for me."

"You mean someone stole it from Mohammed Salameh's apartment?"

"Nah, we didn't steal it," Eddie protested. "We're just borrowing it. I figure we get what we need, make copies maybe, and then put it all back. The dirtbag's gone for the day, so he'll never even know we borrowed it."

I didn't bother to ask how Eddie knew Salameh was gone for the day, assuming he had the so-called dirtbag under surveillance. I like clients who can help with their case, but what Eddie had done wasn't helpful. "There's no way the judge is going to let us use anything in that box at trial."

"Why not?" Eddie wanted to know.

"Because your friend's friend stole it, and judges have this incredibly unreasonable rule about not allowing stolen items to be introduced into evidence at trial."

My sarcasm was lost on Eddie. "Yeah, that is pretty unreasonable, but you'll find a way to do it," he said as he backpedalled to my office door. "You always do. Besides, like I said, this stuff ain't stolen, just borrowed. The dirtbag won't even know it's gone. I'll be back at three o'clock to pick it up and my friend will put everything back were it was." I assumed everything would find its way back to Salameh's apartment. Whether or not it would end up in its original location was another matter.

Eddie disappeared through the door just as Carolyn appeared with my cup of coffee. She was trying hard not to laugh. "You never know what to expect from that guy." She put the coffee on my desk and stood there with arms folded, waiting. "So, are you going to open it?" she asked, nodding toward the box.

"Might as well," I replied. "Too late now. The damage has already been done."

Carolyn and I spent the next two hours going through the contents of the box. Eddie's friend's friend must have vacuumed up every piece of paper in Salameh's apartment, including a bunch of unpaid bills and the instruction manual for a toaster oven. The only thing out of the ordinary was what looked like a memo written in squiggly lines and seemingly random dots that I guessed was Arabic. Since I can't read Arabic, or any language other than English for that matter, I had Carolyn make two copies, put one in Eddie Rizzo's file and send the other to Dr. Stern with a request that he translate it into English. At the time I couldn't have imagined how useful that memo would turn out to be.

15

"Bob Proctor is dead."

As I expected, Emerson Lambert objected to turning over copies of Proctor's tax returns, forcing me to file a motion to compel discovery. I had just arrived at the courthouse in Morristown to argue that motion when my pager chirped. Carolyn, my secretary, needed me to call her ASAP. I went to the bank of pay phones just inside the entrance and called the office.

"Stacey needs you to call her right away," Carolyn said when I got her on the line. "She says it's important." Stacey knew I was in court that morning, so she wouldn't have called unless it really was important. And very few things qualified as important with Stacey, unlike Eddie the Skunk for whom everything was either important or urgent.

I called Stacey and she picked up on the first ring. She skipped the preliminaries and began the conversation with, "Bob Proctor is dead." Just as Stacey was delivering that unexpected news, Emerson Lambert entered the courthouse. I waved him over.

"At the risk of speaking ill of the dead, it couldn't have happened to a nicer guy," I said to Stacey as Lambert made his way through the throng of attorneys and litigants in the lobby. "As a general rule, dead people can't maintain a defamation claim, so you may have gotten rid of one plaintiff. I'll have to do some research to be a hundred percent certain, but I think you're in the clear as far as Billboard Bob is concerned."

"No, Brendan," Stacey said, "I'm not talking about Billboard Bob. I'm talking about the Bob Proctor who worked with Machias Phelps at the ice cream place in Maine. He died in an auto accident the summer before his sophomore year in high school."

"That would explain why he didn't appear in his tenth grade yearbook photo," I said.

By this time Emerson Lambert had arrived by my side. Since I no longer had news about his client, and there was no reason for him to know about Billboard Bob's namesake, I said, "I have to finish this call, but I'll be ready to go in a couple minutes. Sorry for any delay."

Always the gentleman, Lambert said, "Take your time. I'll see you in the courtroom." Then he walked away.

As soon as he was out of hearing range, I asked Stacey, "How do you know the other Proctor died?"

"I called Thomas, the guy we met when we had breakfast in Machias. He seems to know everybody who ever lived in that town. According to him, Proctor was riding in a car with two older boys when the driver lost control and hit a tree. The driver and Proctor, who was sitting in the front seat, were both killed. The third kid ended up in the hospital."

"That was a long time ago," I pointed out. "Are you sure Thomas is right?"

"I called someone I know at the newspaper in Augusta. He went to the records office, got a copy of the death certificate and faxed it to me. I've got it right in front of me. The Bob Proctor that Phelps knew in Maine is dead. No question about it."

Now I only had one reason for getting a copy of Billboard Bob's tax returns. If our imperial mayor had been bribed to re-zone the fairgrounds property, it was unlikely he would have reported the income on his tax return. But if he had received consulting fees or some other type of seemingly legitimate income instead of a briefcase filled with cash, there was an outside chance he reported it to avoid a problem with the IRS. It was a long shot, but I had come this far, so when I finished my conversation with Stacey, I made my way to Judge MacAndrew's courtroom.

When I entered the courtroom, the judge was hearing arguments on a motion that had something to do with a boundary dispute. I took a seat next to Emerson Lambert and whispered, "Any idea where we are on the docket?"

"Next," he said. "You finished your call just in time."

The exciting drama of a misplaced fence continued for another five minutes, at which point the judge announced that he had heard enough and told the attorneys he would rule on the motion the following week. Then it was our turn to be heard.

We did the judge's patented "good-morning-counselors-good-morning-Your-Honor" routine, with Lambert and I delivering our line on cue, unlike the hapless Tinoo Barahi. Then I began my argument. "I'm requesting the court to instruct Mr. Proctor to turn over his tax returns for the last two years."

"Yes," that's evident from your moving papers," Judge MacAndrew said. "Why do you need them?"

"It's our contention that Mayor Proctor arranged for the so-called fairgrounds property to be re-zoned so CIRR could build a mosque. We need the tax returns to find out if he received anything of value for doing that."

"That assumes, first, that he received some sort of remuneration, and, second, that he reported it on his tax return," the judge pointed out. "Do you have a good faith basis for believing he received anything?"

Emerson Lambert answered the question for me. "No, this is another one of Mr. O'Brian's fishing expeditions."

"How do we know what's on those tax returns if we can't see them?" I responded.

"I can represent to the court that Mr. Proctor's tax returns for the years in question show only his salary as Mayor of Troy Forge, dividends from a few hundred shares of stock, and interest on a CD at a local bank."

"Mr. O'Brian," Judge MacAndrew said, "response?"

"I can represent to the court that the statements in the newspaper articles my clients published aren't defamatory."

The judge tried hard not to smile, but didn't succeed. "Point taken, Mr. O'Brian."

"My client has a right to privacy, especially when we're talking about something as personal as his tax returns," Lambert insisted. "After all, my client is the aggrieved party. Making him turn over his tax returns is rubbing salt in the wound."

"And my clients are being sued for a substantial sum of money. They have the right to use the discovery process to obtain the information needed to defend themselves."

"I'm all in favor of broad discovery," the judge said, "but Mr. Lambert does raise a valid point about his client's right to privacy."

"Nobody but me will see his client's tax returns. It's not as though they're going to be made available to the public," I argued.

"Judge, his clients are a newspaper and a newspaper reporter. Giving copies of my client's tax returns to Mr. O'Brian is tantamount to telling the whole world."

Judge MacAndrew held up his hand to signal he had heard enough. "Here's what we'll do. Mr. Lambert will turn over the tax returns to me, and Mr. O'Brian will review them in my chambers. He won't receive copies, he won't be permitted to take notes, and he won't be able to use them in open court unless he can convince me they're essential to his case."

Lambert and I vacated the counsel tables to make way for another set of supplicants on the assembly line of justice. As we headed for the courtroom exit, I tried to figure out the best way to explain the morning's proceedings to Stacey's boss, who would certainly feel I had wasted the *Ledger's* money. At the time, neither of us could have realized that we had just won a resounding victory.

16

"I hate motions to compel discovery."

The uneasy feeling of being followed continued to haunt me. I never actually saw anyone, was never confronted, and had no tangible evidence that I was under surveillance. It was just a creepy feeling that I couldn't shake. The only time I didn't feel that way was when Stacey and I went to Antigua the week after Christmas.

A few days after our return from that getaway I was reviewing the file for *Rizzo v. Salameh* in preparation for the motion hearing scheduled for later that morning when Stacey entered the living room after having spent the last half hour turning my bathroom into a steam room. She was wrapped in a towel with a second, smaller towel on her head. That was one towel too many, but before I could rectify the situation, she pointed to the driver's license photo of Mohammed Salameh laying on top of the paperwork spread out on the coffee table in front of me. "I've think I've seen him at the mosque." She picked up the photo and examined it. "Wait a minute," she said before rushing up the stairs to the second floor.

Stacey returned a moment later carrying a file folder, which she opened to reveal a stack of photographs. She leafed through them until she found the one she was looking for, which she placed on the table next to the photo of Mohammed Salameh. "I thought he looked familiar," she said, pointing first to the photo she had just placed on the table, and then at the one Tony Biffano had gotten from his contact at the Department of Motor Vehicles.

The photo showed five men standing in what appeared to be a large room with a rack of shoes in the background. I recognized Salameh immediately, along with one other person.

I took the file folder from Stacey. "How did you manage to take all these photos?"

"You'd be amazed how much you can hide under a *burqa*," she replied, referring to the head-to-toe garment worn by some Muslim women.

"Can you make me copies of these *burqa* shots?" I asked, coining what I considered a catchy term for Stacey's photos.

"You can keep them," she said. "I have the negatives locked away. I can make additional copies of the ones I need."

I pointed to the two photos on the coffee table. "What can you tell me about this Salameh character?"

"Not much," Stacey said, "except that he seems to be in tight with the bunch running things at the mosque."

"I don't suppose you ever heard him say anything about a fender bender."

Stacey laughed. "I never got close enough to hear him say anything. Women sit in the back of the mosque and men sit in the front. The only thing I ever hear is the imam's harangues and some small talk as people enter and leave." Stacey spent the next ten minutes recounting some of the imam's more frightening, but amusing, sermons before retreating to the bathroom to dry her hair.

She was still drying away when it was time for me to leave. "I'll call you when I get back from Jersey City," I said through the bathroom door. I thought she said, "Fine, talk to you later," or something to that effect, but I couldn't really be certain, the drone of the hair dryer making her words semi-intelligible.

I followed my regular route: down the long, tree-lined boulevard to Route 46, then east toward Troy Forge where I picked up a series of highways that eventually dumped me out on local roads in Jersey City, the county seat of Hudson County. I had the sense of being followed as I had on previous trips, but again, never actually saw anyone, and was never confronted.

Though Jersey City, like many of New Jersey's urban centers, is a shadow of its former self, it boasts what many consider one of the most beautiful courthouses in the Garden State. Constructed in the Beaux-Arts style in the early years of the twentieth century, it fell into disuse in the 1960s, only to be restored to its former glory the following decade.

I parked my Mustang, entered the courthouse from Newark Avenue and walked up the steps to the marble floored rotunda. I've been here many times, but each time I find some little detail that I missed on previous occasions. Today it was the paintings of the symbols of the zodiac encircling the glass dome. The building's grandeur never fails to bring a smile to my face.

My enjoyment abruptly ended when I entered the courtroom of Judge Latisha Washington, an overweight, ill-tempered black woman who hated white people in general, white men in particular, and white male attorneys with a level of animosity that, in a sane world, would have disqualified her as a Superior Court judge.

I was standing in the back of the room, looking for a place to sit, when I spotted Omar Obduhali clambering over other people seated in the back row. "Good morning, my friend," he said as he approached with an outstretched hand and a big smile. As we shook hands – unenthusiastically on my part – he held out a sheaf of papers in his other hand. "This is for you," he said, returning to his seat without another word. I settled into a seat next to a woman in a colorful outfit that would have been more appropriate at Woodstock than in a courtroom, and unfolded the papers Obduhali had just handed me. It was his long over-due answer to the complaint I had filed against his client.

Before I could read the answer, our case was called and we took our places at the counsel tables before Judge Washington. We began not with a "good morning your Honor" routine as in Judge MacAndrew's courtroom, but with Judge Washington wanting to know, "Mr. O'Brian, why are you wasting my time with this motion?"

I've dealt with antagonistic judges before, but never one who assumed I was wasting the court's time before I had said a single word. "Your Honor," I began, "this motion to compel discovery is..."

"I hate motions to compel discovery," the judge said, cutting me off in mid-sentence. "You're not children having a school-yard squabble. You're adults, attorneys. You should be able to settle these kinds of things without running to me."

"I wish that were the case," I said, "but I've been unable to secure Mr. Obduhali's voluntary cooperation." I started to explain how Obduhali had produced the wrong vehicle on two separate occasions.

"Hold on," the judge said, raising one hand like a traffic cop while holding a document in the other hand. I waited while she scanned the document. She flipped to the second page and continued reading. I noted that my adversary was standing with arms crossed, a wide grin on his face that reminded me of Bob Proctor's crocodile smile. The judge finally stopped reading and looked right at me. "You obviously didn't bother to read the answer to the complaint. If you had, you'd realize why the defendant isn't able to produce the vehicle."

"I just got the answer this morning," I said.

"I'll take that to mean you haven't read it," Judge Washington said, "so let me read it for you." She began reading from the document she was holding: "Defendant denies being involved in a motor vehicle accident with plaintiff on the date set forth in the complaint, or at any other time. Defendant asserts that plaintiff is a known criminal who has been arrested on numerous occasions and has filed this complaint against defendant out of racial animus."

I was stunned. While the statements about Eddie Rizzo may have been true, they were wildly inappropriate in the answer to a complaint for personal injury. "I'm sure Your Honor will agree with me that those statements are highly inappropriate. I would ask the court to..."

Before I could finish, Judge Washington said, "It's rather presumptuous of you to think you know whether or not I would agree with you on this or any other matter."

I was starting to get really pissed, at both Obduhali and the judge. "Judge, I agreed to grant Mr. Obduhali additional time to file an answer in exchange for his promise to produce the correct vehicle."

"How can he produce a vehicle that collided with your client's vehicle if there was no collision?" the judge asked.

"I think you're missing the point here," I began, only to be cut off yet again.

"No, I think you negotiated a bad deal with your adversary and now you're expecting me to bail you out, which I'm not going to do. Motion denied."

"Your Honor," I began, "this is..."

Latisha Washington looked right at me and smiled. "I said, motion denied. Have a nice day, counselor." She turned to a court officer and asked, "What's next on my docket?"

"Your Honor," I said, "how about the other part of my motion, an order to make the defendant available for a deposition?"

"What part of 'motion denied' didn't you understand, Mr. O'Brian?"

I was really steamed at that point. "This is highly improper, Your Honor, and I think you know it. You're assuming statements in the defendant's answer are truthful and those in the plaintiff's complaint are false. You're making a determination that should be made by a jury at trial, not by the court at a motion hearing."

"Don't tell me how to run my court," the judge said.

"It's not your court," I shot back. "It belongs to the people of the State of New Jersey, and it should be run in accordance with the law, not your personal whims or animosities. The Rules of Civil Procedure give me the right to depose the defendant and examine the vehicle he was driving the day of the accident."

"But there was no accident, my friend," Obduhali said.

"That's your version of events," I said. "My client says otherwise."

"And when the case comes to trial we'll all find out which version is correct," the judge said. "Now get out of my courtroom. I have a full docket this morning, and you're wasting my time with your frivolous motions." She made it a point to emphasize "my courtroom."

Before I could respond, Omar Obduhali picked up his expensive leather briefcase and made a beeline for the double doors at the back of the courtroom. I hurried after him, but he got to the elevator just before the door closed, leaving me standing there, feeling both angry and foolish. So much for playing by the rules.

I got to the ground floor in time to see Obduhali cross the street, apparently heading for the parking lot down the block where I had parked my Mustang. Just before reaching the sidewalk on the other side of the street, he called out to a man who appeared to be scanning the contents of a newsstand. The man turned around, and I could see it was Tinoo Barahi, the attorney representing the Council for Islamic Religious Respect. The two shook hands and laughed, then continued to the parking lot. I followed at a leisurely pace to ensure they wouldn't see me. I wanted to throttle Obduhali for his little stunt, but I didn't want him to know I had seen him with Barahi. One of the keys to success in the courtroom is never letting your adversary know how much you actually know.

When they reached the parking lot, Obduhali and Barahi got into a black Lincoln, which immediately backed out of the parking space and turned toward the exit. I got a good look at the driver. It was the Troy Forge cop I had nicknamed Scarface, Bob Proctor's personal bodyguard.

17

"You have an interesting caseload at the moment."

I arrived home that evening to find a dark colored sedan parked in the circular driveway in front of the house, and smoke coming from the chimney. Stacey and Rick were the only people who would conceivably be in my house in my absence, but Stacey was having dinner with her mother, and Rick was still at the office. I had no idea who was waiting inside, but reasoned that someone who meant me harm wouldn't advertise his presence. So instead of heading for a neighbor's house and calling 911, I parked behind the mystery sedan, opened the unlocked front door and went inside.

I passed through the entry hall into the living room where I found Reynaldo Renoir sitting in my favorite chair by the fireplace. Four years ago, Eddie the Skunk, mistakenly believing my wife had hired someone to kill me, arranged through a third party for Reynaldo to watch my back. I hadn't seen the officially deceased Navy-SEAL-turned-gun-for-hire since then.

"I started a fire to take the chill off," Reynaldo said nonchalantly, as though I shouldn't be surprised by his presence. "Hope you don't mind." As I settled into the other chair by the fireplace, Reynaldo said, "You have an interesting caseload at the moment."

"Meaning what?"

"You're defending the *Ledger* in the defamation case filed by the Council for Islamic Religious Respect. Understandable, since your girlfriend is the one who wrote those articles. But you also have a case involving Mohammed Salameh. Could be just a coincidence, or it could be that you know something we don't know."

"Who's 'we'," I wanted to know.

"Uncle Sam."

"Care to be more specific?"

"Above my pay grade," Reynaldo said, quickly adding, "and way above yours."

"Are you telling me you don't know who you're working for?"

"The person who recruited me for this assignment is someone I know from previous jobs."

"Then you must know the agency he represents."

Reynaldo laughed. "You'd think so. But each time he hired me, he told me he worked for a different agency."

"Then how do you know you're working for the government?" I asked.

"Because funds are wired into my bank account by the Treasury Department, and last I checked, Uncle Sam had enough trouble paying his own bills, much less paying someone else's."

Based on what I had just learned, I assumed that Reynaldo or one of his colleagues had been following me, hoping I would lead them to someone or something. But before I could confirm that, Reynaldo leaned forward, put his forearms on his knees and did something completely unexpected: he volunteered information.

"The government has been keeping an eye on CIRR for some time. We know they're a front group for the Muslim

Brotherhood, but we've never been able to convict them of anything."

"How do you know they're connected to the Muslim Brotherhood?"

The Justice Department won a case in Texas last year against another Brotherhood front group, thanks to a particularly diligent prosecutor named Shapiro. He managed to dig up a treasure trove of incriminating documents linking a bunch of seemingly unrelated organizations to the Brotherhood. CIRR was one of them." Reynaldo leaned back in his chair, looked at the ceiling and smiled, as though savoring a private joke. "Shapiro wore a yarmulke to court every day just to piss off the defendants and their attorney."

That was the end of what passed for levity. Reynaldo returned to business. "How much do you know about the Brotherhood?"

"Not much," I admitted. "Learned a little bit when I talked to Daniel Stern, the expert I brought in to consult on the case, but can't say I'm an expert."

"No, but Stern is," Reynaldo said. "One of the few people who really understands Islam and the organizations involved with it."

"You know him?"

"Not personally," Reynaldo said. "I was part of a protection detail when he spoke at the Geller Foundation in New York last year." Apparently Stern wasn't exaggerating about the death threats.

For the next half hour Reynaldo gave me a crash course on the Muslim Brotherhood and its worldwide web of front groups. He explained that although the Brotherhood was founded in Egypt, it now has an extensive network in the United States, consisting of non-profit organizations like CIRR, as well as traditional business corporations. According to Reynaldo, the

Brotherhood moves money between these groups, in the process circumventing a wide range of laws.

"We've long suspected them of money laundering and violation of the Foreign Agent Registration Act," Reynaldo said at one point, "but we've never been able to assemble enough solid evidence to get convictions. The case in Texas is the closest we've come. And the front group that was the defendant in that case was only a minor player."

"Based on what you're telling me, this sounds more like an organized crime syndicate than a religious group," I said.

"Don't let the kumbaya crowd in the State Department hear you say that or they'll brand you a bigot." His tone of voice led me to believe he was speaking from personal experience. "Okay, your turn," Reynaldo said, abruptly sending the conversation in a new direction. "What's the connection between Mohammed Salameh and CIRR? We know he attends the new mosque in Troy Forge, but not much else."

"Before this morning, I would have said there is no connection." I told him about the attorneys for CIRR and Salameh driving off in a car driven by Mayor Proctor's bodyguard.

"Interesting," Reynaldo said, using Stacey's favorite word.

"The only reason I'm involved with Salameh is because one of my long-time clients retained me to file a personal injury case against the guy."

"That would be Eddie Rizzo," Reynaldo said. "He's a real piece of work."

"You should know," I said. "You worked for him."

I thought I saw a flash of anger in Reynaldo's eyes, though his tone of voice never changed. "No way. I don't work for people like Rizzo."

"Who do you think hired you to watch my back four years ago?"

"It sure as hell wasn't Rizzo."

"No," I agreed, "but it was one of his associates who owed him a favor. Eddie may not have hired you, but you were working for him."

"Isn't that interesting," Reynaldo said as he got up to throw another log on the fire. His tone of voice led me to believe he wouldn't be having any future dealings with the person who had hired him for that assignment.

Reynaldo returned to the chair across from me and asked, "What else do you know about this Salameh character?"

"Not much," I replied. "According to his attorney, Salameh is supposed to be a poor handyman, but apparently he owns multiple trucks and has at least one employee. My investigator says there's no record of a business, no phone listing, no business license, nothing. All we know is Salameh immigrated here from Jordan a few years ago and has had a number of fender benders."

"That's it? That's all you know?" Renaldo seemed surprised that I didn't know more. Or perhaps he thought I was withholding information.

"If I learn anything else, I'll let you know. How can I reach you?"

Reynaldo didn't answer my question. Instead, he got up and crossed the room, stopping in front of an abstract painting called *Blowing In The Wind* that my late wife, Aimee, had purchased. "I've been authorized to tell you about the Muslim Brotherhood in exchange for information about Salameh," Reynaldo said. "I think you got the better end of that deal," he added as he reached behind the painting and removed a small black object, which he held up for me to see.

I walked to where he was standing to get a better look. "I haven't been authorized to tell you about this, however" Reynaldo said.

"What is it?"

"A listening device that picks up everything said in this room."

"You bugged my house!"

"Not us," Reynaldo replied. "Someone connected to the Muslim Brotherhood or one of their front groups."

"If it wasn't the people you work for, how did you know it was there?"

"You and your girlfriend were mentioned in a telephone conversation we intercepted with one of our wiretaps," Reynaldo said.

"Whose phone did you tap?" I didn't bother asking which government agency was doing the wiretapping, assuming Reynaldo wouldn't tell me, even if he knew.

As it turned out, he wouldn't even tell me whose phone calls they were monitoring. "Above your pay grade" was all he'd say.

I wasn't convinced. "If that thing was planted by the Muslim Brotherhood, that means they're hearing this conversation, and I doubt you'd want them to hear any of this. More likely, someone you work with is listening to all of this."

"Nobody is hearing anything," Reynaldo assured me, withdrawing a small object from the pocket of his tweed sport coat and holding it up for me to see. "I disconnected the power supply as soon as I found the device. I'll reconnect it before I leave so they won't know we're on to them."

"No, leave it off," I said. "I don't want anyone listening to my private conversations." I ran through a mental list of the things I wished I hadn't already said in this room.

"Can't do that," Reynaldo said. "We don't want them to know we found it. Besides, now that you know it's there, I have a feeling you'll figure out how to use it to your advantage." Before I could say another word, he snapped the two pieces together and tucked the device back behind the painting. Then he began walking toward the front door and motioned for me to follow.

We crossed the foyer, and went out to the porch. "Watch yourself with these guys," Reynaldo said over his shoulder as he walked down the steps. When he got to the bottom, he turned back to face me. "They'll extend the right hand in friendship, and stab you in the back with the left." Omar Obduhali immediately came to mind.

18

"I'm not big on rocket ships either."

After Reynaldo left, I drove to a local diner and used a pay phone to call Stacey. "Be careful," I warned her. "CIRR probably knows you've been to the mosque. Reynaldo thinks these people could be dangerous." Then I called my partners at home. I told them about the listening device and suggested we have Tony Biffano check our offices to ensure they weren't bugged. Everyone agreed, and Scott Woodson, who took over as senior partner a few years ago when Rick's condition worsened, said he'd make the arrangements.

When I arrived at the office shortly after eight o'clock the following morning, Tony was in the waiting room waving some sort of electronic wand. He held up one finger when he saw me, did a few more waves of the wand, and said, "Clean. Nothing here and nothing in any of the other rooms."

Relieved that we were apparently bug-free, I went to my office and began dialing the most recent phone number Eddie Rizzo had provided. His "investment" business apparently requires him to change phone numbers on a regular basis. I wasn't looking forward to his reaction when I told him about the answer Obduhali had filed in response to our complaint, but

I had an ethical obligation to keep him informed about his case. I was about to punch in the last number when Scott appeared at my office door. "Partners meeting in the conference room," he said. I hung up the phone, jotted a quick note for Carolyn, my secretary, to call Eddie and arrange an appointment for later that day, and followed Scott down the hall to the conference room.

Avery Glickman and Rick were already seated at the conference table when Scott and I arrived. Avery was reading a copy of the *Wall Street Journal* and Rick appeared to be scrutinizing the painting of the Ford Mansion that hangs on the conference room wall. Or perhaps he was off in a world of his own. Although his condition appears to have significantly improved in recent months, there are still times when he seems disconnected from reality.

Scott took his seat at the head of the table. "We have three items on the agenda this morning. Let's do the easy ones first." He nodded toward Avery, who slid an object toward each of us that I recognized as a smaller version of the mobile phone Omar Obduhali had used in our parking lot to call his client.

"Put it in your briefcase," Avery said, "and you can stay in touch with the office wherever you go."

I hefted the phone in my hand. "Carrying change for a pay phone would be easier. This thing weighs a ton."

"You can't always find a pay phone when you need one," Avery said. "And in the future, finding a pay phone will become even more difficult. In the long run cell phones will become the most economical way to stay in touch."

I wasn't thinking about economics; I was thinking about inconvenience. "And now clients will be able to call me at all hours of the day and night. How wonderful."

"The only people who will call you on this phone are people who know the number," Avery assured me. I wasn't convinced.

I made a mental note to give the damn thing to Stacey and tell her it was a belated Christmas present.

"Item two on our agenda," Scott said, "is particularly timely considering the listening device that was planted in Brendan's living room." He handed each of us a brochure for a seminar on law firm security scheduled for the end of February in Manhattan. "We can send two people. Any volunteers?"

"Not me," I said. "I've got a full calendar for the next couple months."

"Count me out," Rick said, studying the brochure. "That building has an express elevator that's like riding in a rocket ship. Last time I was there, I ended up on the fiftieth floor while my stomach was still at ground level."

Scott looked at Avery. "I guess that leaves you and me."

"I'm not big on rocket ships, either," Avery said, "but I'll go with you."

With the housekeeping matters concluded, we got down to the real reason for our meeting. "We've had blowback from cases over the years," Scott began, "but I think this is the first time we've had a partner's home bugged."

"Are you sure CIRR is the culprit?" Avery asked. "This is the sort of thing I could see Proctor doing."

"Good point," I said. I recounted my conversation with Reynaldo in as much detail as I could remember, concluding with: "He didn't tell me whose phone the government was tapping, but I got the distinct impression it was someone connected with the Muslim Brotherhood. Of course, according to Reynaldo, CIRR is one of their front groups, so it could have been someone from CIRR."

"And since CIRR and Proctor are both plaintiffs in the case against Miss McCain and the *Ledger*," Scott pointed out, "it's not inconceivable that one of Proctor's people planted the bug."

"The bottom line is, we just don't know," I said. "The real question is, how do we respond?"

"Well, for starters," Scott said, "I've got a locksmith coming this afternoon to change the locks and install a new security system."

"That's all well and good," I said, "but I'm tired of playing defense with these clowns. I'd like to go on offense and give them a dose of their own medicine." I told them about the answer Obduhali filed in Eddie Rizzo's personal injury case.

Rick was aghast that Obduhali had violated the first commandment of the legal profession: *Thou shalt not screw a fellow attorney.* "The guy offers to settle a fender bender for a briefcase filled with cash, without even requesting a medical report, asks for an extension of time to answer the complaint, and then files an answer denying the fender bender even took place?"

"The schmuck sandbagged you," Avery said.

"That's the about the size of it," I said. "And yesterday after the motion hearing in Jersey City, that schmuck met CIRR's attorney, who's also a schmuck, and the two rode away in a car driven by a member of Bob Proctor's personal palace guard."

"Maybe I'm missing something," Scott said, "but I can't see how Eddie Rizzo's personal injury case is related to CIRR's defamation case against the *Ledger.*"

"I don't think they are related," I said, "but the people involved with each case are another matter. There's something going on that we're missing. I just haven't been able to put the pieces together yet."

"So, what do you want to do about all this?" Avery asked.

"What I want to do is depose this Salameh character. I want this guy sitting across from me, face to face, in a small room where I can grill him for hours. I'm hoping I can get him to say something that will allow me to figure out what the hell is going on."

"And how do you propose to do that?" Scott asked. "From what you've told us, it's unlikely Judge Washington is going to force the guy to sit for a deposition."

"You could always appeal her order dismissing your motion," Avery suggested.

I couldn't help myself; I laughed at his suggestion. Avery's a great guy who's responsible for much of the firm's financial success, but he hasn't set foot in a courtroom in years. "Sorry," I said. "I don't mean to offend you, but an interlocutory appeal, an appeal before a case is finally decided, can take forever. I file a notice of motion for leave to appeal, Obduhali files a cross motion, Judge Washington schedules a hearing to reconsider her decision..."

"And at that hearing she comes up with another reason why you can't depose Salameh," Rick interjected.

"Exactly," I said. "By the time the Appellate Division gets the matter, it's July."

"And Judge Washington is even less likely to give you a fair shake when you eventually try the case in her courtroom," Rick added.

"So what's the solution?" Scott asked.

"I add Salameh to my witness list in the *Ledger's* defamation case and depose him as part of that case."

"Assuming you can find him," Rick said.

Scott pointed out another problem. "CIRR's attorney is almost guaranteed to object to questions that have nothing to do with that case."

"I'll sneak them in somehow," I said. "Frankly, I'm less concerned about CIRR's attorney than I am about Stacey's boss at the *Ledger*. He bitches and moans every time I do anything that costs money. He seems to think the case is a slam dunk, and we should just sit back and wait for the jury to rule in our favor. He won't even let me depose the inner circle running the mosque."

"If he's unwilling to foot the bill to depose them, it's unlikely he'll agree to pay for a deposition of Salameh," Scott pointed out.

"I'll pay for it myself, if I have to."

Avery, ever mindful of the firm's finances, suggested an alternative. "Stacey's boss must have a boss. Maybe we should be talking to him."

"I have a contact at the *Ledger*," Scott said. "He's high enough in the organization to countermand instructions from Stacey's boss, and he and I belong to the same country club." Scott buzzed his secretary on the intercom. "See if you can get through to Steve Porter at the Ledger Media Group," he instructed her. "Steve's their vice president and general counsel," he explained as we waited for his secretary to make the call.

A few minutes later a jovial voice boomed out from the conference call speaker Avery had positioned in the middle of the table. "Scott Woodson, are you still cheating at golf?"

"Careful, Steve," Scott warned, "you're on speaker and my partners are listening. One more word about my golf game and I'll tell the world about your fairway mulligans." The two laughed at the private joke and engaged in golf talk for what seemed like an hour, but was only a few minutes. Scott finally got around to the reason for our call. "My partners and I need to talk to you about this defamation case involving the Council for Islamic Religious Respect."

"What about it?" Porter asked.

"Your managing editor is second guessing our every move," Scott said. "We need the flexibility to try the case the right way."

We spent the next several minutes trying to persuade Mr. Porter, never actually mentioning my plan to depose Mohammed Salameh, but kept getting the same response: "It's a garden variety defamation case filed by public figures. Under *Sullivan*, there's no way they can win. You guys just want to run the meter."

We tried to convince him that we weren't trying to run up his company's legal bills, but needed to handle the case as we saw fit. The back and forth continued for a few more minutes until Porter terminated the conversation with an expression I'm used to hearing from judges: "I'll give you some latitude, but I'm going to keep you on a short leash."

I left the meeting feeling we were moving in the right direction, totally unaware that one of the decisions we had just made would have far-reaching consequences for our firm.

19

"As many as you need."

After the meeting, I prepared a subpoena for Mohammed Salameh to appear for a deposition and had Carolyn, my secretary, arrange for one of Tony Biffano's associates, whose fees are considerably lower than Tony's, to serve it on the elusive Mr. Salameh.

I spent the rest of the morning reading a book called *Reliance of the Traveler* that Dr. Stern had recommended. It was a modern translation of a fourteenth century text written in Arabic by Shihabuddin Abu al-'Abbas Ahmad ibn an-Naqib al-Misri. Subtitled "a classic manual of Islamic sacred law," Muslims regard it as an authoritative work covering pretty much every aspect of life.

Although Scott handles most of the firm's divorce cases, out of curiosity, I skimmed the chapter devoted to Islamic marriage law to see how it compared to the law in New Jersey. I discovered that under Islamic law, a husband can apparently divorce his wife simply by telling her, "I divorce you." And if someone asks him if he's married and he says no, that also results in a divorce. I'm guessing divorce lawyers in Muslims countries don't make a very good living.

I was just beginning the chapter entitled "Justice" when Carolyn entered the office to drop off the mail. She turned her head sideways to read the book's spine. "Ten bucks says you can't pronounce the author's name." A minute later she returned to her desk with an unplanned ten-dollar bonus.

Shortly after noon, I unwrapped the tuna on rye I had brought from home while learning why fasting Muslims are prohibited from using toothpaste. According to the learned Mr. al-Misri, toothpaste use at that time is *haram*, or prohibited, lest some of the paste find its way to the stomach. Apparently toothpaste is considered food in Muslim countries. That should come as good news to impoverished Muslim divorce lawyers, who can eat dinner and brush their teeth at the same time.

I had just finished the last bite of my sandwich when Carolyn buzzed to inform me that Eddie the Skunk was in the waiting room. It was a meeting I was dreading, but one I couldn't avoid.

Eddie sauntered in a moment later, dressed in his customary jeans and white polo shirt. He tossed his navy pea jacket on my sofa and settled into the chair across from my desk. "So, how did that thing in Jersey City go yesterday?" Eddie asked. I assumed he already knew the answer and was asking to see if my version of events matched the report from one of his associates who was most likely hiding in plain sight in the crowded courtroom.

I decided there was no point in sugar coating it. "I've got bad news and bad news. Which would you like to hear first?"

"Give me the bad news first," Eddie said. I wasn't sure whether he didn't get the lame joke or was playing along with it.

"The other driver's lawyer finally got around to filing his answer to the complaint. Apparently, he filed it right before yesterday's hearing and then gave me a copy the minute I walked into the courtroom."

"Don't sound kosher," Eddie said.

"It's not, not really, but it's consistent with court rules."

"So what's his answer say?" Eddie wanted to know.

"He denies the accident ever took place."

I thought the news would infuriate Eddie, but it didn't seem to disturb him at all. A moment later I discovered why. "No problem," he said. "All you gotta do is tell the judge they offered to settle for a bunch of cash. They wouldn't offer to settle if the accident didn't happen."

"It's not that simple," I said.

"Why not?"

"One of the rules of evidence, Rule 408 to be precise, says an offer to settle is inadmissible in court to prove liability."

"That's a stupid rule," Eddie said. "Like that other rule about us not being able to use any of the stuff we got from the scumbag's apartment."

Instead of pointing out that "we" hadn't broken into Mohammed Salameh's apartment, or explaining the reasoning behind Rule 408, I said, "I don't make the rules; I just have to follow them."

"So, what's this do to my case?" Eddie asked.

"Since there were no witnesses, it means you tell your version of events and Salameh tells his and we see who the jury believes."

"What do you mean no witnesses?" Eddie asked. "Why didn't you say we need witnesses? We got witnesses."

During our initial meeting Eddie had told me he was alone. Now that we needed witnesses, Eddie would most likely tell me he had an entire church choir in the back seat. "How many witnesses do you need?" he asked.

"How many do you have?"

"As many as you need," Eddie said as he checked his watch. Apparently he had a "business meeting" that was more important than his personal injury case. "So what's the other bad news?"

I hesitated, trying to figure out the best way to tell him that he had been called a common criminal in open court. Eddie saved me the trouble of answering his question, confirming my suspicion that one of his associates had been in the courtroom. "Don't sweat it, counselor, I know what the scumbag said about me. You take care of the fucker in court and I'll deal with him another way."

Eddie retrieved his navy pea jacket from the sofa and headed for the door. He was halfway across the room when I made the decision to ask for his help. "Can I ask you about something unrelated to your case?"

"Sure, counselor, what do you need?"

"What do you know about creating a new identity?" I asked as I leaned forward and rested my forearms on the desk.

"Don't worry, counselor, you won't have to get a new identity and skip town if you blow my case." I took that as a veiled warning until Eddie laughed and added, "Don't be so serious, counselor. I'm just kidding." I hoped he was just kidding. With Eddie the Skunk, you never really know. "There are two ways to do it," Eddie said as he resumed his seat across the desk from me. "The easy way is to buy fake ID. There are plenty of guys who'll sell you a fake driver's license or practically any kind of fake paperwork you want. Some of it looks like the real thing, but some looks like crap." Eddie shrugged his shoulders. "You get what you pay for."

"How does someone go about buying a fake ID?" I asked. "I assume you can't just look in the classified ads."

"It's like anything else," Eddie said. "You gotta know who to ask. Practically every town has someone who'll hook you up with a fake ID for the right price."

"Is there someone like that here in Troy Forge?" I asked, assuming that would be the source of Bob Proctor's phony credentials.

"Probably," Eddie said.

"Probably, but you don't know for sure?"

"I know a lot of people," Eddie said, "but it's not like I know everybody."

He seemed offended, so I decided to move on. "You said buying fake ID is the easy way. I assume that means there's a hard way?"

"Yeah," Eddie said. "It's called ghosting. You take over the identity of someone who died. This is the best way to go, if you do it right."

"How does ghosting work?" I wanted to know.

"First thing you gotta do," Eddie said, "is get the dead person's birth certificate. Tough to do here in Jersey, but easier in some other states." *Much easier*, I thought, recalling my conversation with the winking woman of Vital Records in Maine. "Once you have the stiff's birth certificate, you use that to get a driver's license, a replacement social security card, pretty much anything you want."

"You said ghosting works if you do it right. What do you mean by that?"

"You gotta use the identity of someone from another part of the country," Eddie explained. "That way there's less chance of running into somebody who knew the dead guy. So if you're living in, say, Jersey or Connecticut, you get the identity of someone from Alaska or Hawaii."

For the better part of an hour Eddie filled me in on the details of ghosting, taking great pains to assure me he was speaking hypothetically. "No one I know is involved with this kinda thing," he told me several times during the course of our conversation.

After Eddie left, I called Tony Biffano to verify what Eddie had told me. Although Biff approached the topic from the perspective of a former cop, rather than a "businessman" like Eddie Rizzo, his description of ghosting was very similar to Eddie's. "It can work for a surprisingly long time," he told me, "as long as someone else isn't using the same stolen identity." He recounted a story from his days as a cop in Paterson. "Guy goes into a bank to open an account and shows his ID. Turns out a wanted bank robber is using the same stolen identity. The bank contacts us and we pick the guy up. Irony is the guy was a law-abiding citizen, other than stealing someone else's identity."

Biff was on his third story from his days as a cop when I interrupted him. "So, the bottom line is, ghosting can work as long as someone else isn't using the same stolen identity, right?"

"Yeah, it can work," Biff said. "At least for now. Some day birth and death records are all going to be computerized. That'll make it a whole lot tougher for ghosting to work."

"You sound like Avery Glickman," I said, referring to my partner who swears computers are going to change the world. Avery and Biff might have the same opinion about computers, but that's probably the only thing they agree on. I suppose that's to be expected since they have a conflicting agenda. Biff's goal is to bill our firm for as much as he can get away with, and Avery's goal is to pay Biff as little as possible.

I was about to end the conversation when Biff said, "By the way, remember that woman at town hall I told you about, Cecilia Marcus?"

"I remember you told me you thought she might know something, but that's about it."

"Well, I managed to talk to her in private as she was leaving work the other day, and convinced her to meet with you," Biff said.

"What does she know?"

"She told me a story about your buddy Machias Phelps that may or may not be something. I'll let you decide."

Biff told me he'd arrange a meeting with Ms. Marcus, and concluded the conversation with, "I'll add this telephone consult to my next invoice."

20

"I found the proverbial smoking gun."

" **A** fax from Dr. Stern," Carolyn, my secretary, announced as she entered my office and placed a small stack of paper-clipped pages on my desk. "His translation of that document Eddie Rizzo took from Mohammed Salameh's apartment."

I picked up the pages, leaned back in my chair, and began to read. The first page was a title sheet telling me I was holding *An Explanatory Memorandum on the Strategic Goals of the Group in North America*. On the next page I learned that "the Group" was the Muslim Brotherhood, and the author of the memo was someone named Muhammed Akrami. That page also contained a long list of recipients, identified by name and the organization they represented. There were dozens of people named Mohammed or Muhammed, plus a handful of Ahmads, Husseins, and Ibrahims thrown in for the sake of variety. Three quarters of the way down the list I found Rashid Mohammed, president of the Council for Islamic Religious Respect.

The memo left no doubt that the Muslim Brotherhood was engaging in what Dr. Stern had called *al-hijra*, or the Islamic doctrine of immigration, to increase their presence and influence in the U.S. and Canada. In the first section of the document, captioned "Our Sacred Duty," Akrami invoked passages from the Qur'an and the writings of Islamic scholars to justify the Brotherhood's actions. It took him six pages of flowery language to say what could have been said in one sentence: Muslims believe they have a duty to their god to move to non-Muslim countries to spread Islam. By the time I finished the first section of the memo, I was convinced of two things: Muhammed Akrami was a terrible writer, and Stacey's characterization of Islam as a dangerous ideology might be more accurate than I had thought.

The second section of the memo, captioned "Plan of Action," was a surprisingly detailed battle plan for implementing the Brotherhood's agenda. Seemingly unconnected Muslim groups, each assigned a specific goal, were to work together, but to never acknowledge the connection. For example, one organization with a seemingly benevolent name, was tasked with lobbying for changes to public school programs and textbooks to "portray Islam in a positive light" and to "highlight Islam's contribution to America since its founding." I laughed when I read that, remembering from my reading how much the Founding Fathers despised Islam and its adherents. John Adams, I recalled, had referred to Mohammed as a military fanatic. I would have thought this brazen attempt to re-write history was doomed to fail if it weren't for the memorandum writer's uncomfortably accurate observation that "Americans are shockingly ignorant of their own history." Akrami's understanding of our society's weakness was unnerving.

He was equally contemptuous of our understanding of religion, contending, "the most devout Christians tend to be the least informed." This, he suggested, opened the door for the Brotherhood's so-called outreach organizations to convince the public that "Islam is one of three great Abrahamic faiths." I chuckled when I read that. I knew from my research that Islam claims the Old Testament Abraham was a Muslim. What I don't know is how Abraham could have belonged to a religion centuries before it was invented. Maybe he had a time machine.

The next six pages outlined the devious role each organization was slated to play in the Brotherhood's grand scheme. I was repelled by the story unfolding before me, but transfixed like a motorist who can't turn away from a highway crash scene. The ingenuity and thought that went into the plan was remarkable. What was particularly disturbing was the reference in each case to "our friends in high places" who could be called upon to help implement the Brotherhood's overall plan. This suggested that people like Billboard Bob Proctor might be fairly common. Left unsaid was whether these individuals acted out of ideological sympathy or for more worldly reasons.

On the tenth page I came to the section outlining the role of the Council for Islamic Religious Respect. That group had two tasks. The first was to popularize "Islamaphobia" as a term that could be used to stifle opposition to the Brotherhood's agenda. CIRR's second task was to establish, through its local affiliates, a nationwide network of mosques and Islamic Centers that could be used to facilitate "the group's ultimate objective."

I turned to the last page, which contained a single paragraph explaining that objective. I read that paragraph three times to ensure I wasn't mistaken.

"Find anything useful?" I looked up to find Carolyn holding a stack of telephone message slips.

"I found the proverbial smoking gun. If I could get this memo into evidence it would destroy a major part of CIRR's case. Unfortunately, Judge MacAndrew isn't going to let me use stolen property in his courtroom."

"Speaking of Judge MacAndrew," Carolyn said, holding up one of the message slips, "you're expected in his chambers first thing tomorrow morning to review Mayor Proctor's tax returns."

21

"Bob Proctor is perpetrating a fraud on the court."

I contacted Carolyn from a pay phone in the courthouse lobby and arranged for her to call me in Judge MacAndrew's chambers in exactly ten minutes. I reasoned that ten minutes after entering the judge's chambers, I'd have a copy of Bob Proctor's tax return in front of me. The plan was for Carolyn to read me the social security number from the tax return we found in the garage in Maine so I could compare it to the one on Mayor Proctor's return. It would have been a lot easier to simply write the Maine social security number on a legal pad, but since the judge had ruled I wouldn't be permitted to take notes, I'd have a hard time justifying the legal pad. And since I haven't even been able to memorize my own social security number, it was doubtful I'd be able to memorize the one from Maine long enough to make a comparison.

Emerson Lambert was already in the judge's chambers when I arrived. "Not discussing the case," he assured me, "just comparing vacation plans."

"No problem," I replied, sliding into the chair next to him. Unlike Obduhali, Emerson wouldn't think of doing anything unethical.

Before we could get down to business, the judge's secretary appeared carrying a tray, which she placed on the desk before him. "I hope you don't mind," he said, "but I haven't had breakfast yet." He removed the lid from a small plate to reveal a single piece of toast. Then he unwrapped a pat of butter and carefully divided it into four smaller pieces, placing one on each corner of the toast. Next, he poured tea from a small, blue pot into a matching cup, stopping when the cup was almost two-thirds full. He reconsidered the contents, and added more tea. Sugar came next, a heaping teaspoonful carefully removed from a blue sugar bowl. The judge selected a paper napkin from the stack next to the teapot and wiped the blade of the butter knife, which he then used to carefully level the mound of sugar on the spoon. Satisfied that he had exactly the right amount of sugar, Judge MacAndrew dumped the contents into his cup and slowly stirred, first in a clockwise direction, then counterclockwise.

Now that his tea was properly sweetened, the judge returned his attention to the toast. The four small pieces of butter were still neatly positioned in each corner. Lyrics from a Beatles song popped into my head: *the butter wouldn't melt, so he put it in the pie.* As I tried to remember whether it was Uncle Albert or Admiral Halsey who put the butter in the pie, Judge MacAndrew began the process of buttering his toast. He started in the northwest quadrant, working his way clockwise around the toast, ensuring that the butter was evenly spread on his culinary canvas. The close order buttering drill completed, the judge assaulted a jar of strawberry jam, using a different spoon than the one he had employed to stir his tea. He neatly positioned a spoonful of jam in the center of the toast before spreading it, dutifully ensuring every square inch was properly covered, right up to the very edge.

He was in the process of cutting his toast into two triangular pieces when there was a gentle tapping on the door, and his secretary entered the room. "There's a call from Mr. O'Brian's secretary on line two. She apologizes for interrupting, but says it's important that she speak with him." I surreptitiously checked my watch. Carolyn was right on time, exactly ten minutes from when I had called her from the pay phone in the lobby. Unfortunately, I hadn't yet seen Proctor's tax return.

Judge MacAndrew punched a button on his phone, picked up the receiver and handed it to me with his right hand while reaching for his tea with the left. The judge apparently wasn't ambidextrous. Instead of picking up the teacup, his left hand knocked it over, spilling the contents onto the desk where it inundated his perfectly buttered and jellied toast. "I'll call you back," I said to Carolyn, hanging up the phone and using the remaining napkins to intercept the wayward tea before it reached file folders neatly stacked on the corner of the desk.

The judge called for his secretary, who scurried into his office muttering, "Oh my, oh my." She took over the cleanup duties as Emerson Lambert, Judge MacAndrew and I relocated to the sofa and two chairs at the other end of the room. When we were comfortably seated, the judge said, "Remember the ground rules, Mr. O'Brian, you can examine Mr. Proctor's most recent tax returns, but you may not retain them, may not take notes, and may not use them in open court unless you can convince me they're essential to your case."

"I understand," I said, holding out my hand to receive the documents the judge had removed from a file folder. I scanned the first page of one return, noting that Proctor resided on a street in a very nice section of town. Not necessarily too expensive for someone living on a public servant's salary, but something to look into nonetheless. The first three digits of the social security number on the form were 006, telling me Proctor's "poor boy from the Jersey Pine Barrens" routine was a sham. After returning from Maine, I had done some research and discovered that the first three digits of a social security number designate its owner's state of residence at the time the number is issued. Maine residents have a social security number beginning with 004 through 007. New Jersey residents have social security numbers that begin with 135 through 158. If Proctor had been born in southern New Jersey as he claimed, he wouldn't have a social security number beginning with 006.

It was time to feign forgetfulness. "Oh heck," I said. "I almost forgot. I hung up on my secretary before she could tell me why she was calling." I pointed to the phone on the judge's desk. "Do you mind if I call her back? Knowing her, she wouldn't have called if it weren't important."

Always the proper gentleman, Judge MacAndrew said, "Of course, of course. Go right ahead."

Still holding the tax return, I walked to the cherry desk, now nice and clean from its tea bath, and dialed the office.

Carolyn must have been waiting for my call because she picked up on the first ring.

"Everything okay?" she asked.

"Yes, sorry about hanging up like that. The judge's tea hopped out of its cup and made a beeline for the phone, so I hung up before I got electrocuted." I heard Emerson Lambert snicker behind me.

Carolyn ignored my smart aleck remark. "You ready for the number from the Maine tax form?"

"Yes," I said, putting Proctor's tax return on the judge's desk. I camouflaged the purpose of our call by adding, "What did the tests show?"

Carolyn read off the social security number, which matched the one shown on Billboard Bob's tax return. "That's a relief," I said to keep the charade going. "Thanks for calling me."

I hung up and returned to my seat across from Judge MacAndrew.

"Everything okay?" the judge asked.

"Yes, everything's fine. Sorry for the delay." I turned my attention back to Proctor's tax return, flipping through the pages, then doing the same thing with the second return. Nothing on those pages was really relevant. I already had what I needed, but I wanted to go through the motions to keep Emerson Lambert in the dark about what I was really up to.

"Nothing but his salary, interest from a CD and some dividends," Emerson Lambert said, "just as I told you at the motion hearing."

"Yes, you're right about that. But these tax returns confirm my suspicion that Bob Proctor is perpetrating a fraud on the court." Uttering "fraud on the court" to a judge is like waving a red flag in front of a bull. It's a legal phrase that means a litigant is trying to make the judge look foolish – something no judge will stand for. "In fact, Proctor is working a fraud on his own attorney," I added, looking directly at Emerson Lambert.

"What sort of fraud are you talking about?" Lambert demanded to know.

"Rather than discuss it here, I suggest we schedule an evidentiary hearing and put it on the record."

Lambert started to object, but the judge said, "Yes, this is something that definitely needs to be on the record. But fair warning, Mr. O'Brian, you're making a pretty serious charge. I hope you have the evidence to back it up."

"I do, indeed," I said. That wasn't exactly true. The tax returns were a start, but I needed more. The question was whether or not I could get what I needed in time for the hearing.

I called Tony Biffano as soon as I got back to my office and explained what I wanted him to do. His immediate response was, "You've got to be kidding." I assured him I wasn't. "It's going to cost you," he warned. "I don't want any grief when I render my bill." I assured him that if he succeeded, money was no object. In retrospect, that was the wrong thing to have said to a guy who can pad a bill better than any attorney I know. The last thing he said before hanging up with a sigh was, "Couldn't this wait for a couple months?" I assured him it couldn't.

22

"I have proof."

Two days later, I had a return engagement with Judge MacAndrew, this time in the courtroom rather than his chambers. I was there to argue in support of my motion to compel Tinoo Barahi to provide long overdue answers to the interrogatories I had served on his client, the Council for Islamic Religious Respect. Dr. Stern's prediction that CIRR would engage in what he called "lawfare," dragging things out as much as possible to run up the *Ledger's* legal expenses, had proven correct. Barahi first requested additional time to provide answers. Next he supplied partial answers to some of my questions. Then he ignored my repeated demands for complete answers to all my questions, forcing me to file a motion to compel discovery.

The hearing began with the judge's "good-morning-counselors-good-morning-Your-Honor" routine, with Barahi getting his line right this time. I initially thought I was about to experience a replay of my appearance in Jersey City before Judge Washington when MacAndrew began, "I don't like to see motions to compel discovery." But instead of claiming I was wasting his time, the judge addressed his comments to my adversary. "As a member of the bar, you're obligated to follow the Rules of Civil Procedure, which are quite clear on how and when interrogatories are to be answered. The court shouldn't have to order you to do something court rules clearly require you to do."

"I am very sorry, Your Honor," Barahi began, "but I believe there has been a misunderstanding."

"What misunderstanding?" the judged wanted to know.

"My client has already provided answers to all of Mr. O'Brian's questions."

The judge looked at me for a response. I shook my head. "Mr. Barahi's client has answered less than half the questions, not all of them, and hasn't produced copies of any of the documents I requested."

"No, we have answered all of the questions," Barahi insisted. He withdrew papers from a file folder and waved them in the air. "I have proof."

Judge MacAndrew motioned to a court officer, who retrieved the document from Barahi and brought it to the bench. The judge flipped through the pages, and gave the document back to the court officer, who brought it to me to examine. At first glance, it appeared to be the interrogatories I had served on the Council for Islamic Religious Respect, with an answer neatly typed under each question. But I quickly realized what Barahi had done. He had brazenly created a shortened version of my interrogatories using just the questions he chose to answer, deleting the rest. "This is not the complete set of interrogatories I served on Mr. Barahi's client. Mr. Barahi is attempting to work a fraud on the court."

"There seems to be a lot of that going around," the judge said. "Must be contagious." He leaned back in his chair and looked at the ceiling, apparently contemplating how to handle a decidedly unusual situation. He lowered his gaze and scanned the courtroom. Although the public gallery was three-quarters full, there was total silence from the attorneys waiting their turn to argue. Hushed conversations might be the norm in some courtrooms, but not in one presided over by Judge Duncan MacAndrew.

"Mr. Lambert," the judge said after a few seconds, "I didn't see you back there." I turned to find Emerson Lambert seated in the back row of the gallery. Although I hadn't seen him earlier, I wasn't surprised he was there. I had made it a point to notify him of this morning's hearing, even though it didn't directly affect his client, Bob Proctor. I had also mailed him a copy of the interrogatories I had sent to Barahi, even though court rules only required me to supply them after they were answered by CIRR. That courtesy was about to pay off.

"Can you shed some light on this matter?" the judge asked Lambert. It was an unusual request – about as unusual as Barahi's claim that I had created two different sets of inter-rogatories – but understandable in view of Lambert's status as a respected figure in the legal community.

Emerson got to his feet. "Mr. O'Brian provided me with a copy of the interrogatories he served on CIRR, as well as the answers he received."

"Did you bring them with you?" the judge asked.

"Yes, Your Honor," Lambert said. Those were the last words he uttered in the courtroom that morning, but his body lan-guage throughout the remainder of the hearing spoke volumes.

MacAndrew motioned Lambert to come forward. "Please join Mr. Barahi at the counsel table."

Emerson took a seat next to Tinoo Barahi, but pointedly ignored him. He placed his briefcase on the table, opened it, and rummaged through the contents, eventually withdrawing two documents, which a court officer collected and brought to the bench. Judge MacAndrew methodically examined both before addressing Barahi. "There appear to be two different set of interrogatories. The one Mr. Emerson says he received from Mr. O'Brian has twenty-eight pages, and the one you claim you received from him has only thirteen pages. Can you explain the discrepancy?"

"Certainly, Your Honor," Barahi said without hesitation. "Mr. O'Brian sent one document to me and a different one to Mr. Lambert." It was a blatant lie, a maneuver right out of Omar Obduhali's playbook. Judge MacAndrew may have suspected as much, but there was no way he could know for sure.

"Why would he do that?" the judge wanted to know.

"To make me and my client look bad."

Judge MacAndrew turned his attention back to me. "Did you do that, Mr. O'Brian?"

"No, Your Honor," I said. "The interrogatories I served on Mr. Barahi as the attorney for CIRR had twenty-eight pages." Although I had blown my credibility with some of the judge's colleagues, I was still on reasonably good terms with him, so I was hoping he would take me at my word.

My adversary wasn't backing down. "I respectfully disagree. I do not wish to impugn the integrity of a fellow attorney, but what Mr. O'Brian says is a lie."

Barahi's use of "lie" rather than "inaccurate" or "incorrect" or "mistaken" seemed to offend the judge's sense of decorum. "Be careful, Mr. Barahi. You're making a serious accusation."

CIRR's attorney didn't respond. He stood defiantly with arms crossed. Emerson Lambert, on the other hand, remained seated next to Barahi, his body turned ever so slightly away from his supposed colleague as though making a concerted effort to distance himself from the proceedings.

We waited while Judge MacAndrew considered the situation. I'll probably never know for sure, but I'm reasonably certain Emerson Lambert's body language swayed the judge's decision. "I don't know for certain what's going on here, but I have my suspicions," he finally said. "So, here's what we'll do. I'll have my secretary make two copies of the interrogatories Mr.

O'Brian sent to Mr. Lambert. I'll put one copy in my file and give the other to Mr. Barahi, who will then provide answers to all the questions within seventy-two hours and provide copies of all the documents requested. If Mr. Barahi fails to fully answer all the questions and provide copies of the requested documents within that time period, I will entertain a motion from Mr. O'Brian for sanctions, and will hold a hearing on the matter on an expedited basis."

The judge might have considered that a reasonable way to handle the situation, but Barahi didn't. "I cannot accept the court's ruling. As Your Honor pointed out, the Rules of Civil Procedure specify when answers to interrogatories are required. If I remember correctly, my client has thirty-five days to provide answers, not seventy-two hours."

Tinoo Barahi hadn't remembered correctly, but I wasn't about to point that out. Judge MacAndrew did, however. "Your reference to thirty-five days is incorrect. You would be well advised to re-read the rules of court. You would also be well advised not to accuse another attorney of lying, absent proof. And you would especially be well advised not to tell a Superior Court judge, or any judge for that matter, that you will not accept the court's ruling." Morris County's most even-tempered judge was clearly annoyed. Before gaveling the hearing to a conclusion, he warned Barahi, "If you don't comply with the court's ruling within seventy-two hours, I won't hesitate to impose sanctions."

23

"I seen the whole thing."

Eddie the Skunk showed up at my office, this time by appointment, with four witnesses in tow. Although I interviewed them individually about Eddie's auto accident with Mohammed Salameh, I could have saved everyone a lot of time by doing it as a group effort. Each witness told the exact same story, often in the same exact words, frequently describing things he couldn't possibly have seen from his supposed vantage point.

Just as Eddie had been coached by Dr. D'Amico about how to describe his injuries, these witnesses had been well prepared, presumably by Eddie, for our meeting. "I seen the whole thing and the Arab was clearly wrong," was the way three of the ersatz witnesses began. The fourth, apparently the group's resident grammarian, substituted "saw" for "seen."

When I had finished interviewing the last of Eddie's witnesses, I let them cool their heels in the waiting room while I explained to Eddie, as gently as I could, why his witnesses would do more harm than good. I could only imagine what Obduhali, whom I had apparently underestimated, would do to this foursome on cross-examination. I briefly considered having just the group grammarian testify, but decided even that was too dangerous. Eddie wasn't particularly happy, but to his credit, he grudgingly agreed that I was right. "You're the one with the law degree," he said. "No point paying you for advice if I don't take it." If only all my clients thought that way.

A few minutes after Eddie and his entourage left, Carolyn appeared at my office door to announce that the answers to the interrogatories I had served on CIRR had just arrived. Tinoo Barahi had apparently taken Judge MacAndrew's threat to impose sanctions seriously.

"Let's see what Barahi has come up with," I said, extending my hand to take the file folder Carolyn was holding.

"This is the Johnson file you asked for," she said, placing the file on my desk. "I'll be right back with CIRR's answers."

She disappeared into the outer office and returned a moment later carrying a cardboard file box, which she placed on my desk. I removed the lid and saw that the box was stuffed with individual papers. My interrogatories included requests for the production of various documents, but the box contained much more than I was expecting. Carolyn returned to the outer office as I began pulling individual pages from the box, being careful to keep everything in order. I needn't have bothered. Although the first page in the pile was the first page of my interrogatories, it quickly became apparent that there was no order. Barahi had simply tossed everything into the box, leaving it up to me to sort through the mess.

Carolyn reappeared carrying a second box, which she placed on my desk. "More answers from CIRR," she said before once again returning to the outer office. She repeated the process three more times until I had five boxes of documents on my desk.

Tinoo Barahi was clearly inundating me with so much information, most of it extraneous, that finding relevant material would be a laborious, time-consuming process. It was on old trick used by large law firms to make life difficult for smaller adversaries. As a solo practitioner, Tinoo Barahi lacked the army of junior associates and paralegals big firms have at their disposal, but according to Dr. Stern, CIRR reputedly had virtually unlimited financial backing from Muslim countries like Saudi Arabia and Pakistan. If that were true, Barahi could likely hire whatever manpower he needed.

Carolyn and I spent the rest of the day sifting through the mountain of paperwork Barahi had supplied. As we pulled individual pages out of the boxes, we created three separate piles. In the first we put the interrogatories I had served on CIRR, their answers now neatly typed under each question. The second pile consisted of tax-related documents, and the third was for everything else. An hour after we started, the "everything else" pile had completely taken over my office sofa and had spilled onto the floor. Barahi had supplied multiple copies of the documents I had requested, as well as many that I hadn't.

The interrogatories pile, on the other hand, had only a handful of pages. Barahi had pulled apart my set of interrogatories and salted the individual pages throughout the five boxes. It was the sort of unprofessional conduct that had earned him the enmity of other attorneys.

Just before five o'clock I found the last page of the interrogatories, stuck between duplicate copies of a flyer announcing a mosque event. I put them in the appropriate stack of papers, then scooped up the armful of tax-related documents and brought them out to Carolyn's desk. "Go home," I told her. "First thing tomorrow morning, messenger all this tax stuff over to Ray Benson." Ray is the accountant for Harvey Berkowitz, who I represented in federal court four years ago after his creative accounting had caused Uncle Sam to charge him with criminal tax fraud. I had gotten to know Ray pretty well during that trial, and had arranged for him to review CIRR's tax documents to see if there was anything there that I could use in court.

After Carolyn left, I returned to my office and began reading CIRR's answers to the interrogatories. They were about what I expected until I got to the questions asking which of Stacey's statements CIRR alleged were defamatory. I read the answers Barahi's client had provided, then re-read them, unwilling to believe what I was seeing. "What sort of idiot," I muttered, stopping mid-sentence when I realized I was violating the first rule of warfare, as applicable in the courtroom as on the battlefield: never underestimate your adversary. Though Tinoo Barahi and his colleague, Omar Obduhali, came across as couple of courtroom clowns, both had so far managed to out-maneuver me.

It was time for that to change.

I spent the next half hour dictating a motion to sanction Barahi and his client for failing to comply with Judge MacAndrew's order.

24

"I can't find him anywhere."

It seemed to take forever to get to the office the following morning, thanks to freezing rain that turned Route 46 into a skating rink. The long downhill section of the highway near the western end of Troy Forge was particularly challenging, as evidenced by the armada of automobiles that had sailed off the road and onto the median or the shoulder.

Carolyn, who lives close to the office, was already at her desk when I arrived. "I've got that motion you left on my desk ready for your signature," she said as I entered the room.

I put down my coffee cup, took the pen she held out for me, and signed the notice of motion. "Think you can get a messenger to deliver that to Judge MacAndrew and Barahi on a day like today?" I asked.

"Already made the call. Jerry's on his way," Carolyn said, referring to the messenger we usually use. "He just got a four wheel drive Jeep," she added, "so the weather shouldn't be a problem. He's also going to take all the tax stuff over to Ray Benson."

Satisfied that Carolyn had everything under control, I retreated to my office and closed the door. I was planning to spend the day doing research for Stacey's defamation case, so after first removing the mountain of paperwork we had piled there the previous afternoon, I stretched out on the sofa with

The Reliance of the Traveler, one of the books Dr. Stern had recommended.

I originally thought what Stacey had written about Islam was a bit crazy. Like most people, I viewed it as just another religion, a bit eccentric perhaps, but essentially harmless. However, after meeting Dr. Stern and beginning to read the material he recommended, texts that Muslims themselves consider authoritative, I began to realize Stacey's crazy views might not be as crazy as I had thought. Her almost visceral hatred for Islam was no doubt due in no small part to the fact that Islam seemed to treat women more like property than people.

For me, the most disturbing aspect of the religion was the way it divides the world into two groups. *Dar al-Islam*, Arabic for "house of Islam," consists of the worldwide Muslim community or *umma*. The rest of us are consigned to *Dar al-Harb* or the house of war. I'm not sure I want to reside in a so-called house of war. Courtroom wars fought with words are fine with me. Wars fought with bullets are another matter.

My recent dealings with Omar Obduhali and Tinoo Barahi, both of whom I assumed were Muslims, convinced me that I needed to up my game if I was going to win a courtroom war with them. Both had brazenly lied to a judge and apparently thought nothing of it. Massaging the facts to make your case look good is a time honored practice in our profession, but outright lying to a judge just isn't done.

An hour into my reading that morning, I came across something that may have explained my adversaries' mendacity. A passage in *The Reliance of the Traveler*, the 14th century exposition of Islamic law, made it clear that wine, gambling and fortune telling are "the Devil's handiwork," as is lying to a fellow Muslim. Lying to a non-Muslim, on the other hand, is completely acceptable if it's necessary to achieve an objective. Seeking clarification, I turned to Dr. Stern's most recent book, which explained that Islamic lies come in two varieties, *taqiyya* and *kitman*. I read that section of his book several times, but eventually decided I was dealing with a distinction without a difference. As far as I'm concerned, a lie is a lie. I also decided that the safest way to deal with Obduhali and Barahi was to assume everything they said was a lie.

I had just gotten up to re-fill my coffee mug when Carolyn appeared at my office door. "Tony Biffano is on line one," she said, taking my empty mug, hopefully to re-fill it.

"Just checking in," Biff said when I picked up the phone.

"Did you get what I need?"

"One is a definite; I'm still working on the second."

"What do you think your chances are on the second?" I asked.

"I'll know later today. I'm following up on something I learned from that guy at the restaurant you told me about. He's been real helpful, so I slipped him a hundred for his trouble. I assumed you wouldn't mind."

Of course, I wouldn't mind; it wasn't my money. Stacey's boss, however, would probably mind plenty. I didn't say that to Biff since his unauthorized largesse was already a done deal. Instead, I said, "Do what you have to, just get me what I need for this hearing."

"Will do," he said before hanging up.

Carolyn reappeared with my refilled coffee mug. "Are we the only ones in the office today?" I asked her.

"Avery came in a few minutes ago," she replied. "He has a four wheel drive Subaru so the ice wasn't a problem. Scott is working at home, and Rick and Elaine are staying put for the day." I didn't ask why she mentioned Rick and Elaine in the same breath or whether they were staying put in the same place or different places. I was curious, but it was none of my business. Carolyn headed back to her desk, but stopped when she got to my office door. "By the way, Avery says it's getting warmer and the ice is melting. The roads should be fine by the time we're ready to leave." That was good news, as I had planned to have dinner that evening with Stacey and Sean McDermott, my high school buddy who's now a Troy Forge cop.

I resumed my place on the sofa and picked up Dr. Stern's book. It was well organized and written in 20th century English, making it a lot easier to read than the Qur'an, which was written in 7th century Arabic and organized by the length of each chapter, or *sura*, rather than chronologically or thematically. I was reading an English translation of course. Dr. Stern knows Arabic, but English is the only language I understand.

I was in the process of discovering that Islam's version of heaven is filled with "voluptuous women of equal age" when Carolyn appeared at my office door to announce, "Your favorite client is on line one." She delivered the news with a smirk and a sarcastic tone of voice. Apparently it wasn't Stacey on the phone.

"Give me a hint," I said as I got up from the sofa and headed for my desk. "All my clients are my favorite client, just ask any one of them."

"I'll be sure to convey that to Eddie Rizzo the next time he calls," Carolyn said, adding as she pointed to my phone, "or you can tell him yourself."

I picked up the phone and was greeted with the familiar voice of Eddie the Skunk. "Yo, counselor. Wasn't sure you'd be in the office today. Roads are really crappy. Drove to a business meeting this morning and almost skidded off the road."

"Stay safe out there," I said. "Getting injured in another auto accident could complicate your case." I'm not sure why I said it. I wasn't particularly concerned about his health. And given all that had happened, his case had gone from a lucrative contingent fee to a colossal waste of my time.

Eddie ignored my comment and plowed ahead with the reason for his call. "I've been thinking, maybe we should settle with the scumbag after all." *A little late for that.* "I mean, if he was willing to offer half a million before, who knows what he'll go for now." I knew, but couldn't figure out a diplomatic way to tell Eddie. My silence caused Eddie to prompt, "So what do you think? Can we get more than the five hundred thousand he offered that day in your parking lot?"

"Eddie," I said, "he didn't offer to settle for half a million. We demanded half a million and he said he'd discuss it with this client. There's a big difference."

"So he must have talked to his client by now. Call the guy and see how high he'll go."

"When an attorney says he'll discuss something with his client, that doesn't mean he's actually going to talk to his client," I explained. "The expression 'discuss it with my client' is lawyer talk for 'no way in hell'."

That revelation seemed to take Eddie by surprise. "So the scumbag was lying to us?"

I waited to see what else Eddie had to say, but all I heard was angry, undecipherable muttering as though he was talking to himself instead of into the phone. I hoped his anger was directed at Salameh or Obduhali and not at me. "Eddie, are you there?" I finally said.

"Yeah, I'm here," came the reply. He sounded really pissed. "So how long before we go to court and you destroy this scumbag on the witness stand?"

"In Hudson County, it could take a year," I said, adding "even longer" to avoid locking myself into a schedule over which I had no control.

"A year? A whole fuckin' year for a little fender bender case?" I noted that Eddie's "serious permanent injury" case had suddenly become "a little fender bender" case, but didn't dare share that observation with my client. "Do what you can to speed it up," Eddie instructed.

"Not much I can do." New Jersey's court system works on a schedule all its own, a reality my client was unwilling to admit.

"You'll find a way," Eddie said. "You always do." Then he hung up.

I had two more phone calls that afternoon. The first was from Judge MacAndrew's secretary, who called to inform me that the judge had, as promised, scheduled an expedited hearing on my motion to sanction Barahi and his client for failing to comply with the judge's order to make full discovery. The judge was apparently more than a little miffed because the expedited hearing really was expedited.

The second call came from Tony Biffano's associate who was trying to serve a subpoena on Mohammed Salameh to appear for a deposition, supposedly as a witness in the *Ledger's* defamation case. "You sure this Salameh character exists?" were the first words out of his mouth. "I've tried half a dozen times to serve him at his home and the business address you gave me, but I can't find him anywhere."

25

"You might want to tag along."

We had just been seated at our regular corner table at the New Amsterdam Inn when Stacey delivered the opening salvo in her tirade. "My boss is royally pissed at you and your partners." For the next five minutes I received a detailed explanation of why I was an insensitive, uncaring, not-particularly-thoughtful jerk for putting Stacey in an awkward situation with her boss. Scott's call to his golfing buddy at the Ledger Media Group had apparently backfired. Stacey revealed something none of us at the firm had known, namely that her boss was the grandson of the *Ledger's* founder and, as such, had far more power than his position would suggest. I made a mental note to pass this information on to Scott.

There was a lull in the conversation as our overly attentive waiter once again topped off our still half-full water glasses. The lull was short lived. As soon as the waiter was out of hearing range, Stacey continued our war of words. "My boss doesn't understand why you can't try the entire case at once instead of having all these separate motion hearings. It's like we're paying for a dozen separate trials."

"A dozen?" I began. "Aren't you exaggerating just a bit?"

"You've got two different hearings scheduled so far," Stacey said. "And who knows how many more before this thing ends."

"A motion hearing is a lot less expensive than a full blown jury trial," I replied. "And it's a whole lot safer. What do you think will happen if you end up with a couple of Muslims on the jury?"

"You don't know that will happen," Stacey shot back.

"And you don't know that it won't. Do you really want to take that chance?"

"So, you use those challenges, the ones where you don't have to give a reason, to make sure we don't end up with any Muslim jurors."

"They're called peremptory challenges," I said, "and *Gilmore* makes that difficult, if not downright impossible."

"Who or what is Gilmore?" Stacey asked.

"*State v. Gilmore* is a 1986 state supreme court case that says juries have to be drawn from a representative cross section of the community. It prohibits an attorney from using peremptory challenges to exclude people on the basis of race, religion, color, sex, or ancestry. And since we have more and more Muslims moving into the area, there's a very good chance we'll end up with at least one on the jury."

"Even if they belong to the mosque?" Stacey asked. "Wouldn't that be a conflict of interest?"

"Probably," I said, "but all they have to do is say they're not connected to the mosque. And it'll be tough for me to prove they're lying unless your boss is willing to foot the bill for Tony Biffano to do expensive background checks."

Stacey knew from prior conversations that Biff's services don't come cheap, so the mention of paying him to do background checks shifted the conversation to safer topics while we awaited the arrival of Sean McDermott, my high school buddy who's now a Troy Forge cop.

He arrived a few minutes later and before even sitting down said, "Why the heck did you choose this place? After everything that happened here, I'd think this is the last place you two would want to eat."

Four years ago, on our first date, Stacey and I ended up in the middle of a police raid while eating dinner at The New Amsterdam Inn, which was then owned by Martin von Beverwicjk, one of my firm's clients. The raid was ostensibly intended to break up a drug ring being operated on the premises by a restaurant employee. The only thing the cops found was a single joint being smoked by a kitchen worker. Those who know how Mayor Proctor operates realize the raid was really designed to harass Martin and "persuade" him to drop his development plans for the so-called fairgrounds property where the town's first mosque now stands.

Stacey answered Sean's question before I could. "We're just a couple of sentimentalists." He found her answer amusing. I can't imagine why.

I signaled our waiter who was hovering nearby and we placed our drink orders. Stacey had her usual glass of wine, Sean ordered a beer, and I asked for a glass of Jameson Irish Whiskey.

Our drinks arrived a few minutes later as we were discussing basketball. Sean was absolutely convinced a kid from Newark named O'Neal was certain to win NBA Rookie of the Year. I agreed the seven foot center was pretty darned impressive on the court, but reminded Sean of the line attributed to Yogi Berra: It ain't over till it's over. Stacey listened politely, but didn't join the conversation. She has as much interest in basketball as I have in sewing.

Stacey eventually grew tired of basketball talk and forced a change of topic. "So, tell us about these special rules Proctor put in place for dealing with the Muslim community," she said to Sean.

"Well, for starters, everyone in the police department has to take so-called sensitivity training so we can learn how to not offend Muslims. It's conducted by the guy Proctor appointed to head up the town's Office of Diversity," Sean said, using his fingers to make quotation marks in the air as he said "Office of Diversity."

"And what did you learn that made you more sensitive?" I asked.

Before Sean could reply, our waiter reappeared to top off our water glasses, all of which were almost full. I held up my hand to signal Sean to wait for the waiter to complete what I considered a completely unnecessary task. "Do you mind giving us a little privacy?" I said to the waiter, whose blank look led me to believe he didn't speak English.

After the waiter had moved out of hearing range, I told Sean about the listening device Reynaldo had found in my living room. "I'm probably just being paranoid," I said, "but I don't need a nosy waiter listening to our conversation."

"So, what did your sensitivity training teach you?" Stacey asked, getting the conversation back on track.

"Oh, things like not making a Muslim woman take off her headgear or dropping a Qur'an on the ground. My favorite is the requirement that we take our shoes off before entering their mosque. Things like that." He took a sip of beer before adding, "Of course, we can't go into their mosque, even if we're in pursuit of a suspect, without first getting permission from the town's Diversity Director."

"But you don't need permission to chase a suspect into a church or synagogue, do you?" Stacey asked.

Sean was about to answer when something in his sport coat began chirping. He reached into a pocket and retrieved a pager.

"When did you go high tech?" I asked.

"When I started moonlighting for a private security company." He read the short message on the pager's screen. "Look's like dinner's over before it even began," he said as he got up from the table. "A silent alarm just went off. I have to check this out." He nodded in my direction. "You might want to tag along."

"Why would I want to do that?" I asked.

"Because the alarm that went off is at your office."

26

"You're such a Luddite."

At Sean's insistence, Stacey and I stayed in my car while he checked the firm's office suite. "If someone is in there, you don't want to be the one to confront him," he explained.

According to my watch, five minutes elapsed, but it seemed much longer. We had a good view of the building from the parking lot behind it, and could see the lights in our third floor office suite come on one at a time as Sean methodically worked his way from room to room.

"I don't hear any gunshots," I said as I turned up the heat in the car. "Whoever was there is probably long gone." According to my clients who have experience with these things, any burglar worth his salt can get what he wants and be gone in less than five minutes.

"Keep cranking the heat up and I'll give you gunshots," Stacey said. "It's like an oven in here." She cracked her window a couple inches and a blast of winter air hit me in the face.

"You seem to have an interesting relationship with your partners," Stacey said from out of the blue.

"What's that supposed to mean?"

"I just mean that for a guy who's not particularly good with relationships, you seem to get along really well with your partners. And they're such a diverse bunch of people."

"Since when am I not good with relationships?"

Stacey gave me her arched eyebrow look. "Your marriage to Aimee bombed. Sean's your only friend from high school. You don't have any friends from college or law school. In fact, other than Sean, you don't have any friends."

"How about Rick? Doesn't he count?"

"Rick's more of a mentor than a friend," Stacey said. "That's what I'm talking about. You spend more time with your three partners than anyone else, but they're not your friends."

"How about you? Don't you count as a friend?"

"That's different. You know what I mean."

I wasn't sure I did know, but I decided to drop the subject before our discussion turned into one of those arguments that I invariably end up losing, in large part because I'm never really clear what we're arguing about.

Fortunately, Sean appeared at the building's back door, my cue to turn off the Mustang's engine and get out. "Damn, it's cold," I said as I wrapped my scarf around my neck.

"That's probably because it's winter," Stacey said as she exited the passenger's side. "And, yes, I know you hate winter. You tell me at every opportunity."

I ignored her remark, preventing our nascent argument from veering off in a new direction. "I assume nobody was there," I said to Sean.

"Place is empty and nothing looks disturbed. Let's go in and have a look around. Maybe you'll see something I missed."

We took the elevator to the third floor and entered the double glass doors to the firm's offices. Sean was right. Nothing seemed out of place in the waiting room. I started to say that, but instead of finishing the sentence I held a single finger to my lips, signaling them not to speak. I crossed the room to Elaine's reception desk and retrieved a legal pad on which I wrote "office bugged?" before holding the pad up for Sean and Stacey to see it.

We proceeded in silence through the offices, checking each one for anything that seemed out of place. I was reasonably certain my own office was just as I left it, but couldn't be certain about my partners' offices. There was nothing that jumped out at me, but that didn't necessarily mean anything. Rick's office overlooking the parking lot was the last one we checked. By that point I was convinced we weren't accomplishing anything meaningful, so I signaled Sean and Stacey to follow me out of the building and back to the parking lot. "I need to call Scott and have him get someone to check the offices for listening devices," I said as soon as we were outside.

"While you're at it, tell him to line up a different company to monitor your security system," Sean said.

His comment took me by surprise. "What are you talking about? You work for the company."

"Yes, and so do a bunch of other off duty Troy Forge cops, some of whom are part of Proctor's private army."

"You think one of them broke into our office?" I asked Sean.

"Probably not," he replied. "One of our guys would have gotten in without tripping the silent alarm."

"It was probably someone who didn't know there was an alarm system," Stacey said.

"Or they knew and didn't care," I said. Stacey looked at me as though I had said something nonsensical, so I elaborated. "Whoever did this could have wanted us to know he was there, just to mess with us. Or what he wanted was important enough that it didn't matter that we knew."

"Or it could just have been a false alarm," Sean interjected. "That's not uncommon, especially with a new system. I'm not sure we'll ever know what happened here, but what I do know is you probably don't want your system monitored by a company that uses off duty Troy Forge cops. I was on call tonight, but next time, if there is a next time, it could be one of Proctor's people."

Sean drove home and Stacey and I retreated to the warmth of my Mustang. "Let's go across the highway to the diner," I suggested. "We can get something to eat and I'll use their pay phone to call Scott."

"You're such a Luddite," Stacey said, reaching into her purse and removing what I recognized as the portable phone Avery had given me, and which I had given to Stacey, supposedly as a belated Christmas present. She handed me the phone. "Here, use this."

I put the phone to my ear. "It must be broken."

"What do you mean, broken?" Stacey said.

"There's no dial tone."

She grabbed the phone out of my hand. "You're such a Luddite. What's Scott's phone number?"

I gave her the number, which she punched into the phone before handing it back to me. "You speak into the little holes in the bottom and Scott's voice comes out the little holes in the top. The magic phone fairy does the rest." Stacey can be even more sarcastic than me when she wants to be.

"It's ringing," I said.

"Oh, good," Stacey gushed with mock enthusiasm. "I was afraid the magic phone fairy might have been asleep at this hour."

When Scott came on the line, I filled him in on what had happened. The following day he lined up a different company to monitor the security system and had our offices re-checked for listening devices. They found four, which were promptly destroyed. In retrospect, I probably should have suggested turning them over to Reynaldo Renoir.

27

"It is in your constitution."

The following morning I once again appeared before Judge Duncan MacAndrew, this time in support of my motion to compel Tinoo Barahi's client, the Council for Islamic Religious Respect, to provide proper answers to my interrogatories that had been the subject of a prior motion hearing.

An obviously annoyed Judge MacAndrew skipped his customary "good-morning-counselors-good-morning-Your-Honor" routine and got right down to business. "Mr. Barahi, you apparently didn't take me seriously when I told you the last time you were in my courtroom that there would be consequences for failing to make full discovery."

If Barahi had offered the judge a sincere apology (or at least one that sounded sincere), a plausible explanation for his actions, and a promise to provide complete answers to my interrogatories within a reasonable period of time, the hearing would probably have ended thirty seconds after it began. Judge MacAndrew is the kind of jurist who bends over backward to ensure litigants can't run to the Appellate Division and argue they weren't treated fairly in his courtroom.

But Barahi was anything but contrite. In fact, he was downright defiant. "My client has answered all of Mr. O'Brian's questions, even those seeking information he has no right to know, like the names of CIRR's officers and board members."

"Mr. Barahi," the judge said, "you know that in cases involving any type of organization, it's routine for an attorney to ask for the names of officers and board members."

"But Mr. O'Brian's clients only want this information so they can persecute the Muslims," Barahi said, perhaps a bit too vehemently.

Someone in the back of the courtroom snorted, most likely in an effort to stifle outright laughter.

Judge MacAndrew didn't lose his cool, but it was obvious he was losing patience with my adversary. "Nobody is persecuting anyone. The question you're referring to is routine, and besides, the issue here is..."

Barahi interrupted the judge, something even a first year law student knows just isn't done. "This is not a routine case involving a routine organization. My client is a religious organization that has been grievously wronged by Mr. O'Brian's clients. There is no reason why my client..."

Now it was the judge's turn to interrupt. "Please don't interrupt me when I'm speaking, Mr. Barahi. You're not here to argue your case. You're here today to respond to Mr. O'Brian's motion to compel your client to provide full and complete answers to his interrogatories."

Barahi started to respond, but the judge raised one finger to his lips, signaling CIRR's attorney to remain silent. This time he did.

The judge held up what I recognized as my notice of motion. Looking directly at Barahi, he said, "I've compared the interrogatories attached to Mr. O'Brian's notice of motion to the set I instructed you to answer the last time you were in my courtroom. They're identical, correct?"

"I do not know," Barahi answered.

"How can you not know?" the judge asked.

"I have not seen the interrogatories Mr. O'Brian attached to the notice of motion he sent to you."

"You were provided with a copy, weren't you?" the judge asked, obviously expecting Barahi to respond in the affirmative.

But that's not the response my adversary gave. Instead, he said, "I do not know if the moving papers you received match the ones Mr. O'Brian sent to me. As you will recall, the last time we were before Your Honor, there were two different sets of interrogatories."

I started to respond to Barahi's ridiculous accusation, but Judge MacAndrew beat me to it. "No, Mr. Barahi, you contended there were two different sets of interrogatories. Whether or not that contention is correct is beside the point. Your client failed to properly answer..." The judge leafed through the paperwork. "Your client failed to answer question 32, which reads: 'List the specific statements in defendant's news articles that plaintiff contends constitute defamation.' Your client..."

"My client answered that question," Barahi said defiantly, once again interrupting the judge.

It was one interruption too many. "Enough!" the judge yelled, slamming his hand on the bench. Emerson Lambert, who had been sitting in the back of the courtroom, told me later it was the first time he had ever heard the normally soft-spoken Duncan MacAndrew raise his voice.

The courtroom became even quieter than usual. There was no rustling of papers or shuffling of feet. Not a cough, nor a sneeze. It was as though everyone in the room was holding his breath, waiting to see what would happen next.

The judge leaned forward and barely above a whisper said, "Your answer to that question reads: 'All of the defendant's statements are slanderous and insulting to the Muslims in general and to plaintiff, which represents the Muslims in this litigation.' Is that correct?"

"Yes, that is correct," Barahi said. "You do not understand how offensive those newspaper articles are to the Muslims. It is not permissible to insult our beloved prophet. What they have written..."

"I've heard enough," the judge said. "Here's what we're going to do. Mr. Barahi, your client will answer question 32 with specificity, and deliver that answer to Mr. O'Brian's office by noon tomorrow. If you fail to do so, or if your answer is not specific, I will entertain Mr. O'Brian's motion to dismiss your case."

"You cannot do that," Barahi said.

"I beg your pardon?"

"You cannot dismiss my case. You do not have that right."

Superior Court judges, or judges of any court for that matter, don't like to be told what they can and can't do, especially by attorneys who don't know what they're talking about. "Mr. Barahi, I gather from your remarks that you're unfamiliar with Rule 4:23-5, which makes it quite clear that I can, in fact, dismiss your case for failing to make discovery. I would strongly recommend that you review the rules of court before making another appearance in my courtroom."

"I am unfamiliar with that rule," Barahi conceded, "but it does not matter. My client has a right to a jury trial. It is in your constitution."

MacAndrew shook his head as though he couldn't believe what he had just heard. "In *my* constitution?"

The judge's emphasis on "my" was lost on Barahi, who responded, "Yes, that is correct. My client has a right to a jury trial. You cannot deny that just because you do not like the answer my client gave to Mr. O'Brian's question. That answer is the correct answer. My client has told the truth."

The judge leaned back and looked at the ceiling, apparently deciding how to deal with Tinoo Barahi.

I waited. Barahi waiting. Everyone in the courtroom waited to see how the county's most even-tempered judge was going to deal with an attorney who was either clueless or pretending to be clueless.

Judge MacAndrew began to drum his fingers on the bench. After what felt like ten minutes, but was really less than one, the judge leaned forward, fixed his gaze on my adversary, and said, "Here's how we're going to proceed. By noon tomorrow, Mr. Barahi will fax his client's answer to question 32 to Mr. O'Brian's office, with a copy to my chambers. That answer will consist of no more than three specific examples of what the plaintiff contends are defamatory statements. Each example will consist of no more than one sentence, and each sentence will be quoted verbatim from the newspaper articles referred to in the complaint."

The judge leaned back and took a deep breath before continuing. "If Mr. Barahi fails to comply with this order, I will entertain Mr. O'Brian's motion to dismiss the complaint filed by the Council for Islamic Religious Respect." The judge banged his gavel, something he rarely does. "We're done here." He got up and headed for his chambers.

"It's a wonder Barahi passed the bar exam," Emerson Lambert said as I walked by him on the way out of the courtroom.

"Indeed," I replied. But I was worried. Barahi had to be up to something. Nobody could be that dense. Or could they?

28

"Not a snowball's chance in hell."

Cecilia Marcus, the only town hall employee Tony Biffano located who was willing to talk to me, was waiting when I got back to the office. I had asked Rick to sit in on the meeting since he knew Miss Marcus back when he was doing a lot of land use work in town and she was a clerk for the planning board. For the last twelve years she had been employed in the mayor's office, her final stop on the employment express before retiring someplace warm.

It was during her time working in the mayor's office that she met Machias Phelps. Based on appearances, the aging, rotund Miss Marcus and the diminutive Phelps would seem to have had little in common. Yet the two were remarkably similar in many respects. Neither had ever married. Both lived in the same apartment complex near Town Hall. Neither had a driver's license. And both walked to and from work, except on cold winter days when they would share a cab. Of course, from my perspective, the most important thing they had in common was a willingness to talk about what went on behind closed doors in the office of His Highness, Proctor the Great.

"Machias was a good person," I said to get the conversation started. "He certainly didn't deserve to die in that car crash."

"Car crash, my eyeball," Miss Marcus shot back. "Machias never drove a car in his life. He was blind as a bat."

"Yes, that's our take on things, too," Rick said. "Which is why we need your help. We'd like to find out what really happened."

"I'll do what I can," she replied, "but there's not much I can tell you."

"For starters," I said, "what can you tell us about Machias' relationship with Mayor Proctor? We know that he had a habit of trying to avoid the mayor."

"Yes, that's true. Of course, it wasn't always like that. When I first started working in the mayor's office, Machias and Mayor Proctor were actually pretty close." Rick and I exchanged glances. What we were hearing was hard to believe. Cecilia Marcus picked up on our body language. "No, it's true. In fact, Machias used to help Mayor Proctor with his taxes. Machias was a whiz with numbers."

If Stacey and I hadn't found a tax return among the items Machias Phelps left with his aunt in Maine, I probably wouldn't have pursued the matter. Of course, it could have been just a coincidence, but my gut told me otherwise.

Rick apparently agreed. "Are you telling us that Machias did Proctor's tax return for him?"

"Oh, he didn't do the actual tax return," she replied, "just the calculations. The mayor insisted on that because it's a crime to fill out someone else's tax form unless you're a licensed tax preparer." That didn't sound right, but rather than interrupt her story, I made a mental note to ask Ray Benson when we met to review the tax-related documents Tinoo Barahi had provided in response to my interrogatories.

"So Machias never saw the actual tax return that Proctor filed?" I asked.

"Only once," Miss Marcus said. "And that's when everything seemed to change." She looked off into space as if conjuring up a mental image of that event before continuing. "I was in the mayor's private office talking to him about something – I don't remember exactly what it was – and Machias came in with a document that needed Mayor Proctor's signature. The mayor's tax return was right there on the desk, and Machias obviously saw it. Mayor Proctor didn't say anything. He just moved some papers around on his desk to cover up the tax return. He tried to make it look casual, but it was pretty obvious. After that, everything changed."

"Changed how?" I prompted.

"The mayor's relationship with Machias changed. The whole atmosphere in the office changed. Everything was different. It's tough to describe."

There was a long pause. I didn't know if she had said all she intended to say or if she was simply collecting her thoughts, searching for a way to explain what she meant.

"Can you give us an example?" Rick finally asked.

"Well, that afternoon, the mayor circulated a memo forbidding employees to assist other employees with their taxes, ostensibly because people's salaries were confidential. But it was much more than that. Everyone seemed to become more careful, more suspicious."

There was another pause, longer this time. Then, finally, "I'm sorry. I know this doesn't help you find out what happened to Machias, but I really don't know any more than what I've told you."

I would have liked more details, but it seemed pretty clear that Cecelia Marcus had said all she was going to say. Perhaps she had forgotten the details. Maybe she couldn't figure out a way to explain how things in the mayor's office had changed. Or perhaps she was having second thoughts about talking to us. Whatever the reason, our meeting was finished. I thanked Miss Marcus, assured her that she had been a big help, and gave her twenty bucks for a taxi.

"So what do you think?" Rick asked as soon as Cecelia Marcus had left.

"I think if you combine what we just learned with what we already know, it's possible to come up with an explanation for what happened to Machias Phelps."

"Okay," Rick said, "let's hear it."

"As a kid growing up in Maine, Phelps and his classmate, Bob Proctor, work at a local ice cream place called Dempsey's Dairy Delight. We know this because Machias' aunt, who still lives in Maine, confirmed that, and because we've seen a copy of Bob Proctor's tax return."

"And Proctor's tax return was apparently filled out by Phelps," Rick interjected.

"Yes, the handwriting seems to match the journal that Machias' New Jersey aunt says was his. We'd have to get a handwriting expert to be sure, but it certainly looks like a match."

"I'm with you so far," Rick said.

"Years later, Machias find himself working for another person named Bob Proctor here in Troy Forge. And just as he helped the Bob Proctor in Maine with his taxes, he ends up doing the same thing for his boss here in New Jersey. Only he never actually sees Mayor Proctor's actual tax return."

"Until one day he does," Rick added.

"Right, and because of what he saw on the mayor's tax return, he went from being the mayor's trusted lieutenant to lying low and staying out of Proctor's way."

"And he saw?" Rick prodded.

"He saw that the first three digits of Proctor's social security number meant he was from Maine, not from the Pine Barrens in southern New Jersey as Billboard Bob has long maintained. And if that ever became public knowledge, it would put a serious dent in Proctor's credibility and damage his political career."

"So Proctor arranged for Phelps to die in a phony auto accident to ensure he would never reveal that information?" Rick asked.

"That would be my guess," I said, "but it's only a guess. I'm not sure we'll ever be able to prove it."

The conversation came to a momentary pause as we contemplated the all too real possibility that Billboard Bob might get away with murder. Eventually, Rick said, "Take it a step further. Suppose the social security number Phelps saw on the mayor's tax return looked familiar. At some point he gets a copy of his childhood friend's old tax return and realizes that Mayor Proctor has stolen his long-dead classmate's identity."

"That would explain something Billy Kane told me," I said. "According to Kane, Machias once said that Proctor wasn't who people thought he was. Kane also told me he remembered Machias taking a trip to Maine."

A soft tapping on my office door interrupted our conversation. Carolyn entered, holding something behind her back. "So, this morning you're in court here in Morris County to force CIRR to answer the interrogatories you served on them, and..." She withdrew a document from behind her back and held it up for me to see. "And a couple hours later, Mohammed Salameh's attorney files a motion in Hudson County alleging you failed to provide complete answers to his interrogatories."

"What are you talking about?" I said, perhaps a bit too forcefully. "We sent answers to his interrogatories weeks ago."

"Don't shoot the messenger," Carolyn said, handing me Obduhali's notice of motion. "I'm just telling you what's in his moving papers."

"Well, you suspected Obduhali and Barahi were working together," Rick said. "I don't think there's any doubt now."

"It's lawfare," I said.

"Lawfare?"

"Legal warfare. According to Dr. Stern, CIRR uses maneuvers like this to run up their opponents' legal costs and force a settlement on their terms."

"I'm guessing that's not likely to happen this time," Rick said.

"Not a snowball's chance in hell."

29

"Just like Machias Phelps."

The following day I met Ray Benson at his office on the second floor of a small commercial building owned by Harvey Berkowitz, one of our firm's longtime clients. Ray had been Harvey's accountant for years when I first worked with him to prepare for Harvey's criminal tax fraud trial back in 1988. Ever since, I've turned to him whenever I have tax-related questions. Ray might not have been able to curb Harvey's penchant for creative accounting, but he understands the nation's convoluted tax laws better than anyone I've ever met.

When I entered Ray's private office, the conference table he uses for a desk was covered with what I recognized as the tax-related documents CIRR had provided in response to my interrogatories. "Find anything useful in that mess?" I asked.

"A few interesting things," he said. "Whether or not they'll help your case remains to be seen."

"Enlighten me."

"Well, for starters," he began, "I discovered that apparently the *Ledger* is being sued by the wrong plaintiff. The complaint names the Council for Islamic Religious Respect as the plaintiff, but the correct name is Council for Islamic Religious Respect of New Jersey. Maybe you could move to dismiss their case on the ground that they named the wrong plaintiff."

I laughed. "If you think that would work, you don't know Judge MacAndrew. The last thing he's going to do is toss a case because Tinoo Barahi was sloppy and left "of New Jersey" off his client's name. The judge will just deem the complaint amended to properly identify the plaintiff, just as he amended the complaint to accuse Stacey and the *Ledger* of libel instead of slander." It wasn't until later that day that I realized how I could use Barahi's apparent drafting error to answer a question that had been nagging at me since I first learned my living room was bugged.

Ray wasn't giving up. "What if I were to tell you that the Council for Islamic Religious Respect and the Council for Islamic Religious Respect of New Jersey are two different organizations?"

I didn't think it would make a difference, but I wanted to hear more, so I said, "It all depends."

"I did a little digging," Ray continued, "and discovered that there are a bunch of connected organizations with similar names. The parent organization, Council for Islamic Religious Respect, is a 501(c)(4) non-profit based in Washington, D.C. There are also separate 501(c)(3) organizations all around the country that operate local mosques."

"So what?" I said. "Isn't that the way a lot of non-profits are set up?"

"Having a national organization with local chapters isn't unusual, but the way money seems to flow between CIRR in Washington and the local non-profits is unusual."

"Go on," I prompted.

"To understand what I'm talking about," Ray continued, "you have to know two things. First, contributions to a 501(c)(3) organization are tax-deductible, but contributions to a 501(c)(4) usually aren't. Secondly, a 501(c)(3) organization can't have any significant involvement in politics, whereas a 501(c)(4) can." Ray paused to allow me to absorb that information before continuing. "It looks to me like the local chapters solicit tax-deductible contributions, and then funnel the money to the national organization, which uses the funds to conduct political activities that the local chapters can't. I'm willing to bet that an in-depth forensic audit would show that the people behind CIRR are operating what amounts to a money laundering operation." I immediately thought back to Reynaldo Renoir's statement that Uncle Sam long suspected the Muslim Brotherhood of using its front groups to launder funds.

"How could you possibly know this just from looking at the paperwork I gave you?"

"I couldn't" Ray said, "not from just the New Jersey chapter's documents. But I called some of my colleagues around the country and asked them to get the tax returns of the local CIRR chapter in their area."

"What, they just walked in and asked for the tax returns, and CIRR handed them over?"

"The local CIRR chapters had no choice," Ray said. "Section 6104(e)(1) of the Internal Revenue Code requires tax exempt organizations to make copies of their tax returns available for public inspection."

I wanted to ask him if he had memorized the entire Tax Code or just its most obscure sections, but instead, I said, "You mean I didn't have to serve interrogatories to get those copies?"

Ray smiled and shook his head. "You should have come to me sooner." It was a phrase he and I have uttered countless times to clients who discovered too late that some things are best left to an expert. He took a sip from a coffee mug emblazoned with "World's Best Accountant" before asking, "Want me to contact people I know at IRS and pass this on?"

"No," I said, "I have a better idea. I'm going to use it as a bargaining chip."

"You're going to use this information to negotiate a settlement with CIRR?" Ray asked.

"Not exactly."

Before I could explain what I had in mind, there was a knock on the door and Ray's secretary appeared. "Sorry to interrupt," she said, "but there's a call for Mr. O'Brian on line three."

Ray punched a button on the phone on his conference table desk and handed me the handset. "I tried calling you on the cell phone Avery gave you," Carolyn, my secretary said, "but I got Stacey, instead."

"I gave Stacey the phone," I replied. "Don't tell Avery."

"My lips are sealed, but if you were carrying the phone like Avery intended, it would have been a lot easier to reach you."

"Well, you've got me now. What's up?"

"Rick asked me to call you," Carolyn began. "You're not going to believe this, but that woman you met with yesterday, Cecilia Marcus?" My stomach knotted up, and I knew that Carolyn was about to deliver bad news. "She's dead."

"How?"

"According to a news report Rick heard on the radio, she borrowed a neighbor's car and drove it into a tree."

"Just like Machias Phelps," I said.

"Just like Machias Phelps," Carolyn agreed.

30

"You're all brains and no heart."

That evening, on our way to pick up dinner at a Chinese restaurant operated by a recent immigrant from Korea, I told Stacey about Cecilia Marcus. "I can't believe Proctor's people think they can get away with two obviously staged auto accidents."

"It's actually pretty clever when you stop to think about it." Stacey replied. "If someone claims Marcus and Phelps both died under unusual circumstances, Proctor's allies in the media will paint them as a nutcase peddling conspiracy theories. It's like Hitler's observation that the bigger the lie, the more people will believe it."

Back at the house we dined on entrees I couldn't pronounce, but did enjoy. As we were cracking open our fortune cookies, Stacey began the conversation we had concocted about my nonexistent friends from law school. "So, tell me about this reunion you're having with your law school buddies."

"It's not really a reunion," I said. "Just a few guys from my law school study group getting together to catch up."

"I don't think I've met any of them, have I?" Stacey asked as planned.

"No, none of them are living in New Jersey. Mark joined a firm out in Ohio, Garry hung out his shingle in Massachusetts, and Reynaldo went to work for the government."

"Reynaldo," Stacey said. "Interesting name."

"Interesting guy," I said, beginning the little speech I had come up with, hoping it would find its way to the government agency tapping the phone of whomever had planted the listening device in my living room. "After law school Reynaldo enlisted in the army and worked for the Judge Advocate General's Corps. Last I heard he was doing some sort of top-secret legal work for a government agency."

"Which one?" Stacey asked, sticking to the script.

"I once made the mistake of asking him that. He told me that information was, to use his exact words, above my pay grade." Using Reynaldo's own words would hopefully get his attention, assuming that our conversation was actually relayed to him. It remained to be seen if he would realize I was signaling him to contact me. It wasn't exactly a foolproof plan, but it was the best I could come up with.

"I'm surprised you kept in touch with these guys," Stacey said, "I mean with your busy schedule and all."

That comment wasn't part of our script, so I wasn't sure how to respond. But someone was apparently listening to our conversation, so I had to say something that sounded plausible. "I didn't really keep in touch. This is our first get-together since law school."

"Oh, that's more like you," Stacey replied. "Far too busy to worry about other people. You're such a busy little bee." She made a buzzing sound and waved her hand in what I assumed was her interpretation of a bee in flight.

I gave her the outstretched arms with palms up gesture that's universally interpreted to mean *what the hell are you doing?* "You're all brains and no heart," she said. Then she flashed a big, phony smile that was far too similar to Billboard Bob's crocodile grin.

Stacey and I seemed to be at odds on a regular basis in recent weeks, which I attributed to the stress of preparing for the upcoming trial. So rather than ask what she meant by that crack, I steered the conversation in what I thought, incorrectly as it turned out, was a safer direction. "Tomorrow I'm filing a new motion in CIRR's case against you and the *Ledger*. I'm going to ask the court to dismiss their complaint on the grounds..."

That was as far as I got before Stacey exploded. "Another motion? Come on, Brendan. My boss will be pissed when he finds out about this. I'm already in enough trouble without you padding your bill even more." There was genuine anger in her big, green eyes.

This was the first time I realized Stacey's job might really be in jeopardy. But it wasn't a subject I wanted to discuss in a room that I knew was bugged. So instead of pursuing the matter, I said, "Your boss is going to love this motion if it succeeds in getting the case thrown out without a trial." As I had explained to Ray Benson earlier that day, that was never going to happen in Judge MacAndrew's courtroom, but that was the message I wanted to convey to whomever was listening to our conversation.

Stacey's skepticism was palpable. "And just how do you propose to pull that off?"

"Turns out CIRR's nitwit attorney, Tinoo Barahi, named the wrong organization as plaintiff." I had begun to suspect that Barahi was just pretending to be a courtroom fool, but I couldn't help taking a jab at my adversary.

Before Stacey could ask me to explain what I meant, I put my index finger to my lips to signal her not to say anything. Then I pointed toward the ceiling, a non-verbal suggestion that we move to the second floor, out of range of the listening device in the living room.

She dismissed the idea with a wave of her hand, apparently assuming I was suggesting something more physical than a discussion. "File your damn motion and I'll be in more trouble with my boss, but go ahead and do it," she said, snatching up her coat and heading for the door. "Even if I asked you not to, you'd do it anyway."

She slammed the door on her way out.

31

"These guys are dangerous."

The following morning on my way to the office, I once again had the weird feeling of being followed. I had attributed previous incidents to an overactive imagination, but today's encounter turned out to be real.

It all began when a black Lincoln appeared in my rear view mirror as I made my way down the tree-lined boulevard in Mountain Springs that leads to Route 46. Lincolns are fairly common in upscale suburban communities like Mountain Springs, so I thought nothing of it at first. But when the Lincoln ran a red light, narrowly missing cross traffic, to doggedly remain three car lengths behind me, I suspected something wasn't right.

My suspicion was confirmed a few minutes later when I got to the traffic light at Route 46. I glided to a stop at the red light and immediately put on my right turn signal, though I really intended to turn left. The driver of the Lincoln put on his right turn signal. We waited as traffic streamed in front of us, heavier in the eastbound direction toward Troy Forge and my office.

When the light turned green, I eased into the intersection and turned the Mustang's front wheels slightly to the right, making it appear that I was about to make a right turn into the farthest westbound lane. But instead of completing a right turn, I yanked the steering wheel to the left and hit the accelerator.

This resulted in a somewhat ungraceful left turn on pavement that was a bit slicker than I had anticipated. My Mustang fishtailed and I ended up in the left lane of eastbound traffic.

As soon as I cleared the intersection I looked in my mirror and saw that the black Lincoln was right behind me, proof that my clever plan to lose my pursuer apparently wasn't clever enough. I put on my right turn signal, but instead of moving into the right hand lane, I stepped on the gas, and the Mustang shot forward. The Lincoln followed. I slipped into a gap in the right lane, this time without signaling, sandwiched between a battered pickup truck in front of me and a white Chevy to my rear. The Lincoln held its position in the left lane, put on its right turn signal, and a moment later eased in behind me, thanks to the overly courteous, out-of-state Chevy driver who flashed his headlights to signal he was leaving space for my pursuer.

I slowed down. The Lincoln slowed down. I speeded up, and the Lincoln accelerated to stay behind me. I moved to the left lane, and the Lincoln followed. I moved back to the right lane. So did the Lincoln.

We continued our lane-changing, speed-changing dance for another mile, with the Lincoln matching my every move, but never doing anything more menacing than following at a comfortable distance. There was no attempt to tap my bumper, run me off the road, or take any of the other maneuvers that are the staple of car chase scenes in the movies.

As we crossed the town line into Troy Forge I once again checked my mirror, hoping to catch a glimpse of the Lincoln's driver, but the morning sun, which was directly ahead of us, reflected off the pursuing car's windshield, making it impossible for me to see inside. What I saw instead were flashing red and blue lights behind the Lincoln's front grill. That was when I knew an unmarked police car was tailing me. And the fact that the driver waited to put on his lights until we had crossed the town line suggested he was a member of Mayor Proctor's private palace guard.

I pulled into the parking lot of a small, freestanding building that over the years has been everything from a butcher shop to a lawnmower repair facility. The current occupant, according to a sign in the front window, was Madame Elvira, Psychic Card Reader. I've passed this building on my way to the office for years, but have never seen any cars in the parking lot. Today was no exception. I assume there's not much demand for psychic card readings in the suburbs of northern New Jersey. Or perhaps Madame Elvira's clients are vampires and only come out at night.

As I was fishing in my wallet for my license and registration, I heard a car horn. Looking up I saw an arm extending from the Lincoln's window pointing toward the back of the building. Proctor's storm trooper apparently wanted our rendezvous to take place out of the view of passing vehicles.

There was no way I was going to let that happen. I just sat in my car and waited.

He pointed again, this time more forcefully.

I refused to budge, determined that whatever was about to happen would play out near the highway, in full view of passing motorists.

The pointing hand disappeared, the door of the Lincoln opened, and the driver partially emerged, his right hand on the car's roof and his left on the partially opened door. It was Reynaldo Renoir.

Reynaldo again pointed to the back of the building, and this time I complied. He followed, parking the Lincoln next to my car. "Novel use of turn signals," he said as he slipped into the Mustang's passenger's seat.

"Novel way to respond to my message," I replied. "You could have just knocked on my door."

"Right, and had a lengthy discussion in your living room that's bugged."

"You could have just picked up the phone and called."

"You mean call the phone in your bugged living room?"

"No, I mean the phone in my non-bugged office."

"Your office was bugged too," Reynaldo pointed out.

In retrospect, I realize I should have asked him how he knew that, but I didn't think to at the time. Instead, I said, "It was, but it isn't now. My partner had the listening devices removed."

"So now you assume the problem's solved and you stop checking," Reynaldo said in the tone of voice a teacher uses when speaking to the class idiot. "What if someone put them back, but this time didn't trip the alarm?"

"You're telling me my office is bugged again?"

"No," Reynaldo said with mock patience, "I'm telling you that you don't know whether or not your office is bugged if you don't continue to check for listening devices."

"Who's putting these gadgets in my home and my office?"

"Not me," Reynaldo said, his carefully chosen words not ruling out the possibility that one of his colleagues had done it.

I briefly considered pressing the issue, but decided there was nothing to be gained. I needed Reynaldo's cooperation, and antagonizing him wasn't likely to help my cause. So I moved the conversation in a different direction. "I'm not particularly thrilled with your tactics, but I appreciate your responding to my message. I wasn't sure our little performance would work, but I'm glad it did."

"I told you you'd figure out a way to use the listening device to your advantage. Of course, this meeting today would have happened even without your little performance."

"Why's that?" I wanted to know.

"Because you're interfering with our investigation, and that's something my superiors won't tolerate." My protestation that I had no idea what he was talking about elicited an angry response. "You know damn well I'm talking about that little surveillance operation of yours."

"What surveillance operation?"

Reynaldo fixed his gaze on me, apparently trying to determine if I was really in the dark or just playing dumb. After an uncomfortably long interval he finally said, "According to our phone intercepts, the Muslim Brotherhood knows they're under surveillance."

"How does that involve me?" I asked. "I assume the people you work for, whoever that might be, are keeping tabs on the Brotherhood. They probably just spotted one of your guys."

"If we had them under direct surveillance," Reynaldo began, "and I'm not saying we do, they wouldn't know it." I wanted to ask if there was a difference between direct surveillance and indirect surveillance, but decided it would be a waste of time. Reynaldo had mastered the art of answering a question without actually providing an answer. If he ever quit the gun-for-hire business, he'd make a great politician.

"I spotted you back on the boulevard in Mountain Springs," I pointed out.

"You spotted me because I wanted you to spot me," Reynaldo said. "What I didn't want was for you to play a bunch of stupid games with turn signals after you spotted me."

"Sorry," I said. I wasn't really, but it seemed the polite thing to say. And since I needed a favor, being polite – or at least appearing to be polite – was the way to go.

"When we want to keep an eye on somebody," Reynaldo continued, "they never know we're there. The clowns you hired must have learned surveillance from watching television."

"I didn't hire anybody to do surveillance," I insisted. "I don't even know who we're talking about. Who, exactly, do you think I hired someone to watch?"

As usual, Reynaldo didn't answer my question, but he did provide information that was to prove useful later that day. "Two guys who look like thugs right out of central casting sitting in a limo in a poor neighborhood. Ring any bells?"

"I have no idea what you're talking about," I said. And I didn't.

"And every four hours they're replaced by two other guys, all of them white, in an area where there aren't a lot of white people. Sound familiar?"

"Reynaldo," I said, "I honestly don't know what you're talking about. I haven't hired anyone to do surveillance work. I don't even know who you think I'm spying on. And, give me a little credit, if I was going to set up a surveillance operation, don't you think I'd be a little less obvious than what you're describing?"

I don't know if he decided I was telling the truth, or if he decided I wasn't going to tell him the truth, but for whatever the reason, Reynaldo dropped the matter. "So what was it you wanted to talk to me about?"

"I thought we might be able to help each other out," I said, retrieving a large envelope from the Mustang's back seat and handing it to Reynaldo.

"What's this?" he asked.

"When we first met, you told me the government thinks CIRR is engaging in money laundering. The material in that envelope contains information that my forensic accounting expert came up with that shows how they're doing it." That wasn't entirely accurate. Ray Benson was a CPA, not a forensic accountant. And the material he put together raised more questions than answers. Whatever government agency Reynaldo was working for probably already had what was in the envelope. After all, if Ray's colleagues could walk into a local CIRR chapter and get copies of the organization's tax returns, Uncle Sam could do the same. Hopefully Reynaldo would make the phone call I wanted him to make before he realized what I delivered fell a bit short of what I had promised.

Reynaldo hefted the envelope, which was several inches thick. Inspired by the paper avalanche Tinoo Barahi had supplied in response to my interrogatories, I had enclosed two copies of every document. He looked inside, then pulled out the contents and fanned it like an oversized deck of cards, presumably to ensure I wasn't giving him a bunch of blank sheets. He put everything back in the envelope and said, "So, what is it you want from me?"

"I want you to make a phone call to Shapiro, the federal prosecutor in Texas you told me about, and ask him to send me his file."

"What, specifically, is it you want from that file?"

"Anything that would help me in my case with CIRR. Having never seen the file, I don't know what's in it."

"And explain to me why you need me to do this," Reynaldo said. "You can't just pick up the phone and call him?"

"I have called him, four times. I also sent him a letter and faxed a second letter."

"When you called, what did he say?" Reynaldo asked.

"I never actually spoke to him. Every time I called he was either in court, in a meeting, or otherwise unavailable. I left messages with his secretary."

"Okay, what did his secretary say?"

"That he'd get back to me."

Reynaldo looked through the windshield at the grey sky. I assumed he was formulating a response, but perhaps he was just assessing the odds of snow later that morning. "I'm guessing there are things in his file that he can't send you, like things that would compromise sources."

"I'm not asking for anything like that," I said.

Reynaldo continued to gaze through the windshield.

"Look," I said to break the silence, "you've told me Uncle Sam wants to nail the Muslim Brotherhood and that CIRR is one of their front groups. We have a common enemy here. I've given you information you can use to go after the Brotherhood. Return the favor by helping me deal with CIRR."

"Get me copies of those photos your girlfriend took in the mosque and I'll see what I can do," Renaldo said as he abruptly opened the car door. I was about to ask him why he wanted the photos when he added, "If the Muslim Brotherhood is interested in those photos, we are too."

Before I could ask how he knew the Brotherhood was interested in Stacey's *burqa* shots, Reynaldo got out of the car and began to close the door. He stopped while the door was still half open, leaned down and poked his head back inside the Mustang. "And by the way, Mr. Barahi may be a nitwit, but the people he works for aren't. So watch yourself. These guys are dangerous."

32

"Are you sure this Obduhali character is a real attorney?"

As usual, Carolyn, my secretary, was hard at work when I arrived at the office. "This was sitting in the fax machine when I got here," she said, holding out a document as I passed her desk. It was an amended complaint that Tinoo Barahi was filing to correct the name of his client, confirmation that CIRR, or someone acting for CIRR, had planted the listening device in my living room.

My first order of business that morning, after my obligatory cup of coffee, was calling Eddie Rizzo to inform him about the motion Omar Obduhali had filed. Ordinarily, I wouldn't bother a client with something like that, but Eddie was no ordinary client. There was a very good chance that Eddie already knew about the motion my adversary had filed, so failing to tell him about it would look like I was attempting to hide something from him. And while attorneys have been known to hide unpleasant information from clients, I wasn't about to try that with Eddie the Skunk. Eddie would certainly never be my friend, but I never want him as an enemy.

I dialed the most recent phone number Eddie had given me, and a moment later a recorded voice told me the number had been changed. I dialed the new number and got a similar recording. I dialed that number. Same result.

The fourth number I called was answered by a baritone voice. "Yeah."

"I'm trying to reach Eddie Rizzo," I said. "Do I have the right number?"

"Just a minute."

A new voice came on the line, asking in quick succession, "Who's this? What do want?"

I identified myself and asked to speak with Eddie. "Just a minute."

I cradled the phone between my ear and shoulder, and waited. And waited. And then I waited some more. I was just about to hang up when a familiar voice came on the line. "Counselor, I'm glad you called. I need to see you." I assumed that meant Eddie knew about the motion Salameh's attorney had filed and wasn't happy about it. As it turned out, I was wrong.

"You and I got something we need to talk about," Eddie said. "I'm sending a car to pick you up. Should be there in about fifteen minutes."

"Eddie," I said. "I've got to prepare for a meeting this afternoon. I can't leave the office. Can you come here?"

"No, that won't work," Eddie said. I waited for an explanation, but none was forthcoming. "Car will be there in fifteen minutes." Then he hung up.

In all the years I've represented Eddie Rizzo, I've never been to his home or office, which is just fine with me. And I've sure as heck never had him send a car to pick me up and deliver me to an undisclosed destination. Was he so unhappy about how his case was going that I was about to feel his wrath? I had visions of two oversized thugs named Vito and Luigi taking me on a one-way trip to visit Jimmy Hoffa.

Eddie's car – a limousine actually – arrived twenty minutes later. And instead of Vito and Luigi, my driver was an older, black gentleman named Earl, who kept up a running conversation about basketball all the way from Troy Forge to Passaic. Shortly after passing the diner on Route 3 with a sign inviting travelers to stop in and "eat heavy," we took an exit that brought us into the Third Ward of Passaic. Like so many of New Jersey's urban centers, Passaic is a shadow of its former self. In the 19th century the city was a thriving textile and metalworking center. And in 1931, Passaic became home to DuMont Laboratories, which manufactured some of the nation's first television sets. Today, the Third Ward, which the locals refer to as Passaic Park, is the last vestige of the city's former grandeur.

We drove past tree-lined streets and soon found ourselves in a part of town that reminded me of European cities after World War II. The best maintained buildings could only be described as decrepit. The worst looked as though they had an upcoming appointment with the wrecking ball. The building Earl stopped in front of fell somewhere in between. It appeared to be structurally sound, but the wooden trim looked as though it hadn't had a coat of pain in years, the red brick walls were covered with green mold, and the windows were either boarded over or covered by a metal grate.

Earl honked the limo's horn, then drove around the side of the building and entered a narrow alley blocked by a metal fence topped with razor wire and two closed circuit cameras. In the center of the fence was a gate that looked secure enough to stop anyone who attempted to enter – or leave – without permission.

A door opened halfway down the alley and a head appeared, then disappeared. A moment later, the gate swung open and Earl drove down the alleyway, the gate silently closing behind us. He stopped the car by the door that had just opened, and turned off the ignition. I started to open my door, but stopped when Earl said, "Hold on." He got out, walked around the limo, and opened the car door for me. "Mr. Rizzo is waiting for you inside," he said. I had an uneasy feeling that Vito and Luigi were waiting as well.

I went inside and found myself in a room with a bare concrete floor and walls painted hospital green. A faded sign on the far wall informed me that I was at the corporate headquarters of Rizzo's Ritzy Limo Service. Four very large gentlemen were playing cards at a table in the corner. The shoulder holster each man wore suggested they were probably not corporate executives. Although in Eddie the Skunk's world, perhaps they were.

"One of you guys Vito?" I asked, throwing caution to the wind.

All four of the "executives," who had thus far ignored me, looked up from their card game. One of them, a guy who I'm guessing spent most of the day lifting weights, said "yeah" in a deep baritone voice before turning his attention back to the cards in his hand.

I stood there, unsure what I was supposed to do or where I was supposed to go. I had just decided to ask my buddy Vito for directions when a door on the far side of the room opened and Eddie Rizzo appeared. "Counselor," he said. "This way."

I followed Eddie into a private office. I assumed it was his, but couldn't be sure. There were no photos of Eddie with dignitaries hanging on the wall to identify the space as his exclusive domain. "I didn't know you ran a limo service," I said as I crossed the room and sat down in a chair across the desk from Eddie.

"Yeah, it's one of my investments," Eddie said. "I don't really run it though. One of my cousins does that for me. I just stop in from time to time to check the books and make sure everything is on the up and up."

Although I had a hard time believing anyone would dare to cheat Eddie the Skunk, I said, "Good idea. Trust, but verify."

Eddie apparently didn't recognize one of President Reagan's favorite Russian proverbs. "Trust, but verify. I like that. You're a smart guy, counselor." He picked up the phone, pressed a button, and told the person on the other end of the line, "Vito, come in here." Then he repeated, "Trust, but verify. I like that."

I assumed that having Vito join us didn't bode well for my health, but all I could do was sit there and await my fate. Although Carolyn, my secretary, knew I was meeting Eddie, nobody at the office had any idea where the meeting was taking place.

Vito entered the room a moment later. Standing up, he was even more menacing than sitting at the card table with his fellow gun-toting executives. "Yeah, boss?" he said to Eddie.

Instead of ordering Vito to whack me, wipe me out, take me for a ride or whatever term is used in this kind of situation, Eddie said, "Get us a couple of coffees. Black for me; cream and sugar for Counselor O'Brian." Vito apparently didn't know how the boss liked his coffee, but Eddie knew how I liked mine. It's downright creepy how much Eddie the Skunk knows about other people, especially me. I was beginning to think maybe he was the one who planted the listening device in my living room.

Vito returned with two cups of coffee, placed them on Eddie's desk, and left the room without saying a word. As soon as the door closed behind him, Eddie said, "Counselor, we gotta talk about my case." I settled back in my chair, preparing myself for the tirade that I was certain was coming.

I was wrong. Instead of complaining about how I was handling his personal injury case, Eddie said something that caught me completely by surprise. "Are you sure this Obduhali character is a real attorney? Cause I had some of my people keep an eye on him, and it don't look like he's running a law office."

"You had Omar Obduhali under surveillance?"

"Not me personally," Eddie explained, "but some of my people."

"You had people watching his office?"

"Yeah," Eddie said. "That's right."

My conversation with Reynaldo Renoir earlier that morning was starting to make sense. "Obduhali's office is in an area where there aren't a lot of white people, right?"

"Yeah, I guess so," Eddie said.

"So you had a couple of white guys sit in a car and watch the office? Like, maybe the guys in the outer office?"

"Yeah," Eddie said again, his tone of voice a bit defensive.

"And the car they sat in was a limo, not exactly the sort of car seen in that kind of neighborhood?"

Eddie didn't respond, at least not verbally. Instead, he leaned back in his chair, crossed his arms, and cocked his head. His body language told me he was trying to figure out if I knew something he didn't think I should know or if I was just making some lucky guesses. A few seconds later, having apparently made his decision, Eddie leaned forward, smiled, and wagged his finger at me. "Good guess, counselor. You see I got a limo service, guys sitting around playing cards, and you put two and two together."

"And I'll guess they worked in four-hour shifts."

Eddie realized that detail required something more than guesswork. "How the fuck you know that? You keeping tabs on me and my people? Cause if you are, you and me need to have a talk. I mean, a serious talk." Eddie was clearly angry.

I realized I needed to defuse the situation, and quickly. "No, I'm not keeping tabs on you and your people," I said in a calm, measured tone, "but the government is."

"The Feds are watching me?" Eddie was genuinely surprised, but surprise quickly turned back to anger. "When the fuck were you going to tell me?"

"Why do you think I called you this morning? A federal agent pulled me over on my way to the office and gave me the third degree because he knows I represent you. The first thing I did when I got to the office was pick up the phone and call you. But before I could tell you, you said you were sending a car to get me, and then you hung up."

My slightly altered version of events had the desired effect. "I'm sorry, counselor. I shoulda known better. You always done right by me. I was way off base. Forgive me." Eddie was genuinely contrite.

"It's okay," I said. "But do us both a favor and call off the surveillance. It's going to get you in trouble and it's not going to help your case."

"Whatever you say, counselor, but don't you wanna know what my guys found out?"

"What?"

"This Obduhali character don't seem to have any clients. The same bunch of Arabs come to his office every day, leave and come back, leave and come back, all day long. It's like they're running errands or something. Don't look like any law office I've ever seen." I wondered how many law offices he had seen besides ours.

"That's interesting," I said, using Stacey's favorite all-purpose word. "Let me see if I can use this information to get the Feds off your back."

"You think you can do that?" Eddie asked. He sounded impressed.

Based on what Reynaldo had told me that morning, Uncle Sam – or at least the agency, bureau, division or department Reynaldo was currently working for – apparently had no idea Eddie was involved. But Eddie didn't know that, and I wasn't about to tell him. Instead, I said, "Don't worry, I'll get them off your back, but I need a favor from you."

"Sure, anything, counselor."

Eddie was surprised when I explained what I needed. "You sure, counselor? I mean, I'll do it if that's what you want, but I thought you told me not to do stuff life that."

I wasn't really sure, and part of me realized it was probably a bad idea that could go wrong a dozen different ways, but Vito and his fellow gun-toting corporate executives seemed ideally suited to the task.

33

"I broke that promise a couple hours later."

On the ride back to my office, instead of talking basketball, I discretely pumped Earl for information about Rizzo's Ritzy Limo Service. I learned that Earl routinely drove corporate fat cats from their home in New Jersey to their office in Manhattan. I also learned that Vito and the rest of his card-playing group served as bodyguards for high-profile passengers. I asked Earl to name one of his high-profile passengers, but he refused, citing confidentiality. Apparently there's a driver/passenger privilege that's even more sacrosanct than the attorney/client privilege. Nothing Earl said led me to believe he was anything other than an ordinary limo driver working for a perfectly legitimate limousine service. But having known Eddie the Skunk for years, I'm reasonably certain there's more here than meets the eye.

My meeting with Stacey and her boss, Ezra Bramfield, was considerably less pleasant than my conversation with Earl. When I arrived at the office, I found them seated at opposite ends of the waiting room. "About time," Bramfield said as I entered, "We've been cooling our heels for twenty minutes." Elaine, our receptionist, who was sitting behind them, held up ten fingers to signal they had been waiting only half as long.

We walked back to my office in silence. Once there, Stacey and her boss, the *Ledger's* managing editor, took a seat on the sofa, and I sat across from them in one of two wing chairs my late wife, Aimee, had selected for my office. "Can I get you something?" I asked in an effort to be hospitable.

I was offering a beverage, but Ezra Bramfield had something else in mind. "Yes, an explanation for this new motion you told Stacey about last night. What should have been an easily winnable defamation case has turned into seemingly endless depositions and motion hearings, each costing the paper a small fortune." Bramfield used his fingers to count the ways my firm, in his view, was wasting the *Ledger's* money. "First you deposed Proctor, which produced nothing useful. Then you deposed the head of the planning board. Again, nothing useful. Next you filed a motion for summary judgment, which required another court appearance, which cost the paper still more money."

I stopped him before he could get to money-waster number four. "My motion for summary judgment was a cross motion in response to CIRR's motion for summary judgment. I would have had to appear before Judge MacAndrew to respond to CIRR's motion, even if I hadn't filed a cross motion."

Bramfield wasn't interested in my explanation. "And in addition to denying your cross motion, the judge scheduled yet another motion hearing, which will cost the *Ledger* still more money."

"Actually," I said, "the judge didn't deny my motion. In fact, he agreed with my argument that it's impossible to defame a belief system like Islam."

"If that's the case," Bramfield shot back, "why did he schedule another hearing?"

"He ruled that because Stacey's articles dealt with one particular mosque operated by CIRR, defaming Islam could be considered tantamount to defaming CIRR."

"That's absurd," Stacey said.

"That may be," I said, "but that's what he ruled. And at that hearing, if he decides your statements are truthful, he'll dismiss the second count of CIRR's complaint because truth is an absolute defense in defamation cases. I wanted to meet with you today to go over the statements CIRR claims are defamatory. There are only three because CIRR's attorney managed to anger Judge MacAndrew, which is no small feat, and the judge limited them to just three specific examples. That makes our job a whole lot easier."

"Perhaps," Bramfield said, "but we still have to go to trial on the first count of CIRR's complaint as well as Proctor's complaint, which will cost the *Ledger* still more money."

"Actually," I said. "I think the upcoming evidentiary hearing will dispose of Proctor's complaint and put a dent in his political career at the same time."

"Right, another opportunity for your firm to make money," Bramfield said, holding up another finger and continuing the count. "There's also your appearance at the hearing to get copies of Mayor Proctor's tax returns, the hearing to get CIRR's answers to interrogatories, another one to sanction CIRR for not providing answers, and now the new motion hearing you told Stacey about last night."

"No new motion," I assured him. I told him about the listening device in my living room and explained that my comment was intended to find out who was eavesdropping on my conversations. "My little gambit produced quick results. This morning CIRR's attorney faxed a copy of the amended complaint he's filing to correct the name of the plaintiff. That tells me that someone connected with CIRR planted the bug."

"Listening devices, indeed," Bramfield fumed. "What should have been a quick and easy trial has turned into a dog and pony show. We're dealing with public figures, Brendan.

Under *Sullivan*, they have to prove actual malice to win. You and I know they can't do that. We win, they lose. Case closed."

Bramfield was really trying my patience. "Every first year law school student knows the holding in *Times v. Sullivan*, but here's something only experienced litigators know: juries routinely return verdicts that have nothing to do with the law or the facts. And if I try your case before a jury with one or more Muslims, there's no telling how things will turn out." My words were perhaps a bit more forceful than they could have been, but they had the intended effect of putting Stacey's boss on the defensive.

"Well, you may be right," he conceded, "but this case is costing the *Ledger* a small fortune."

"I'll make you a deal," I said. "If we can move on and focus on the three statements CIRR claims are defamatory, I'll handle the upcoming Proctor hearing and the deposition of Mohammed Salameh *gratis*." I hadn't planned to charge the paper for either, but Bramfield didn't know that. I wasn't even sure he knew I was planning to depose Salameh.

The thought of getting something for nothing calmed Bramfield down, and he nodded his agreement.

I sorted through the stack of clippings I had on the coffee table in front of me, and picked up an article with the headline *New mosque brings religion of hate to Troy Forge.* "Okay, the first statement CIRR claims is defamatory is from the first article you published."

Before passing the article to Stacey, I read the sentence I had underlined: "Although most Westerners think of Islam as a religion, it is perhaps better characterized as a political system with a thin veneer of theology."

"Absolutely true," Stacey said.

"But just your opinion unless you've got facts to back that up," I responded.

My comment didn't sit well with Stacey. "Whose side are you on?" You're supposed to be representing us."

"I do represent you, but the best way to prepare for this hearing is to put ourselves in CIRR's shoes so we can anticipate what they'll throw at us in the courtroom. And, trust me, they'll label that statement as nothing more than your opinion – your defamatory opinion - unless we have facts to back it up."

"All you have to do is read some of the literature they hand out in the mosque to realize what I wrote is true," Stacey said. She withdrew a stack of brochures, pamphlets, and paperbacks from her briefcase and stacked them on the coffee table between us. "There's your evidence."

"Care to be more specific?" I asked, thumbing through a pamphlet entitled *Jihad in Islam* by someone named Abul A'la Maududi.

"Virtually every page of everything they pass out at the mosque contains something to back up what I wrote."

I waited, hoping Stacey would provide me with actual examples, but she leaned back and crossed her arms, apparently satisfied that I had everything I would need for the hearing.

"Okay," I finally said. "Let's move on. The second statement CIRR contends is defamatory comes from the second article you wrote. It reads: Muslims revere Mohammed as a prophet, but based on his actual deeds, he could be more accurately described as a criminal." I looked directly at Ezra Bramfield. "Can you imagine how a Muslim juror would react to that?"

"All you have to do is read the Qur'an to realize that state-ment is one hundred percent accurate," Stacey said.

"That may well be true," I said, "but I think you're missing the point. A Muslim juror is likely to go ballistic when he hears you refer to his prophet as a criminal. That's not going to help our case."

"So, you're suggesting reporters shouldn't tell the truth to avoid offending Muslims?" Stacey asked in a tone of voice that made it clear our discussion was about to escalate into an argument.

"That's not what I'm saying, and you know it." It came out a bit more strident than I intended. I took a deep breath and said more calmly, "What I'm saying is we're better off having Judge MacAndrew decide all this than a jury that may have one of more Muslims on it."

Perhaps Ezra Bramfield realized I was right, or perhaps he just wanted to speed up our meeting, which I was billing at my usual hourly rate. Regardless of the reason, he said to Stacey, "Brendan has a point. Let's move on to the third statement we have to deal with." He nodded in my direction, a signal for me to proceed.

"The third statement that CIRR alleges is defamatory appears in this article," I said, picking up another clipping from the coffee table. I read the sentence I had previously underlined: "Muslims would like the world to believe that *jihad* means a personal struggle against evil, but, in reality, the term more often means armed combat against non-Muslims." I picked up the copy of *Jihad in Islam* I had thumbed through moments before. "I'm guessing I'll find what I need in here?"

"Yes, that's helpful," Stacey said as she began sorting through the stack of pamphlets and paperbacks, "but there's something that's even better." I waited while she went through the material. "Damn," she finally said. "It's not here. I'll have to get you a copy."

It was becoming apparent that this meeting wasn't providing me with the information I'd need for the upcoming hearing, so I announced that it was time to wrap things up. Ezra Bramfield readily agreed, but only after making me promise that I wouldn't schedule any new motion hearings or depositions before the trial.

I broke that promise a couple of hours later.

34

"There's something about this case you're not telling me."

I was still sitting in the wing chair, sifting through the stack of material from our meeting, when Stacey appeared at my door. "Forget something?" I asked as she reclaimed her seat on the sofa across from me.

"We need to talk," she said. In my experience, conversations that begin with those four words tend to go rapidly downhill. "I get the distinct impression you just don't appreciate the importance of this case. To you it's just a routine defamation case."

"I think you're confusing me with your boss. He thinks it's routine. Any case in which you're a defendant isn't routine in my book." I thought that was a pretty good response, but apparently I was wrong.

"Just as I thought. You don't get it. This case isn't about me. It's about the ability to sound a warning about Islam without being attacked by Muslim pressure groups."

"You really seem to have a problem with immigrants," I said, thinking back to our conversation during the trip to Maine to find Machias Phelps' aunt.

It was the wrong thing to have said. Stacey went from annoyed to downright angry. "If you heard what's being preached in this mosque, you'd understand what I'm talking about. These people have absolutely no respect or tolerance for anyone who's not a Muslim. They're not immigrants, Brendan, they're invaders."

"It's only one mosque with a few hundred people. A pretty puny invading army."

"A few hundred in this mosque," Stacey countered, "and a few hundred in the ones in Jersey City, Union City, Paramus, New Brunswick, Camden, and dozens of other places. And that's just here in New Jersey. Muslims are pouring into Western countries at record rates, and nobody is even bothering to ask the obvious question: why are they coming here if they hate our way of life?"

I could sense that this was about to turn into one of those epic arguments I never win. It was time to shut things down. "If you want to play Paula Revere and ride through the streets shouting 'the Muslims are coming,' that's fine with me. My job is winning your case so you can do that. As you said, the case is about press freedom."

I thought that would satisfy her and end the conversation. I was wrong, yet again.

"You just don't get it," Stacey insisted. "Islam isn't just another religion. It's an entire way of life that's the polar opposite of everything we believe in. Publicly, groups like CIRR say all they want is to be treated equally, but in private they admit their real aim is supremacy." She picked up the *Jihad in Islam* pamphlet from the coffee table, flipped though it and began to read. "Islam wishes to destroy all states and governments anywhere on the face of the earth which are opposed to the ideology and program of Islam regardless of the country or the nation which rules it." She stopped reading and looked me in the eye. "Does that sound like any other religion you've ever encountered?"

"That's just one pamphlet from one mosque."

"There are dozens more just like it in this mosque and every other mosque," Stacey shot back.

I was tempted to ask how she knew what was in other mosques, but decided that was probably a bad idea. Instead, I said, "Just because this kind of stuff is handed out at a mosque doesn't mean everyone who attends reads it. And even if they do read it, that doesn't mean they believe it. Catholics are told not to use contraceptives, but many do. Jews aren't supposed to eat pork, but many do. Heck, Avery has bacon and eggs for breakfast seven days a week."

My observation made Stacey narrow her blazing green eyes like an angry cat. "A Catholic who obeys church doctrine by not using contraceptives doesn't hurt anyone. A Jew who follows Jewish dietary laws by not eating pork doesn't hurt anyone. But a Muslim who follows Islamic law to convert, subjugate, or kill non-Muslims can cause a lot of mayhem."

"Last I heard, none of the Muslims from the Troy Forge mosque has gone on a killing spree." It seemed like a sensible thing to say at the time. Of course, had I known then what I know now, I wouldn't have said it.

Stacey unleashed one of her most potent weapons: the exasperated sigh.

I played a hunch. "There's something about this case you're not telling me."

"What do you mean?"

"You know perfectly well what I mean." I leaned back in my chair, folded my arms and waited, an old litigator's trick that forces the other party to fill the uncomfortable silence.

"My job is on the line," Stacey finally said. "When I pitched my idea for a series of articles about the new mosque, Ezra turned me down flat. Other papers in the Ledger Media Group had already taken flak from CIRR for things they published. I convinced Ezra to publish my series by telling him that if we got sued, as we both assumed would happen, you'd wage one of your notorious courtroom battles that would cause CIRR and other Muslim pressure groups to think twice about coming after us in the future."

Everything suddenly became clear. "And instead of a widely followed show trial, you're ending up with a bunch of low-profile hearings."

"And they're costing a whole lot more than we expected." Stacey said, snatching up her coat and briefcase and heading for the door.

"Wait up," I said, not wanting things to end that way.

"No, I have to go."

When she was halfway across the room, Stacey stopped and slowly turned back to where I was sitting. "Do you remember when we first met?" She didn't wait for an answer. "It was at the Berkowitz tax fraud trial in Newark. You were amazing. You broke every rule in the book to defend your client. You were passionate. Now you're..." She paused, searching for the right word. "Pedestrian." In retrospect, I should have explained that every trial is different and, perhaps more importantly, every judge is different. Antagonizing Judge Abrams was part of my trial strategy in the Berkowitz case. In this case, it was best to let Tinoo Barahi annoy the judge. Unfortunately, I was so surprised and, truth be told, a bit hurt by Stacey's comment that I didn't say anything. I'll always wonder if my silence played a part in what eventually happened.

Stacey turned and continued to the door, arriving just as Carolyn appeared. Seeing them standing side-by-side, I realized how much they resembled one another. They were both petite, green-eyed redheads with a figure to rival that of any of the models who had graced the cover of *Sports Illustrated*. Stacey took one last look in my direction, then turned on her heel and walked away.

Carolyn, who had obviously overheard my conversation with Stacey, but who was far too circumspect to admit having heard it, much less comment on it, said, "You'll never guess what just came over the fax machine." Realizing I wasn't in the mood to play guessing games, she handed me a stack of papers and retreated to the outer office.

I returned to my comfortable wing chair, propped my legs up on the coffee table, and began reading. The first page was a letter from Shapiro, the prosecutor in Texas who, according to Reynaldo Renoir, had won the Justice Department's sole victory against one of the Muslim Brotherhood front groups. Shapiro's letter was short and to the point. Most of the material in his file, he wrote, pertained to the local organization that was the defendant in that case, and consequently wouldn't do me any good. However, he was including a copy of two government exhibits from that trial that he thought could be useful in defending my clients in the defamation case brought by the Council for Islamic Religious Respect. As a trial attorney who understood the process of admitting documents into evidence, Mr. Shapiro concluded his letter with a promise to mail me certified copies of those exhibits.

The second of the faxed pages looked like it might have been some sort of cover sheet. There were three lines of large type in the middle of the page, with three lines of smaller type in the bottom right corner. I had no idea what it said since it was written in what I assumed was Arabic, but it looked vaguely familiar. At the very bottom of the page was the outline of a sticker used to mark exhibits at trial. The sticker told me I was holding Government Exhibit 003-0085 submitted into evidence in a case captioned *U.S. v. HLF, et al.* The same sticker appeared on the next thirteen pages, all written in Arabic. Fortunately, when I got to the fourteenth page, Arabic gave way to English.

These pages were labeled as Government Exhibit 003-0086, telling me they were introduced into evidence in federal court right after the thirteen-page document written in Arabic. That, combined with the layout, suggested it was a translation of the first document.

I hadn't read more than the first paragraph when I realized why the document looked familiar. It was the same memo that Eddie Rizzo's associate had stolen from Mohammed Salameh's apartment. And while I couldn't use stolen property in court, a document already admitted into evidence in a federal court was a different matter. I called Carolyn into my office and dictated a motion for summary judgment on the first count of CIRR's complaint alleging Stacey and the *Ledger* had defamed that organization by linking it to terrorism.

Then I began preparing for the following morning's hearing in Jersey City.

35

"The most dangerous enemy is the one who hides in plain sight."

Snowflakes had just started falling as I walked to my car in the parking lot behind our office building that evening. If it continued snowing through the night, my drive to Jersey City the following morning would be even more tedious than usual. No sooner had I gotten in and turned on the radio than a voice from behind me asked, "How was your trip to Passaic?"

I looked in the rear view mirror to find Reynaldo Renoir lounging in the Mustang's back seat. His body language suggested that appearing unannounced and uninvited in someone's car was an everyday occurrence. "I always liked this car," he said. "Nicely restored, but you really should get the locks repaired."

"To what do I owe the pleasure?"

"Just checking to see how fruitful your limo drive to Passaic was."

"How do you know I went to Passaic?" I asked.

"We keep tabs on things."

"So, your people have been following me." It was more a statement than a question.

"Sometimes we follow you. Sometimes we follow the people who follow you."

"And who are the people who follow me?" I asked.

"Sometimes it's Proctor's people," Reynaldo said. "Sometimes its people we know are connected to the Muslim Brotherhood. Sometimes it's people we think are connected to the Brotherhood, but we don't know for sure. And sometimes it's people we don't know."

That was something I didn't want to hear. "You've got all the resources of the FBI, CIA, DIA, and who knows how many other government agencies at your disposal and you don't know who's following me? That's reassuring."

"I only work for one agency," Reynaldo said, "and an underfunded one at that. Besides, we're not your personal body guards." He changed the subject before I could ask questions about my unknown pursuers. "I assume you received a fax from Shapiro down in Texas."

"I assume that was your doing," I said, trading assumptions. "Thanks."

"You're welcome. Now return the favor by telling me about your limo trip to Passaic and how Eddie Rizzo is involved in all this."

"I already paid for the favor by giving you the information my forensic accountant dug up about CIRR and its local affiliates." Ray Benson wasn't really a forensic accountant, but Reynaldo didn't need to know that.

"That stuff wasn't worth the paper it was printed on. And giving me duplicates of every document didn't make the information twice as valuable."

Rather than debate the value of the material I had provided, which I knew was a losing proposition, I decided to come clean, or at least reasonably clean. "I'll make you a deal. I'll tell you everything I know, including some interesting things I learned since the last time we spoke, if you'll agree to leave Eddie

Rizzo alone. His involvement in all this is nothing more than a coincidence."

"Rizzo's not on our radar," Reynaldo assured me. "We don't have the resources to chase after petty crooks and shady businessmen. We leave those for local law enforcement. We want Mohammed Salameh. We have intelligence that he's up to something, perhaps something big. We can't find him, and that has us worried."

"I can't find him, either. I've been trying to subpoena him to appear at a deposition, but I can't find him to make service. I asked Eddie Rizzo to have his people keep an eye out for Salameh."

"That's why you went to Passaic?"

"Not exactly." I told Reynaldo about Eddie's surveillance of Obduhali's office and his conclusion that it didn't look like the typical law practice. I also told him that I had made Eddie promise to stop his ham-fisted surveillance operation. "I assume this is what you were referring to in our conversation behind Madame Elvira's card reading parlor on Route 46."

"Would appear to be," Reynaldo said.

"Okay for Rizzo's people to keep looking for Salameh? We're not trying to interfere with your investigation, but I want to find the guy as much as you do. I want him to sit for a deposition."

Reynaldo thought for a moment before answering, apparently weighing the pros and cons of having outside help from so-called petty crooks with surveillance skills that had thus far proven deficient. "Have them keep looking, but discretely this time. And make it clear all you want them to do is find the guy. We want to know where he is, not take him out of play. And it's crucial that he not know we found him."

I assumed that meant Reynaldo's people wanted to follow Salameh to someone else. I also assumed it meant Reynaldo was desperate to find Salameh. "I'll make sure Eddie Rizzo understands."

For the next half hour, I traded information with Reynaldo. It was probably the most cordial conversation I had ever had with the man, so cordial, in fact, that he provided me with a phone number where I could reach him if I learned the whereabouts of the elusive Mohammed Salameh. Our discussion eventually circled back to the Muslim Brotherhood and the Akrami memo used in the Texas federal court trial. "I'm guessing that memo was a wakeup call for Uncle Sam," I said.

"For some people in government it was," Reynaldo explained. "For others, not so much. The guy who recruited me for this assignment thinks the Muslim Brotherhood is a major threat. Other people in high places think the Brotherhood is composed of non-violent moderates." His comment reminded me of the memo's reference to "our friends in high places."

"What do you think?"

"I think the most dangerous enemy is the one who hides in plain sight."

36

"Mohammed Salameh isn't in Michigan."

"Not you two again," Judge Latisha Washington said as Omar Obduhali and I made our way to the counsel tables in her Jersey City courtroom. "What have you come up with to waste my time this morning?"

"Good morning, Your Honor," I replied pleasantly, hoping that would buy me some goodwill.

I needn't have bothered.

The judge looked right at me and smiled. It was the smile of a predator sizing up its prey. She held up one finger to signal we were to wait while she reviewed the case file. When she finished, Judge Washington said, "Take a seat." I began to sit down at the counsel table. "Not there." She pointed to the public gallery. "Back there. You're not the only one who can waste other people's time." I was tempted to point out that my adversary was the one wasting her time by filing a frivolous motion and that I was simply there to respond to it, but decided that would only make things worse.

Obduhali and I took seats in the public gallery. I made it a point to sit as far from him as possible. He removed a newspaper from his briefcase and began to read. He didn't seem particularly upset to wait. Perhaps he had a light schedule that day. Or perhaps he was being paid by the hour. I was more than a little perturbed by this turn of events, however, since I had other things to do. Besides, I had taken Eddie Rizzo's personal injury case on a contingent fee basis, meaning I wasn't being paid to sit and wait. My fee would be thirty percent of a judgment or settlement. And the way things were going with this case, I was pretty certain I'd end up with thirty percent of nothing.

We were still waiting when noon arrived and the judge recessed for lunch. After paying way too much for a mediocre tuna on rye, I made my way to a pay phone and called the office. "I have a handful of phone messages for you," Carolyn said. She went through them, concluding with, "Stacey called to tell you she can't keep her dinner date with you this evening."

I waited for an explanation, but none was forthcoming. "Is she working on a tight deadline?" I finally asked.

Carolyn hesitated. She had overheard my overheated conversation with Stacey the day before and apparently assumed, incorrectly as it turned out, that that was the reason for Stacey's decision to cancel our dinner date. She eventually said, "I don't know; she didn't say."

After the lunch recess I returned to the courtroom, and resumed watching the parade of supplicants marching to the throne of Queen Latisha. After an hour of listening to arguments, I learned how to predict, with almost one hundred percent accuracy, which attorney would prevail. It didn't matter what kind of case it was. It didn't matter what the law was. And it sure as hell didn't matter which attorney had the better argument. What mattered in Latisha Washington's courtroom was the attorney's place in a well-defined pecking order. Black attorneys routinely won arguments against white attorneys. Female attorneys almost always beat male attorneys, unless the female attorney was white and the male attorney was black. Attorneys who shared a last name with a president, like Washington or Jefferson, had a tough time losing, but attorneys with names like Goldberg, Goldfarb, or Goldstein never won. Judge Washington was apparently very fond of the executive branch, but had something against the letter "G." Perhaps she had a bad childhood experience with Sesame Street.

I entertained myself picking winners for another hour, but grew bored when my predictions proved correct almost every time. It's no fun to always lose, but it's equally boring to always win. Assuming Judge Washington planned to keep us waiting as long as possible, I left the courtroom and wandered out to the elevator lobby where I found a window that looked out over a rooftop now covered with a light dusting of snow. The dreary gray sky I had encountered on my drive to Jersey City that morning was even darker, making mid-afternoon seem like dusk.

After stretching my legs, I returned to my seat in the court-room in time to see a white attorney named Goldfarb make a compelling argument in support of his motion, only to be vanquished by a black attorney whose argument consisted of repeating "it just ain't right" over and over.

Despite the scintillating rhetoric, I found myself nodding off. The next thing I knew, I was a reporter at a White House press conference. President Muhammed Hussain had just explained his plan to invade Israel and increase foreign aid to Saudi Arabia. Now he was pointing at me and saying, "Mr. O'Brian, you're up." I assumed that meant it was my turn to ask a question until I realized the shrill voice calling my name was that of Latisha Washington.

"Glad you could join us," Judge Washington said as I roused myself from my daydream and made my way to the front of the courtroom, which was now almost empty. Omar Obduhali was already seated at one counsel table. I had just started to take my seat at the other table when the judge fired the first salvo in what was to be a prolonged tongue lashing. "I'm sick and tired of attorneys who squabble like school children. I shouldn't have to waste my time settling your petty disputes." She went on in similar fashion for the better part of five minutes before addressing Obduhali. "What's your problem today?"

My adversary got to his feet, buttoned his suit coat and said, "I am respectfully asking the court to compel Mr. O'Brian's client to answer all of the questions in the interrogatories I served on him."

Judge Washington nodded in my direction, and I responded by explaining, "My client has provided complete answers in timely fashion." I held up the set of answered interrogatories I had returned to Obduhali.

A court officer retrieved the document I displayed and brought it to the bench where the judge leafed through it. She handed it back to the court officer, who walked it over to Obduhali. "Now you have your answers," the judge said.

Judge Washington was about to gavel the proceedings to a close when Obduhali said, "I would ask the court to sanction Mr. O'Brian for not providing answers in timely fashion."

"Don't push your luck, Mr. Obduhali. You got your answers, now get out of my courtroom."

Obduhali wouldn't quit while he was ahead. "This is not acceptable. Mr. O'Brian has violated the rules of court and Your Honor must do something about it."

That was the wrong thing to have said to someone like Latisha Washington. "Don't you dare tell me what I *must* do. In my courtroom I decide what I must do, not you or anyone else."

"I sincerely apologize," Obduhali said in a tone of voice that suggested he was neither sincere nor apologetic. "What I meant to say is that I *request* Your Honor to sanction Mr. O'Brian for his blatant violation of the rules."

"You just won't quit, will you?" the judge said. She pointed to the answered interrogatories the court officer had given to Obduhali. "Let me see those again."

The same court officer retrieved the document and brought it to the judge, who flipped through the pages. "Let's see what we have here. Question six asks for the name and address of all persons in plaintiff's vehicle at the time of the accident. Now, if I remember correctly, and in my courtroom I always remember correctly, the answer you filed in response to the complaint states that your client wasn't involved in an auto accident with the plaintiff. If that's the case, why would you ask for the names of people in a car that was involved in an accident?"

I was elated at the judge's reaction, but disappointed that my foolproof system for predicting winners in Latisha Washington's courtroom was about to be proven unreliable. I crossed my arms and waited, curious to see what kind of answer Obduhali would come up with.

He never got the chance. The judge rose from her seat, leaned forward, put both hands on the bench, looked down at my adversary and said, "I'm sick and tired of attorneys who waste my time. Perhaps I should sanction you for wasting Mr. O'Brian's time as well as mine."

I took advantage of the opening the judge's anger afforded me. "Perhaps Your Honor might consider sanctioning Mr. Obduhali by requiring him to produce his client for a deposition?" I purposely phrased it as a question rather than a request.

To my surprise, the judge said, "Mr. Obduhali will produce the defendant for a deposition within five days at a mutually convenient place and time."

Knowing how Obduhali operates, I assumed it would be impossible to arrive at anything that was mutually convenient. While I was considering whether or not to raise that issue, Obduhali said. "I'm afraid that will be impossible."

"It will be possible if I say it will be possible," the judge shot back.

"You do not understand," Obduhali said, "my client is not in New Jersey. He is visiting a sick brother in Dearborn, Michigan."

"When will he return?" the judge asked.

"This I do not know. All I know is he has a brother who is in hospital."

"How long has he been gone?"

"I believe it has been about a week."

"That's long enough for a hospital visit," Judge Washington said. "Get him back here."

"I will see what can be done," Obduhali replied.

"No, you'll get him back here," the judge instructed.

A dowdy woman in a too-colorful-for-court dashiki appeared at the door to the judge's chambers, waddled up to the bench, leaned down and whispered something into Judge Washington's ear before hastily retracing her steps.

"The snow is starting to accumulate," the judge said, "and roads are getting slippery." She looked directly at Obduhali. "You have my instructions. I expect you to follow them." She gaveled the proceedings to a close and made a beeline for her chambers.

Obduhali packed up his briefcase and headed for the exit in the back of the courtroom, deliberately avoiding eye contact with me. I sat there savoring my unexpected victory before making my way to the pay phones in the elevator lobby. I had promised Reynaldo that I'd let him know if I learned the whereabouts of Mohammed Salameh, and that was a promise I intended to keep. Unfortunately, I had used the last of my change to call the office during the lunch recess so it was a promise that would have to wait. Maybe I should have kept the cell phone Avery gave me instead of giving it to Stacey.

Instead of making a phone call, I got on the elevator and was joined by a distinguished, middle-aged man in a three-piece suit as the doors were closing. I had seen him in the courtroom earlier and assumed he was a fellow attorney. He proved me wrong a moment later when he said, "Mohammed Salameh isn't in Michigan. We followed him to an industrial park in Secaucus earlier today. Unfortunately, he slipped away and we don't know where he went."

"Sorry to hear that," I said.

"Mr. Rizzo wasn't particularly happy either."

37

"I came to see the mini-bar."

The drive home from Jersey City took almost twice as long as usual because of the snow. Fortunately, I made it in one piece, unlike the driver of a BMW who flew by me on Interstate 280 before combining his car with a guardrail to create a grotesque parody of a shish kabob. I forced that image out of my mind by focusing on what awaited me at the end of my drive: a comfortable chair by the fireplace, a tuna sandwich, the latest Nelson DeMille novel, and a glass or two of my favorite Irish whiskey.

By the time I got off I-280 in Troy Forge the snow had stopped falling, but the roads were still slick. I made it home without incident and managed to get the fireplace started and the tuna sandwich made. Unfortunately, the phone rang before I could pour the Jameson.

"Brendan." It was a female voice on the other end of the line, speaking so softly I wasn't sure who it was until she added, "it's me, Stacey."

"Why are you whispering? Do you have a sore throat?"

I thought that was a perfectly reasonable question, but apparently I was wrong. "No, I don't have a sore throat." She sounded angry.

"Then why are you whispering?"

I thought that was also a reasonable question, but I was wrong again. "I'm whispering because I don't want anyone to hear me." She didn't actually tack on "you idiot" to the end of the sentence, but her tone of voice did it for her. I waited for an explanation, which was soon delivered in the same hushed voice. "I'm in the ladies' room at the mosque."

"Why are you in the mosque."

"I came here to get a copy of that pamphlet I told you about when Ezra and I were in your office." That explained why she was in the mosque, but not why she was whispering. I can understand the need for whispering in a mosque or a church. But a restroom? Stacey supplied the explanation. "I'm hiding from two large, scary men who saw me take the pamphlet. I think they realize I'm an outsider."

"So, why not just walk out the door?" It seemed like another perfectly reasonable question. Wrong again.

"Are you out of your mind?" Stacey hissed. "Do you have any idea what these people would do to me if they caught me?"

I didn't, and I suspect she didn't either, but there was no point in arguing. "So, what do you want me to do?"

"Come get me," she said. "If I'm with a man, they'll probably leave me alone. If I'm by myself, who knows what they'll do."

Rather than point out she had just admitted she didn't really know what would happen if she simply walked away, or remind her she was in suburban New Jersey rather than the Middle East, I took the path of least resistance. "I'll be there as soon as I can."

After Stacey told me exactly where she was inside the mosque, I donned my suit of shining armor and hopped on my white horse. Actually, I put on my topcoat and hopped into my Mustang.

The snow had stopped falling, but the roads were still slippery, and it took me longer than usual to get to the mosque in

Troy Forge. Friday evening services were apparently in full swing when I arrived, as the well-lighted parking lot was almost full. I pulled the Mustang into an empty space in the back corner of the lot, weaved through the parked cars, and trudged up the steps to the mosque's main entrance. I passed through an ornately carved door and found myself in a lobby with a rack of shoes to my right, restrooms to my left, and three sets of double doors straight ahead. Judging from the sounds I was hearing, the doors in front of me led to the main prayer hall or *musalla*. Two bearded men in suits stood in front of the doors on the right. Rather than risk a confrontation, just in case Stacey's fears were justified, I decided to create a diversion that would allow her to slip away undetected.

"I came to see the mini-bar," I said in a voice loud enough for Stacey to hear. Striding toward the two men, I added, "One of my buddies told me you guys had a mini-bar in your church. I know Catholics serve wine, but I never heard of a church with a mini-bar."

Both men moved toward me. "I believe you are misinformed, my friend," the larger of the two said. "We have no mini-bar here. And this is not a church; it is a mosque."

"Mosque, church, same difference," I said just as we met in the middle of the lobby. Instead of stopping, I walked by them and turned around. They spun around with military precision to face me, putting their backs to the rest rooms on the far side of the lobby. Pointing to the main prayer room, I said, "My buddy says your priest walks up some stairs to a mini-bar. I want to see this for myself."

"You cannot go in there," the bigger of the two informed me.

The smaller guy said something to his compatriot in a language I didn't understand, causing both to break into laughter. Good. The more entertaining they found my absurd performance, the less likely they'd notice Stacey when she made her move. They conversed in the unknown language for a few seconds before the larger man said, "My friend, I believe you are referring to the *minbar*, which is where the imam stands to speak." As he said this, a figure dressed in a black *burqa* emerged from the ladies' room on the other side of the lobby and made a beeline for the exit. She disappeared through the front doors of the mosque, my cue to wrap up the dumb infidel routine and leave.

I took a step toward the door. Well, if there's no mini-bar, then there's nothing for me to see."

The larger of the two men moved to block my path. "Wait a minute. Who are you?" His accusatory tone suggested he wasn't buying my routine. I can't understand why.

Unwilling to give him my real name, I introduced myself as Eric Stratton, extended my hand for a handshake and added, "Damn glad to meet you."

Instead of shaking my hand, he stepped aside and pointed to the exit. "Get out and do not come back." I shrugged my shoulders and complied.

As I emerged from the mosque I was greeted by a gust of cold air rather than Stacey, who was nowhere to be seen. I stood on the top step and scanned the parking lot, eventually spotting a hand waving at me from behind a minivan to my left. I walked to the minivan where I discovered a *burqa*-clad woman whose penetrating green eyes told me I had found Stacey.

"Very fashionable," I said. "Always thought you looked good in black." She responded by grabbing my arm and yanking me behind the minivan. I was about to suggest she was being more than a little paranoid, but she put her finger to her lips to signal me to be quiet, and pointed back in the direction of the mosque.

I peeked around the minivan and saw the two men I had engaged inside the mosque. They were standing on the steps surveying the parking lot, each holding a pistol. A moment later they were joined by two more bearded men, also brandishing weapons. Judging from their hand signals, it appeared they were about to search the parking lot. Since four-legged game is usually hunted with rifles, I had to assume these guys were gunning for two-legged prey. And while I found it difficult to believe they'd actually start shooting, I didn't plan to stick around and find out. "We have to get out of here," I said.

"No shit, Sherlock," Stacey whispered.

Walking in a crouch, we worked our way down the line of parked cars until we came to the end of the row. An open space of about twenty feet separated us from the next row. I was in the process of calculating our chances of crossing that expanse unseen when I heard a noise behind me. I turned around and found myself face to face with a clean-shaven, baby-faced guy in a dark coat. He couldn't have been more than twenty-five, if that. And like the four bearded men, he was armed with a very dangerous looking pistol.

38

"It was a close call, but Uncle Sam won."

The baby-faced kid, who identified himself as Special Agent Phillips, turned out to be part of a task force headed by Reynaldo Renoir. I had always thought of Reynaldo as a lone wolf, and was a bit surprised to discover he was part of an organized group, perhaps even its supervisor. Phillips didn't provide details or explain why he happened to be in the mosque's parking lot, but he did drive Stacey and me home. He even arranged for someone to retrieve our cars and return them to our respective homes so we wouldn't have to venture back into what I had come to regard as enemy territory.

Agent Phillips and I had another bizarre encounter the following week in the Jersey City courtroom of Judge Latisha Washington. He was already there when I arrived, casually reading a newspaper in the back row of the public gallery. I was making a return appearance before Judge Washington because the judge, true to her word, had ordered a hearing to find out why Omar Obduhali had failed to produce his client for a deposition as she had instructed the last time we appeared before her.

That morning we were the fifth act in the judicial circus, the first four warm-up performances involving everything from misaligned fences to misappropriated funds. By the time it was our turn, the judge was in an even more cantankerous mood than usual. Fortunately, her ire was directed at my adversary.

She fired the opening shot of her tirade just as Obduhali and I were about to be seated at our respective counsel tables. "Mr. Obduhali, the last time you were in my courtroom, I told you to make your client available for a deposition, didn't I?" She didn't wait for an answer. "You apparently didn't take my instructions seriously. What do I have to do to convince you I'm serious?" It looked as though Obduhali was about to make the mistake of supplying an answer to a question that clearly didn't anticipate one, but before he could say anything, the judge continued her tirade in a voice that grew increasingly louder and more vitriolic. "When I tell an attorney in my courtroom to do something, I expect it to be done. I'm in charge here, not you. My instructions aren't suggestions, they're orders. I expect them to be carried out. You didn't carry them out."

Five minutes later, Hurricane Latisha finally blew itself out, and Obduhali, who had remained quiet throughout the judge's tirade, responded in a tone of voice that was entirely too calm under the circumstances. "I have been unable to reach my client, Your Honor."

"What do you mean you can't reach your client? The last time you were in my courtroom wasting my time, you told me your client was in..." She stopped to consult her file before continuing. "Michigan. Dearborn, Michigan to be exact. This is 1993, Mr. Obduhali. They have telephones in Michigan. All you have to do is pick up the phone and call your client."

"I have tried to reach Mr. Salameh on the telephone," Obduhali explained, "but I have been unsuccessful."

It looked as though Obduhali was about to go down in flames without any help from me, but just to be sure, I decided to add fuel to the fire. "Your Honor, if I may," I said deferentially, requesting permission to speak. My groveling paid off with a nod in my direction, my cue to proceed. "The last time we appeared before Your Honor, Mr. Obduhali told the court that his client had been gone for about a week. Yet he told me on previous occasions that his client was in Michigan visiting a sick brother. Either my adversary's representation to the court was inaccurate, or Mr. Salameh has gone to Michigan on more than one occasion. If the latter, one would think that Mr. Obduhali has established a way to communicate with his client." I decided to add a bit of flattery. "As Your Honor correctly pointed out, it is 1993 and they do have telephones in Michigan."

"What about it, counselor?" the judge asked, turning to Obduhali.

My adversary never flinched. "Mr. O'Brian is correct. Mr. Salameh has made several trips to Michigan to visit a sick brother. And I do have the phone number for his brother's home in Dearborn. I have been calling that number every day, but the phone is never answered."

Then he dropped the bombshell. "Since I am unable to communicate with Mr. Salameh, I can no longer represent him."

That didn't sit well with the judge. "You're the attorney of record on this case, and you'll continue to represent the defendant until I say otherwise." Under New Jersey court rules, an attorney must first secure the client's consent before walking away. That, of course, assumes the client hasn't pulled a disappearing act as Mohammed Salameh had supposedly done.

"Your Honor, it's impossible for me to..." That's as far as Obduhali got before the judge cut him off.

"It's impossible for me to run my courtroom if an attorney can simply walk away in the middle of a case. I let you withdraw for no good reason and soon every attorney who can't collect his fee from a client will want to do the same. I'd never get anything done in this courtroom."

"I have a good reason," Obduhali said, but before he could elaborate, the judge held up her hand to signal she didn't want to hear any more.

"I think you're playing games, counselor, wasting my time and Mr. O'Brian's time as well." The fact that Latisha Washington even pretended to care about wasting my time was a sign that my adversary was in deep trouble. "Before I would even consider allowing you to withdraw, you'd have to secure Mr. O'Brian's consent." She was looking right at me as she said that, which is why I was taken by surprise when she added, "Who the hell are you?"

Someone tapped me on the shoulder. I turned around to find Agent Phillips standing behind me, waving a piece of paper in the air.

"I'm an associate at Mr. O'Brian's firm," he said in response to Judge Washington's question. It was an obvious lie, but the judge wouldn't know that, and I wasn't about to tell her, at least not until I discovered what was going on. "My apologies to the court," Reynaldo's associate continued, "but I have an urgent message for Mr. O'Brian from a federal judge."

The mention of a federal judge had its intended effect. "Very well," Judge Washington said with a hand gesture that signaled permission for Phillips to give me the folded piece of paper he was holding.

I took it from him and read the handwritten message: *Don't pursue this. You might undermine our investigation.*

Now I had a quandary. If I fought to keep Obduhali in the case, I'd incur the wrath of Reynaldo Renoir and who-knew-how-many federal agents working for some shadowy agency, bureau, or task force. On the other hand, if Obduhali were no longer representing Salameh, I'd find myself in a procedural no man's land that would turn a money-losing case into an even bigger disaster, and piss off one of the firm's most profitable clients. It all boiled down to whether Uncle Sam or Eddie the Skunk was scarier when crossed or more likely to be helpful when placated.

It was a close call, but Uncle Sam won.

"I have no objection to Mr. Obduhali withdrawing from the case," I said to the judge as I folded the note and put it in my pocket. To justify that position and make it appear that my decision had nothing to do with the note I had just read, I added, "Frankly, Mr. Obduhali has been completely uncooperative throughout this matter. Perhaps I'll be able to secure more cooperation from whomever takes over representation of the defendant." I thought that sounded pretty convincing, so I made a mental note to use that line when it came time to explain things to Eddie Rizzo, who I assumed had an observer hiding in plain sight among the dwindling number of people in the public gallery.

"Very well," the judge said to Obduhali, "I'll take your motion to withdraw under advisement and render a decision in due course." She gaveled the hearing to a close.

My adversary hurried from the courtroom as though he was afraid the judge might change her mind. Or perhaps he simply wanted to avoid a confrontation with me.

By the time I got to the elevator lobby, Obduhali was nowhere to be seen, but Agent Phillips was holding open one of the elevators, apparently waiting for me. "Let's ride," he said, pointing to the open door. We got on, the door closed and the elevator began its descent. "I think you misinterpreted my note," Phillips said, "We don't care who his attorney is. I just didn't want you to say anything more about Salameh's whereabouts. We want him to think we're buying his story about being in Michigan."

"You could have been a bit clearer," I said. "The only reason you know Salameh is here in Jersey is because of me. And the only reason I knew that is because of Eddie Rizzo, whose case you may have just screwed up."

"Sorry about that," Phillips said, "but it's important we find Salameh. We know he's up to something, we just don't know what."

We found that out a few weeks later.

39

"Maybe he likes to grow flowers."

January had been unusually warm, with the temperature reaching sixty-six degrees early in the month. February, unfortunately, didn't follow suit. When I arrived at the office that morning the temperature was below freezing. It was a good day to settle in to my comfortable chair, put my feet up on the coffee table, and read the two items Stacey had retrieved from the mosque the night I first met Reynaldo Renoir's colleague, Agent Phillips.

The first item was a pamphlet called *Words of Faith* by Mohammed Mustapha. According to the answers to my interrogatories that Tinoo Barahi had eventually provided, Mustapha was the mosque's imam, the Muslim equivalent of a priest or minister. Flipping though the pages, I determined that it was a collection of the imam's sermons, what Stacey referred to as harangues.

I put the pamphlet aside and turned my attention to the second item Stacey had filched from the mosque, a paperback containing a collection of hadiths (or *ahadith* to use the Arabic plural), accounts of things purportedly said or done by Mohammed, the man Muslims regard as a prophet. These are considered the most authoritative guidance for Muslims apart from the Qur'an.

According to Dr. Stern, although there are scores of hadith collections, two are considered the most reliable, one assembled by a man conveniently named Muslim and another by a guy whose name is so long he's referred to simply as Bukhari. The book Stacey had obtained was the handiwork of Bukhari. Just over two hundred pages, it consisted of nine "volumes" divided into ninety-three "books" containing sequentially numbered hadiths, each dealing with a specific topic. According to the table of contents, Mohammed took time out from his busy schedule to weigh in on matters ranging from bathing and menstrual periods to taxes, trade, and bankruptcy. He also had something to say about blood money, punishment laws, agriculture and fasting. The guy was a real Renaissance man.

Book 52, which recounted Mohammed's words and deeds relating to jihad, provided some choice nuggets I could use in court. I had spent about half an hour perusing that book when Avery Glickman appeared at my office door. "Got a second?"

"Sure, what do you need?"

"Remember that seminar in New York scheduled for the twenty-sixth, the one about law firm security?"

Actually, I had forgotten all about the seminar, but it seemed bad form to say that. So instead, I said, "What about it?"

"I told Scott I'd go with him, but something's come up. Any chance you could go in my place?"

"I'd like to help you out," I said, "but I'll be in court that day on the *Ledger's* defamation case." That wasn't entirely true. I assumed I might be in court at the end of the month, but I didn't yet have an actual date for the hearing. But using the motion hearing as an excuse was easier than explaining to my partner that I hate the hassle of driving into Manhattan. Avery nodded acknowledgment, rapped the door jamb with his knuckles, and disappeared.

I returned to Bukhari's handiwork, leafing through Book 84, which contains Mohammed's directives for dealing with apostates, people who leave Islam. According to Mohammed, the proper way to deal with apostates is to kill them. Islam is apparently the Hotel California of religions. Once you're in, you can never leave. An image of the four men with guns I had encountered at the Troy Forge mosque popped into my mind.

I was about to read Book 82 to see if Mohammed was equally harsh with disbelievers when Carolyn appeared at my door. "Tony Biffano called. Your witnesses for tomorrow's hearing before Judge MacAndrew have arrived."

"About time," I said. "They were supposed to have been here yesterday so I'd have time to prepare them for the hearing."

Carolyn laughed. "Tony said you'd say that. He told me to tell you he had to drive to Maine and pick them up because they decided at the last minute they didn't want to fly."

"I'm sure that will cost me a small fortune," I said.

"I'm sure it will," Carolyn agreed just as the phone on my desk rang. She crossed the room and picked up the receiver. "Just a moment, Mr. Rizzo," she told the caller before handing me the phone.

Eddie skipped the niceties. "What happened in court?"

Since he most likely had one of his own people in the courtroom, there was no point beating around the bush. "Omar Obduhali is no longer representing Salameh."

"How'd that happen?" Eddie wanted to know.

I fudged the truth a bit. "Part of my arrangement to keep Uncle Sam off your back."

There was a long pause, which I assumed meant my answer came as a surprise to the man who prided himself on knowing everything about everyone.

"Thanks, counselor," Eddie finally said. "But what's that mean for my case?"

"To be perfectly honest, I'm not entirely sure." This time I really was being honest. "Your personal injury case is one of the most bizarre cases I've handled in a long time."

"You got that right," Eddie shot back. "One minute I got half a million bucks, and the next I got bupkis."

"You never actually had half a million dollars," I reminded him. "You asked for half a million, but asking for something doesn't mean you have it."

"Okay, so maybe I didn't have half a million, but I coulda had that suitcase full of cash you told me the scumbag's attorney brought to your office." He was starting to sound a bit belligerent, my cue to implement damage control.

"For starters, it was a briefcase, not a suitcase. And more importantly, he didn't actually offer you that money. He simply plunked it down on my desk to see how I'd react." I had no way of knowing if that was true, but the last thing I needed was Eddie the Skunk thinking I had blown his chance of receiving a cash windfall.

After an uncomfortable silence, Eddie asked, "So where do we go from here?"

"I can't answer that until I see the order the judge enters. I'm hoping she'll require Omar Obduhali to substitute in another attorney before she actually releases him from representing Salameh. That's the way these things usually work. But as I said, this is one truly bizarre case, so I don't know what's going to happen." I decided it was only fair to reassure Eddie I would handle things. "Regardless of what happens, I'll protect your interests."

That seemed to placate him. "I know you will, counselor," Eddie said. "You been handling stuff for me for years and you never once let me down. You're the only guy I know I can always count on."

I was touched - not a lot, but touched nonetheless.

Apparently satisfied that I had his case under control, Eddie switched topics. "So, I still got my people looking for Salameh. He's one slippery S-O-B."

"So I gather."

"My guys spotted him at a garden center in Paramus, but they lost him in traffic when he left."

"Any idea what he was doing at a garden center?" I asked.

"I sent the guys back to find out. The manager was a prick, but one of the sales clerks opened up after we slipped him a hundred bucks. He said Salameh bought bags of fertilizer."

"Wonder what he wants with fertilizer."

"I don't know," Eddie said. "Maybe he likes to grow flowers when he's not driving like a maniac."

Later that month we found out why Salameh had bought fertilizer, and it had nothing to do with growing flowers.

40

"Billboard Bob is the one who should be worried."

When I arrived at the courthouse in Morristown the following morning, Emerson Lambert and his client, Bob Proctor, were already there. As usual, Billboard Bob was flanked by two members of the Troy Forge police department, a short, stocky guy and the man I had nicknamed Scarface. Proctor and his bodyguards had positioned themselves in the corner of the lobby with their backs against the wall, allowing them to keep an eye on everyone threading their way through the busy room.

As I entered the building, Emerson Lambert began walking toward me. We met in the middle of the lobby. "I don't know what you've got up your sleeve," Lambert said, "but it better be good or Judge MacAndrew will skin you alive." It was his latest attempt to find out what I had in store for his client. Ever since the day in Judge MacAndrew's chambers when I accused Bob Proctor of working a fraud on the court, Emerson Lambert had tried to find out what I knew. It started with a phone call, progressed to a friendly letter, then a not-so-friendly letter, and culminated in a formal application to the court. In the typical case, he probably would have succeeded in convincing the judge that he was entitled to details about my allegation so he could prepare a response. But this was anything but a typical case, and Judge MacAndrew declined to order me to turn over information prior to the hearing, agreeing with my admittedly insincere contention that doing so would allow Proctor to perpetuate his fraud on the court. It was probably the first time in his career that Duncan MacAndrew issued a ruling that wouldn't sit well with the Appellate Division.

"I'm not worried," I said nonchalantly as I looked around the lobby. "Billboard Bob is the one who should be worried."

"We'll see," Lambert responded before heading toward the hallway leading to Judge MacAndrew's courtroom. He signaled to Proctor, who fell into step beside him, his private praetorian guard bringing up the rear.

Truth be told, I was worried. The hearing was scheduled to begin in five minutes, and Tony Biffano still hadn't arrived with my witnesses. I waited a couple minutes and then headed to the courtroom.

When I got there, I found Rick and Carolyn seated in the front row of the public gallery, flanking three empty seats. They were attempting, with great difficulty, to save those prime properties for Biff and my two witnesses. The *Ledger* had run a story the previous day suggesting this hearing would mark an important turning point not just in the defamation case, but also in the career of the mayor of Troy Forge. As a result, the courtroom was packed to capacity, with people standing along the entire rear wall, many casting a covetous eye on those three empty seats.

As I took my place at the counsel table, a court officer knocked on the door to Judge MacAndrew's chambers. The judge appeared moments later and took the bench. After his customary "good-morning-counselors-good-morning-Your-Honor" routine, Judge MacAndrew began the proceedings by instructing me to call my first witness.

I called Bob Proctor, who jumped to his feet and hurried to the witness stand, smiling his big, toothy politician's smile. He apparently believed that showing an eagerness to testify would lend credence to what he was about to say.

As Proctor stated his name, spelled it for the benefit of the court reporter, and identified himself as the mayor of Troy Forge, Judge MacAndrew handed me the two tax returns I had reviewed in his chambers the day I accused Proctor of working a fraud on the court. By prior agreement, I would not ask any questions that would reveal financial information on the tax returns. Emerson Lambert apparently thought that restriction would protect his client. He was about to learn otherwise.

I handed the tax returns to Proctor and asked, "Can you identify the two documents I just handed you?"

Proctor took his time leafing through each document, perhaps because he was afraid I had made some alteration to trap him, or more likely just to annoy me. He finished his inspection and handed the documents back to me. "Yes."

"And what are these documents?"

"Tax returns," Proctor answered. Emerson Lambert had undoubtedly told him to make his answers as brief as possible, and Proctor was taking that advice seriously.

"Are you the Robert Proctor identified on these returns?"

"Yes."

"And is the address shown on these returns your address?"

"Yes."

"Is the social security number on these returns your social security number?"

"Yes." He said it in the same calm, measured tone he had used to answer my previous questions, but he hesitated ever so slightly before answering. I took that as confirmation of Machias Phelps' pronouncement that Bob Proctor wasn't who he claimed to be.

"Are these, in fact, copies of tax returns you filed with the Internal Revenue Service?"

Once again he answered with a single word. "Yes."

"Is the information on these returns accurate?"

Billboard Bob finally responded with more than one word. "To the best of my knowledge, it is."

"Have you filed tax returns for all previous years when you had reportable income?"

Proctor wasn't expecting that question. "What kind of question is that?" he wanted to know.

That prompted Emerson Lambert to object to my question. "Relevancy?"

Judge MacAndrew looked to me for a response. "The relevancy of that question will become apparent shortly."

"I'll allow it," the judge said. "It seems fairly innocuous."

I repeated the question, and Proctor once again supplied a one-word answer. "Yes."

At that point I had all the testimony I needed from Billboard Bob Proctor. But Tony Biffano and my two witnesses still hadn't arrived, so I had to stall for time. I spent the next few minutes going through the two tax returns, having Proctor testify that each entry was correct as far as he could remember. Emerson Lambert objected several times on the ground that my questions weren't relevant, which they weren't, but the judge let me proceed based on my assurances that everything would shortly become clear.

I had almost run out of questions to ask when Tony Biffano entered the courtroom, pushing a frail woman in a wheelchair. She was wearing a purple dress with a white sweater draped around her shoulders, an oversized purse on her lap. She was clearly nervous, or perhaps frightened, repeatedly tying and untying a floral handkerchief as Tony wheeled her down the aisle to the front row seats Rick and Carolyn had been saving.

Watching her body language, I regretted more than ever not having had an opportunity to prepare her testimony in advance.

The tall gentleman who strode down the aisle at Tony's side, on the other hand, exuded confidence. His weathered, leathery face told me he was older than the woman in the wheelchair, but he stood ramrod straight, with squared back shoulders and a determined set to his jaw. He was dressed in baggy slacks with cuffs, a tweed sport jacket, a plaid flannel shirt, and a bow tie. A pair of rubberized shoes popularized by L.L. Bean completed the outfit.

"Call your next witness," Judge MacAndrew said just as the trio arrived at their seats. I motioned to the man wearing what I assumed was Down East business attire, and instead of taking a seat in the public gallery, he made his way to the witness stand, passing shoulder to shoulder with Bob Proctor as the mayor returned to his chair beside Emerson Lambert.

"Please state your name for the court reporter," I said after the witness had been sworn in.

"Herbert Dempsey," he said in a strong, steady voice. Then, without being asked, he spelled his name for the court reporter. His demeanor suggested he was an old hand at testifying, though I learned later that everything he knew about courtroom decorum was learned from watching television.

I began by asking, "Did you at some point own and operate a chain of ice cream stores in Maine known as Dempsey's Dairy Delight?"

"Yes, sir, I did," he answered.

"And was one of those stores located in Machias, Maine?" I positioned myself so I could see Proctor as I asked the question. My mention of Machias caused him to lean forward in his chair.

"Yes, sir, I had a store in Machias."

"Did you hire local students to work in your stores?"

"Yes," Dempsey responded, adding "during the summer when school was out."

"And did you report their earnings to the IRS?"

"Oh, yes indeed," he answered. "Did everything by the book." He supplied the answer to my next question before I could ask it. "Sent them a W-2 form, just like all my other employees."

Up to this point, no one in the courtroom, with the possible exception of Billboard Bob, could possibly know where this line of questioning was leading. It was time to change that.

I walked back to the counsel table, retrieved a legal pad from my briefcase, and proceeded to study it. The pad was blank, but nobody knew that. The whole routine was nothing more than a pause for dramatic effect. I put the pad facedown on the table and started back to the witness stand. When I was about halfway there, I casually asked, "Did you by any chance ever employ a student named Bob Proctor in your store in Machias?"

"As a matter of fact, I did," Mr. Dempsey said.

Emerson Lambert was halfway out of his chair to object to what appeared at that point to be an irrelevant question when I pointed to Billboard Bob and asked, "Is the gentlemen in the blue suit sitting at that table the Bob Proctor who worked for you in Maine?"

"This is completely irrelevant," Emerson Lambert said before the witness could answer. "It's a well known fact that my client has been a resident of New Jersey his entire life. If the witness hired someone named Bob Proctor to work for him in Maine, it was obviously a different person with the same name, someone who has absolutely nothing to do with this case."

"That's not entirely correct," I said.

My deliberately vague answer must have piqued Judge MacAndrew's curiosity because he said, "I'm not sure where you're going with all this, Mr. O'Brian, but I'll let you ask one more question."

I turned back to face Herbert Dempsey. "Is there some reason why the Bob Proctor sitting at the counsel table in this courtroom, who currently serves as the mayor of Troy Forge, couldn't possibly be the same Bob Proctor who worked for you at Dempsey's Dairy Delight in Maine?"

"Yup," Mr. Dempsey said.

I asked a second question before the judge could stop me. "And what would that reason be?"

"Well, sir, the Bob Proctor who worked for me was a local boy who died in an auto accident the summer before his sophomore year in high school. So unless the Good Lord raised him from the dead, that man can't possibly be the Bob Proctor who worked for me."

Emerson Lambert shot to his feet. "I move the witness' testimony be stricken from the record," he said. "The fact that another person by the same name worked at an ice cream stand in Maine is completely irrelevant to this case."

"The relevancy of this testimony will become apparent when my next witness testifies," I assured the judge.

"Very well," Judge MacAndrew said, "but don't try my patience, Mr. O'Brian." Turning to my adversary, he asked, "Cross examine?"

Lambert shrugged his shoulders. "There's nothing to cross-examine." As he said it, his client tapped him on the elbow to get his attention, whereupon the two began a whispered conversation.

The judge patiently waited while Lambert and Billboard Bob conferred. I couldn't hear what they were saying, and I have no expertise as a lip reader, but at one point I'm reasonably certain Proctor told his attorney, "You work for me. Don't forget that."

When the conversation ended, Lambert told the judge, "There's no way I can effectively cross-examine the witness without time to prepare. I would ask that this hearing be adjourned until tomorrow." Months later, Lambert confided to me that requesting an adjournment was Billboard Bob's idea, a stratagem that took on sinister implications in view of events that unfolded in the Court Street parking lot after the hearing.

"Under the circumstances, I think that's a reasonable request," the judge said. "We'll adjourn until tomorrow at nine o'clock."

Proctor bolted from the courtroom, accompanied by the short, stocky bodyguard who carried on a hushed conversation on his cellular phone as he walked. Scarface, who had been standing in the back of the courtroom, was nowhere to be seen, having apparently slipped away while the hearing was in progress. I didn't think anything of it at the time, but I learned the reason for his disappearance fifteen minutes later.

By the time I got back to the courthouse lobby, Billboard Bob's impromptu news conference was underway. He was in the process of assuring the local media that this hearing was nothing more than a brazen attempt to smear his good name, and a complete waste of the taxpayers' money, when I decided to slip out the Court Street exit and begin my trek to the distant parking lot where I had left the Mustang.

I had just emerged from the building when a well-dressed, middle-aged man approached me. "Mr. O'Brian, a moment of your time, please." I assumed he was a reporter who wanted my take on the morning's proceedings. The first words out of his mouth told me I was wrong. "I have a message from Mr. Rizzo. He said to tell you that his people are still looking for Mohammed Salameh, but haven't been able to catch up with him. We think he must have accomplices who are helping him stay out of sight."

"Interesting," I said, using Stacey's favorite all-purpose word.

"Mr. Rizzo told me to tell you that he'll find the bastard eventually."

"Yes, I'm sure he will," I replied.

As it turned out, Eddie the Skunk was too late.

41

"I'm always happy to get information."

The parking lot at the end of Court Street is a bit of a hike, which probably explains why it's the last one in the vicinity of the courthouse to fill up. It had been almost empty when I arrived, giving me my choice of parking spots. I selected a place in the back of the lot, assuming my restored Mustang would remain surrounded by empty space, thus minimizing the chance of dents and dings from other vehicles. I needn't have bothered. By the time I returned from the hearing, the parking lot had filled.

Cold and wet from the freezing rain and bone-chilling wind, I headed for my car, moving as quickly as I dared on pavement that seemed to be getting slicker with every step I took. I was so focused on getting to the Mustang that I never saw the movement to my left until Scarface suddenly appeared from between two parked cars. At first I thought he was lunging toward me, but when Reynaldo Renoir materialized behind him, I realized Mayor Proctor's favorite bodyguard had been shoved in my direction. Reynaldo confirmed that a second later. "I caught this guy tampering with your brake lines."

I began to shiver, partly from the cold and partly from the thought of meeting the same fate as Machias Phelps. Reynaldo and I were apparently thinking the same thing. "I guess we know what happened to Machias Phelps," he said.

Proctor's bodyguard snickered, prompting Reynaldo to ask, "This is a joke to you?" It was more an accusation than a question.

"Not just Phelps," I said as I carefully made my way to where Scarface and Reynaldo were standing. "Phelps learned something Proctor didn't want the world to know, and he ends of up dead. Cecilia Marcus saw something she wasn't supposed to see, tells me about it, and the next thing you know, she also ends up dead."

Reynaldo gave me a puzzled look. "Tell me about Cecilia Marcus." That prompted another snicker from Scarface.

"Older woman who worked with Phelps in Proctor's office," I said. "Like Phelps, she never had a driver's license, but one day drives someone else's car into a tree and dies."

"Coincidence?" Reynaldo asked.

"Not likely. Both worked for Proctor, both learned something that could end Proctor's political career, and both end up dying in an auto accident even though neither was known to ever drive a car. And now I'm about to reveal what they discovered in open court and you find this clown messing with my brakes. Too many coincidences for my taste."

"Too bad you've got nothing that will convince a jury," Scarface said. It wasn't actually a confession, but it was close.

The word "jury" had barely left his lips when Scarface found himself bent over the hood of the nearest car. "Unfortunately for you," Reynaldo said as he handcuffed Proctor's bodyguard, "he doesn't have to convince a jury, just me."

After unceremoniously depositing Scarface in a nearby vehicle with a metal screen that turned the back seat into a holding cell on wheels, Reynaldo came back to where I was standing. I should have thanked him, but instead, I said, "I gather from your reaction that you didn't know about Cecilia Marcus."

"We knew she died in an auto accident and we knew she worked at the town hall in Troy Forge," he replied, "but we didn't know she had talked to you."

"I thought you guys knew everything."

It was intended as a joke, but Reynaldo didn't seem to find it amusing. "We can't possibly know everything, unless we turn the country into a police state. I don't know about you, but that's not the kind of country I want to live in." He shoved his hands in the pockets of his coat and looked briefly at the darkening sky before continuing. "So, tell me about your conversation with Ms. Marcus."

I did, providing as much detail as I could remember. It was the least I could do, considering he had probably prevented me from meeting the same fate as Cecilia Marcus and Machias Phelps. After I had recounted how Marcus and Phelps had accidently seen Billboard Bob's tax return, Reynaldo asked a series of questions, most which I answered with "we didn't discuss that" or "I'm not sure about that." I concluded our discussion by pointing out, "Our meeting with Cecilia Marcus didn't last more than ten or fifteen minutes."

"I guess we're done here," Reynaldo said as he turned to go. "I have to deliver Mr. Chambers to some people who are considerably less pleasant than me."

"Chambers? That's his name?"

Reynaldo laughed. "One minute I think you're holding out on me, and in the next, I realize how much you don't know."

"Speaking of not knowing things, there's something I can't figure out. Why did you want copies of the photos Stacey took inside the mosque?"

"Why not?" Reynaldo said with a shrug of his shoulders. "I'm always happy to get information. You never know when some of it will turn out to be useful. Those photos your girlfriend took are proving to be very helpful. One in particular sheds a lot of light on how things are connected."

"The one with the five men in front of the shoe rack?"

Reynaldo didn't answer my question, so I asked another one. "But don't you have your own people inside the mosque taking photos?"

"Sorry," Reynaldo said, "but that's above your pay grade." He started back toward his car, but stopped and turned around after he had taken a few steps. "Remember that police state we were just talking about? Some people think putting an operative inside a mosque would be a step in that direction."

"What do you think?

"I think I'm always happy to get information."

42

"Mr. Lambert, we appear to have a problem."

The following morning I was back in Judge MacAndrew's courtroom, which was even more crowded than the day before. Unlike the previous day, my witnesses were already there when I arrived. Herbert Dempsey was sitting ramrod straight in the third row, sandwiched between Rick and Carolyn. The frail woman who had arrived in a wheelchair yesterday was now sitting in an aisle seat in the fourth row, knotting and unknotting a floral handkerchief while Tony Biffano spoke to her in a whisper.

Emerson Lambert and Bob Proctor had also arrived before me, and were seated at their counsel table. Lambert sat motionless, staring straight ahead at the judge's empty bench, while Billboard Bob engaged in a hushed conversation with a man in the front row of the public gallery. From his general appearance, I guessed the guy was a replacement for Scarface, who I learned somewhat later, had spent his first night in captivity having a rather unpleasant conversation with an associate of Reynaldo Renoir.

I motioned to Tony to join me at the counsel table where we could talk without being overheard. "Is she going to be okay?" I asked, nodding toward my witness who continued to knot and unknot the handkerchief.

"This is the first time she's been out of Maine in years, and she's a bit overwhelmed with all this." He made a circular motion with his hand as he spoke to clarify that it was the courtroom setting that was making my witness nervous.

"If I had been able to talk to her last night at the hotel, she'd be prepared to testify and wouldn't be so nervous."

"That wasn't going to happen," Tony said. "She was so exhausted, she ate dinner and went to bed. He patted me on the shoulder. "Don't worry, she'll be fine."

I looked back at the woman, who was still knotting and unknotting the handkerchief, and gave her a reassuring smile. As I did, I caught sight of Tinoo Barahi, CIRR's attorney, making his way down the aisle in search of a place to sit. It's possible Barahi was in the courtroom to watch the morning's proceedings, but more likely, he was there because Judge MacAndrew had informed us he would hold a scheduling conference at the conclusion of the hearing.

Barahi and the judge were no doubt expecting a quick, routine meeting. I had other ideas.

The judge took the bench a few minutes later, and we went through his customary "good-morning-counselors-good-morning-Your-Honor" routine before getting down to business. Judge MacAndrew began by asking Herbert Dempsey to take the stand so Emerson Lambert could cross-examine him. Mr. Dempsey had just gotten out of his seat in the public gallery when my adversary rose to tell the judge, "I have no questions for this witness."

Judge MacAndrew was a bit perturbed. "Mr. Lambert, if I remember correctly, you asked me to adjourn yesterday's session so you'd have time to prepare a cross-examination. Now you're telling me you don't wish to cross-examine the witness?"

Lambert's decision didn't surprise me. There was nothing to be gained by cross-examining Dempsey, and potentially much to lose. What I expected him to do was make a motion, which is exactly what he did.

"Rather than cross-examine, I move to strike the witness' testimony. It has absolutely no probative value. The fact that Mr. Dempsey once employed a teenager who shared the same name as my client has no bearing on this case. In fact, it doesn't appear to have any bearing on anything. It's a complete waste of everyone's time."

The judge looked to me for a response.

"Everything will become clear after my next witness testifies."

Ever cautious, Judge MacAndrew made the only ruling he could under the circumstances. "I'll take your motion under advisement," he told Lambert. Then he instructed me, "Call your next witness."

After momentarily losing her balance getting up from her seat in the public gallery, Agnes Proctor slowly shuffled to the witness stand, using a four-legged cane for support. The ordeal was almost as painful to watch as it must have been for her to accomplish. She wore the same purple dress she had worn the previous day, carried the same floral handkerchief and oversized purse, and had the same white sweater draped over her shoulders. Once seated, she resumed knotting and unknotting the handkerchief.

After being sworn in, she stated her name for the record while looking around the courtroom as though seeing it for the first time. She appeared a bit dazed or bewildered, causing me to once again regret not having had a chance to prepare her testimony in advance.

"Mrs. Proctor," I began, pointing to Billboard Bob, "are you related to Robert Proctor, the gentleman seated at that table?"

"Not that I know of." Her answer elicited laughter from the public gallery.

"Do you currently reside in Machias, Maine?"

"No, no I don't, " she answered hesitantly. That wasn't the answer I was anticipating.

"Where do you currently reside?"

"At the Sunnyview Nursing Home."

"And that's located in Machias, Maine?" I prodded.

"No, it's not in Machias," she answered. "Machias is too small to have a nursing home. Sunnyview is in Lewiston."

The fact that she knew the town was too small to support a nursing home was a good sign. I plowed ahead. "But you lived in Machias at some point, didn't you?"

"Yes, most of my life."

She was still knotting and unknotting the floral handkerchief, so I decided to switch from attorney to tour guide mode in an effort to put her at ease. "I enjoyed visiting Machias last year," I said in what I hoped would sound like a conversational tone. "Unfortunately, I didn't get to see Fort O'Brien, which was named for one of my ancestors." That wasn't true, but Stacey and I were the only ones in the courtroom who would know that.

Agnes Proctor proved me wrong. "Oh, I doubt that. According to your business card, you spell O'Brian with an 'a'. The fort is named after Jeremiah O'Brien, who spelled his name with an 'e'." Her body might be failing, but her mind was still sharp.

"I can't slip anything by you, can I?" I asked playfully.

"Not that sort of blarney," she replied.

Laughter filled the courtroom. Agnes Proctor stopped knotting the handkerchief and joined in. Mission accomplished.

"Did you have a son named Robert?" I asked, switching back to attorney mode.

"Yes," she answered in a whisper. She looked off into space as though attempting to conjure up a mental image of the teenage boy who would never grow into manhood.

"What happened to him?" I asked as gently as I could.

"Bobby died in an auto accident."

"When was that?"

There was a long pause. Perhaps she was trying to remember the date, or maybe she was replaying the events of that tragic day. She finally said, "The summer before his sophomore year in high school."

"Did he ever work at Dempsey's Dairy Delight in Machias, Maine?"

Emerson Lambert objected. "Your Honor, I fail to see where any of this is relevant. We'll stipulate that a person having the same name as my client worked at an ice cream store in a small town in Maine at some point in the past. But, so what? This is a complete waste of the Court's time."

Judge MacAndrew turned to me. "If you can assure me that this line of questioning is going to lead to something relevant, I'll allow you to continue. Otherwise, we're through."

"I absolutely guarantee that when I'm finished, Your Honor, Mr. Lambert, and the public will forever view Billboard Bob Proctor in a different light."

My answer had the desired result. "Very well, proceed."

I retrieved three copies of a document from my file on the counsel table, handed one to Emerson Lambert and another to a court officer, who delivered it to the judge. "This is a copy of a tax return that I found in a filing cabinet in a garage in Machias, Maine belonging to the aunt of the late Machias Phelps. Until his untimely death, Mr. Phelps was employed by the Town of Troy Forge. As you can see, attached to the tax return is a W-2 form issued by Dempsey's Dairy Delight."

I walked to the witness stand and was about to hand the third copy of the document to Agnes Proctor when Emerson Lambert objected. "Best evidence," he said, referring to the rule that requires an original document, rather than a copy.

I was expecting that objection and had prepared for it. "Of course it's a copy. The original was filed with the IRS. That's why we have Rule 1003, which allows the use of duplicates as long as there's no question about the authenticity of the original."

"Well, there is a question," Lambert shot back.

"How do we know that?" I countered. "The witness hasn't even had a chance to identify the document."

Judge MacAndrew interceded. "Keep in mind that this is a hearing. We're not at trial and there is no jury. So let's allow the witness to see the document, and we'll go from there."

I handed the third copy to Agnes Proctor and asked, "Can you identify this document?"

"Yes," she said. "It's a copy of my son's tax return."

"How do you know that?"

"Well, it has his name on it and ..."

Emerson Lambert was on his feet before she could finish the sentence. "The mere fact that her son's name is on that document doesn't establish that it's his tax return. And the fact that Mr. O'Brian found it in someone else's garage makes it even more suspect."

Before the judge could respond, Agnes Proctor dropped a bombshell. "But it looks just like the copy of Bobby's tax return I gave to his friend, Machias, when he came to see me a couple years ago."

With a wave of his hand, the judge signaled Lambert to sit down. "Let's allow Mrs. Proctor to finish." He nodded to me to continue questioning the witness.

"By Machias, do you mean Machias Phelps?"

"Yes, he and Bobby were good friends growing up. In fact, he's the one who filled out Bobby's tax return for him."

"So the document you're holding is a copy of a tax return you had in your possession and gave to Machias Phelps when he visited you?"

"Yes."

Addressing Judge MacAndrew, I said, "The fact that Mrs. Proctor had the tax return in her possession shows that it's her son's return. It's not likely she would have had a copy of a stranger's tax return."

Emerson Lambert still wasn't satisfied. "Nothing the witness has said is sufficient to authenticate that document. And besides, I still fail to see how a tax return from years ago supposedly filed by someone with the same name as my client has anything to do with this case. That tax return has no probative value whatsoever."

Agnes Proctor may not have understood the complexities of authenticating a document under the Rules of Evidence, but she did realize that Lambert was, in effect, questioning her honesty. So before the judge could respond to Lambert, Mrs. Proctor said, "If it's not Bobby's tax return, then why does it have his social security number on it?"

Lambert laughed. "We're supposed to believe that the witness not only knows her late son's social security number, but has remembered it all these years?" He was either incredulous or doing a good job of feigning incredulity.

Agnes Proctor, unschooled in the niceties of courtroom decorum, addressed Lambert directly. "I don't need to *remember* Bobby's social security number," she said in a tone of voice that was equal parts anger and indignation. "All I have to do is look at the card."

"What card are you referring to, Mrs. Proctor?" Judge MacAndrew asked.

"Bobby's social security card."

"Do you have it with you?"

In response to the judge's question, Agnes Proctor began rummaging through her oversized purse, eventually withdrawing a small, blue card that I recognized as a social security card. She placed it in the outstretched hand of the court officer who had approached the witness stand when she began the search, and he delivered it to Judge MacAndrew.

The judge first examined the social security card, then his copy of the tax return I had asked Mrs. Proctor to identify. "The social security numbers match," he said. "In view of the evidence submitted, I'm inclined to admit the tax return into evidence." He looked at Emerson Lambert. "Mr. Lambert?"

"If it will speed things along, we'll stipulate that the document is, in fact, a tax return filed some years ago by the witness' late son who has the same name as my client. But I renew my objection on the ground that the document has no probative value. It has nothing whatsoever to do with my client or this case."

"Oh, but it does," I said before the judge could rule. "I would ask Your Honor to compare the social security number on that tax return to the one that appears on the returns filed by the Robert Proctor who's the plaintiff in this case, and who serves as the mayor of Troy Forge."

The normally quiet courtroom came alive with the murmured discussions of speculating spectators as Judge MacAndrew removed a document from the file folder on his bench and reviewed it. The almost imperceptible back and forth movement of his head told me he was doing what I had requested. As the judge was comparing the documents, I looked over to where Lambert and his client were sitting. Billboard Bob was looking straight ahead, his face expressionless. Emerson Lambert looked confused.

The judge finished his review of the tax returns and looked directly at my adversary. "Mr. Lambert, we appear to have a problem. The social security number on the tax return filed years ago by the witness' deceased son is identical to the one on the returns filed by your client. Do you have an explanation for that?"

Emerson Lambert looked to his client, who continued to stare straight ahead. Then he slowly got to his feet and said, "I would ask for an adjournment so I can review this matter with my client."

"What's to review?" I asked before the judge could respond to Lambert's request. "The numbers match, not just once, but on both of the tax returns the plaintiff turned over to Your Honor. Moreover, I would ask Your Honor to take judicial notice of the fact that the first three digits of the social security number being used by the plaintiff are 006. The first three digits denote the owner's state of residence at the time the number is issued. Social security numbers issued to Maine residents all begin with 004 through 007. Those issued to New Jersey residents all begin with 135 through 158. If the plaintiff had been born in New Jersey as he contends, he wouldn't have a social security number beginning with 006."

The hushed conversations in the public gallery became louder. Although it would take time for the ramifications of this revelation to play out, the observers apparently realized they were watching the beginning of the end of Billboard Bob's political career.

Judge MacAndrew gaveled for silence as I retrieved a document from my file. "I have a certified copy of the death certificate issued by the State of Maine confirming that Mrs. Proctor's son is, indeed, deceased." I waved the document above my head for everyone to see before handing it to a court officer who carried it to the bench. "Since the person using the social security number beginning with 006 died years ago, and it's black letter law that dead people can't sue for defamation, I move that the plaintiff's case against my clients be dismissed."

"Your Honor," Emerson Lambert said, rising to his feet, "the newspaper articles at the heart of this case clearly refer to the mayor of Troy Forge, and my client is universally recognized as that person, regardless of the social security number he uses."

I was about to make the public policy argument, but the judge beat me to it. "You might very well have a point," the judge said to Lambert, "but I'm nonetheless troubled by this revelation. There's a public policy issue here. Shouldn't the public have a right to know the real identity of someone elected to public office?"

The volume in the courtroom increased as everyone awaited the judge's decision. Judge MacAndrew gaveled the room into silence, leaned back in his chair and stared at the ceiling for a few seconds. "I'll take Mr. O'Brian's motion under advisement and render a decision in due course. We're adjourned. Counsel will meet in my chambers in fifteen minutes for a scheduling conference."

I turned to where Stacey and her boss, Ezra Bramfield, were sitting and saw something I had never seen before. Bramfield was smiling.

43

"We are the aggrieved party."

Emerson Lambert and Tinoo Barahi were seated side by side on the sofa in Judge MacAndrew's chambers when I entered carrying an easel and a large poster board covered by a thick sheet of paper obscuring what I had glued to the poster.

"What's that?" the judge asked.

"Something I think you'll find quite interesting," I responded.

"After what just happened in the courtroom, I can only imagine," the judge replied.

I set up the easel and put the poster on it, then took a seat in the chair next to the judge. Barahi stared at the easel, perhaps hoping his X-ray vision would kick in and allow him to preview what I was about to reveal. Lambert, on the other hand, hardly glanced at it. In fact, Emerson seemed to be completely lost in thought. Perhaps that was to be expected after what had just happened in the courtroom.

"I had a call from the Assignment Judge," the judge began, "and he wants me to combine the hearing on Mr. O'Brian's motion for summary judgment on the first count of the complaint with the evidentiary hearing on the second court. His thinking was that combining the hearings will allow us to expedite matters. I tend to agree."

Barahi's response was immediate. "I will have to discuss that with my client."

That clearly annoyed the judge. "There's nothing to discuss, Mr. Barahi. I'm not asking for your permission, I'm telling you what's going to happen."

"Even so, I must discuss this with my client."

"Feel free to discuss whatever you want with your client," the judge replied, "but when you do, tell them to be in my courtroom, ready to proceed, on February twenty-sixth."

"I do not know if that will be possible," Barahi said.

"The twenty-sixth," Judge MacAndrew said, apparently assuming that would end the conversation.

It didn't.

"I know of no rule or law that would allow you to do this," Barahi said.

"Then I suggest you spend some time reviewing the Rules of Civil Procedure," the judge replied.

Barahi wasn't about to give up. "What you are doing is unfair to my client."

The judge ignored Barahi's remark and turned his attention to Emerson Lambert. "In view of what just happened in the courtroom, I'm going to sever your client's claims from those of Mr. Barahi's client. If I don't grant Mr. O'Brian's motion for dismissal, I'll set your client's case down for trial at a later date." Emerson Lambert nodded in acknowledgement, but didn't say a word. Judging from his body language, I surmised that he expected the judge to grant my motion for dismissal. Or perhaps he knew something that I didn't know.

"Now, Mr. O'Brian," Judge MacAndrew said, turning in his chair to face me, "what new surprise do you have in store?"

"Actually, judge, more of a request than a surprise." I withdrew the photo of Mohammed Salameh that Tony Biffano had gotten from the Department of Motor Vehicles and put it on the easel. Pointing to the photo, I said, "I've been trying to depose this man, Mohammed Salameh for some time, but I've haven't been able to locate him to serve him with a subpoena. I have reason to believe Mr. Barahi and his client are keeping Mr. Salameh under wraps and preventing me from making service."

Barahi took the bait immediately. "That is an outrageous accusation. It is totally untrue. I have never set eyes on this Mohammed Salameh."

Judge MacAndrew took a long look at Barahi, but didn't say anything. Then he turned his attention back to me. "Do you have something to back that up?"

I answered the judge's question by removing the paper covering the poster board to reveal Stacey's photo of five men standing in front of the shoe rack in the lobby of the new Troy Forge mosque. "Mohammed Mustapha, the imam at the mosque," I said, pointing to the man on the left in the photo. "The man next to him is Salameh, and next to him, with his arm around Mr. Salameh's shoulder is..."

The judge finished the sentence for me. "Mr. Barahi."

"Precisely," I agreed. "The very same Tinoo Barahi who a moment ago told Your Honor that he had never set eyes on Mohammed Salameh."

Barahi jumped to his feet, pointed at me and angrily shouted, "This is a trick. This man's clients slander Islam and our beloved prophet, peace be upon him, and now he slanders me with this trick photograph."

"Are you suggesting this photograph has been altered?" Judge MacAndrew asked.

Instead of answering the question, Barahi said, "We are the aggrieved party in this case. You must not listen to O'Brian's lies."

"Do you or do you not know Mohammed Salameh?" the judge asked calmly.

"The fact that I am in a photograph does not mean that I know other people in the photo," Barahi said. "I am in many photographs."

Judge MacAndrew repeated the question. This time Barahi said, "I cannot be expected to know everyone who attends the mosque."

"I didn't ask you if you knew everyone who attends the mosque," the judge replied. "I asked if you knew Mohammed Salameh, the man Mr. O'Brian has been trying to depose."

"There is no reason for O'Brian to depose Mr. Salameh. He is not involved with the operation of the mosque."

"So you do know him?" The judge phrased it as a question, but it was clearly an accusation.

"I do not have to answer that," Barahi said defiantly.

The judge finally proved that his patience wasn't unlimited. Looking directly at my adversary, he said, "Mr. Barahi, when you appear before me on the twenty-sixth, you will arrange for Mohammed Salameh to be in the courtroom, at which time Mr. O'Brian will have an opportunity to question him under oath."

Then he arose from his seat. "We're done here."

44

"Have you heard the news about Proctor?"

The days leading up to the hearing on February twenty-sixth were filled with surprises. On Monday of that week, Daniel Stern, my expert witness and consultant on Islam telephoned to inform me that he wouldn't be able to appear at Friday's hearing. "The FBI has informed me of a credible threat on my life," he explained.

"Because of this case?"

"Not sure," came the answer. "All I know for sure is this is more serious than the usual garden variety threats I get on a regular basis."

Dr. Stern outlined how he thought I should proceed at the hearing, apologized repeatedly for leaving me to face CIRR by myself, and assured me that I was up to the challenge.

I had Carolyn contact Judge MacAndrew's chambers to inform him that Dr. Stern would not be in court on Friday. The judge had previously made it clear that both attorneys were to keep him apprised of the witnesses we planned to call and the time we estimated their testimony would take.

In keeping with instructions from the Assignment Judge (who most likely considered *CIRR v. McCain* to be a garden variety defamation case involving public figures), Judge MacAndrew had taken a number of other steps to expedite Friday's hearing. For example, he required both attorneys to provide the court and opposing counsel with a list of exhibits we planned to introduce into evidence. Each attorney was then required to submit any objections he might have to the use of those exhibits, with the caveat that failing to object prior to the hearing would foreclose objections during the hearing. I took a page out of Barahi's playbook and submitted a list that ran nine pages, hiding the exhibits I planned to use among dozens that I had no intention of introducing into evidence. Surprisingly, Barahi didn't object to any of them. The intention of the judge's pre-hearing order was to streamline the entire process and allow it to be disposed of efficiently. As it turned out, Tinoo Barahi had other ideas.

On Tuesday, I received a fax from Judge Latisha Washington, who was presiding over Eddie Rizzo's personal injury case against Mohammed Salameh. It was a copy of a letter the judge had sent to Omar Obduhali informing him that his failure to name a substitute attorney meant he was still the attorney of record for the defendant. I wasn't sure if that was good news or bad news. Of course, if Mohammed Salameh didn't turn up, it really didn't matter who was representing him.

News about Salameh arrived on Wednesday, which turned out to be the most eventful day of the week. It all began just after nine o'clock when Elaine, the firm's receptionist, appeared at my office door to inform me that someone was in the waiting room asking to see me. It's unusual for people to appear at the office without an appointment, and even more unusual for Elaine to deliver the news in person instead of contacting Carolyn on the intercom.

"I didn't want him to overhear me talking to Carolyn," Elaine said by way of explanation for her trip to my office. "He says his name is Leslie Purcell, but I swear I've seen him in wrestling matches on television, and he wasn't called Leslie Purcell."

"Those guys use stage names in the ring," I said. "So, Purcell may be his real name." As Elaine turned to leave, I added, "I wouldn't have pegged you as a wrestling fan."

"I'm not, but Rick loves to watch," she said, shedding more light on their relationship.

As Carolyn retrieved my unexpected visitor, I pondered how much I apparently didn't know about my wrestling-loving partner. A few minutes later, the largest human being I have ever seen appeared at my office door. The guy was so big he had to duck his head and angle his body sideways to get through the doorway. He had long, flowing hair that touched his shoulders, and he was impeccably dressed in a blue, pinstriped, three-piece suit. Instead of a tie, he wore a paisley cravat. A matching pocket square completed the outfit.

"Good morning, Mr. O'Brian. I'm Leslie Purcell," he said with a cultured British accent in a voice that was about two octaves too high for a man his size.

I couldn't help myself; I laughed. "Sorry, but I wasn't expecting the British accent." I also wasn't expecting the squeaky, high-pitched voice, but I didn't mention that. Pissing off guys twice your size is rarely a good idea.

Mr. Purcell was surprisingly forgiving. "Happens all the time. People expect pro wrestlers to sound like truck drivers, and having a name Americans think of as a woman's name doesn't help."

He looked around the office at the available seating, and decided the sofa was the only thing big enough to accommodate his massive frame. I settled into a chair across from him and began the conversation by asking, "What can I do for you?"

"Mr. Rizzo asked me to stop by and report on our progress locating Mohammed Salameh." I had a hard time understanding why Eddie would use a huge guy with flowing locks and an upper class British accent to do surveillance work in the urban enclaves where Salameh was most likely hiding. Before I could formulate a diplomatic way to pursue that, Purcell said, "Of course, I didn't actually look for Salameh myself. I'm just here to tell you what Mr. Rizzo's people discovered."

He withdrew a small notebook from an inner pocket of his suit jacket, flipped it open and began to read. It was a surprisingly detailed report, delivered in clipped sentences that reminded me of the way cops talk when they're testifying in court. According to Purcell, Eddie Rizzo's people had spotted Salameh on six occasions in various places throughout Hudson, Union, and Essex Counties. Each time he slipped away. Either Eddie's people needed to sharpen their skills or, more likely, Salameh was getting help staying one step ahead of them. On four of those occasions, Salameh had been seen going into a garden center. One other time he was spotted entering a Middle Eastern restaurant. The final sighting occurred at the office of Omar Obduhali, his attorney, who professed not to know Salameh's whereabouts. I made a mental note to call Reynaldo Renoir and pass the information on to him.

When Purcell finished his report, I asked Carolyn to walk him back to the waiting room. I assumed she would return with Stacey, who had an appointment to go over her testimony for the hearing on Friday. Carolyn reappeared at my office door a few minutes later, not with Stacy, but with Ezra Bramfield, Stacey's boss.

"Where's Stacey?" I asked as Bramfield took a seat on the sofa that had just been vacated by Purcell.

"Not coming," was his terse reply.

I waited for an explanation, but none was offered. "Why not?" I finally asked. "We were supposed to spend the morning preparing for her testimony on Friday."

"She won't be testifying on Friday," Bramfield said. He was clearly angry, but at whom? "She's been getting threats ever since we published those articles, and they've increased in the last week or so. And last night, she was followed home from work."

"Is she okay?"

"She's fine," Bramfield assured me. "But instead of going home, she drove back to the *Ledger* and slept on the sofa in her office."

"Why didn't she come to my place?"

"You'll have to ask her," Bramfield said. There was an awkward silence while I contemplated what this meant to my relationship with Stacey. Bramfield ended the silence a moment later. "In any event, she won't be testifying on Friday."

"If you want to win this case, I need Stacey's testimony."

"You can do it without her," Bramfield replied. "You've got that very expensive expert witness."

"No, actually I don't." I explained why Dr. Stern wouldn't be at the hearing on Friday.

Ezra Bramfield was clearly less than happy with that news. He muttered something about "a damn waste of money" before abruptly getting up from the sofa. "I'll see what I can do," he said as he left my office.

I must have phoned Stacey a dozen times that day, but never spoke with her. I left messages on her office phone, her home phone, and on the cell phone I had given her.

When six o'clock arrived, I gave up waiting for her to return my calls and headed home.

I had just pulled out of the parking lot onto Route 46 when a voice behind me said, "That shiny thing is called a mirror. It comes in handy for seeing things behind you."

Startled, I yanked the steering wheel to the left and almost sideswiped another vehicle. Looking in the "shiny thing," I saw Reynaldo Renoir lounging in the back seat.

"Didn't mean to startle you," he said.

"Yes, you did."

Reynaldo laughed. "Well, maybe a little."

"After you carted Scarface away, I wasn't sure I'd see you again."

"I got the message you left about Salameh," Reynaldo said. We're following up on that information."

"You're welcome, but you could have just called to thank me."

He leaned forward and put his forearms on the Mustang's bucket seats. "I thought you might like to know what happened to your buddy, Machias Phelps."

"He wasn't my buddy, but yes, I would like to know what happened to him."

"Well, for starters, you were right about Phelps seeing Proctor's tax return. And according to Chambers, the guy you call Scarface, the way Phelps reacted when he saw the mayor's tax return convinced Proctor that your buddy knew something wasn't right."

"Phelps wasn't my buddy; he was my town hall informant."

"Buddy, informant, whatever you want to call him, he was a dead man the minute he saw Proctor's tax return."

"How did they do it?" I asked. I assumed Billy Kane would want to know. And, truth be told, I wanted to know too.

"According to Chambers, a Troy Forge cop drove Phelps to a remote part of town on the pretense that he was needed to notarize a document for an injured member of the fire department."

"And needless to say, there was no injured firefighter."

"No firefighter, injured or otherwise," Reynaldo said. "Just two of Proctor's people who sedated your buddy, buckled him into the driver's seat of the building inspector's car and rolled it down a hill into a tree."

"He wasn't my buddy," I reminded Reynaldo. "So, I assume the building inspector is also a member of Team Proctor?"

"We can't prove it," Reynaldo said, quickly adding, "at least not yet. We assume he is, but we don't have proof. What we do know is that he called in sick that day, leaving his town owned car sitting in the parking lot at town hall."

I laughed, more of a snort, actually. "How convenient."

"You can let me out anywhere along here," Reynaldo said as I passed the Catholic church.

Instead of pulling over, I moved into the left lane to pass a slow moving pickup truck.

Reynaldo didn't seem particularly perturbed by the maneuver. "You do realize that kidnapping a federal agent is a crime, don't you?" he asked calmly.

I answered his question with one of my own. "Did Chambers tell you who actually killed Machias Phelps, and if so, have you arrested them?"

"Yes, he named names, and no, we haven't arrested them, at least not yet. And before you ask, the reason we haven't arrested them is because we're hoping they lead us to bigger fish."

"Proctor?"

"That, my friend, is above your pay grade," Reynaldo said as I pulled back into the right lane and began climbing the hill that marks the western edge of Troy Forge. It was the first time Reynaldo had every referred to me as a friend. Of course, it was probably just an expression. As Stacey has pointed out with increasing frequency, I don't really have friends, just acquaintances.

Reynaldo spent the next five minutes dodging my questions, by which time we had turned onto the main boulevard in Mountain Springs, and then to the street where I live. We pulled into the circular driveway in front of my house and got out.

"Do you want to come inside and call someone to come get you?"

"Not necessary," he said. "Besides, remember, your living room is bugged."

I was about to offer to drive him back to my office when a car appeared from the section of driveway leading to the garage at the back of the property. "My ride's already here," Reynaldo said as walked to where the car had stopped. He opened the door and started to get into the passenger's seat, but stopped, and looked back over his shoulder. Anticipating my question, he said, "We want to make sure you make it to the hearing on Friday."

"Did one of your guys follow Stacey home last night?"

"We started to, but she went back to her office," Renaldo said. "The agent assigned to her sat in the *Ledger's* parking lot all night. Poor guy damn near froze his balls off."

When I got inside the house, the first thing I did was call Stacey. She didn't answer, so I left a message that wouldn't mean much to whomever was listening.

I spent most of Thursday preparing for the hearing before Judge MacAndrew. Late that afternoon Scott stopped by my office to remind me that he and Avery were going to Manhattan the following day to attend a seminar about law firm security. As he was leaving, he stopped at the door and asked, "By the way, have you heard the news about Proctor?"

"What news?"

"A local radio station is reporting that Proctor seems to have disappeared. When he didn't show up at his office this morning, the police went to his home. The place was empty. Proctor's clothes and personal items were gone, and there was food left out in the kitchen as though he left in a hurry. Nobody's seen or heard from him, and calls to his cell phone go to voicemail."

45

"I'm surprised Mr. O'Brian hasn't objected."

The following morning, I arrived at the courthouse early, hoping to speak to Stacey before the hearing began. By the time nine o'clock arrived, the courtroom was packed, with every seat in the public gallery taken and spectators lining the walls. Stacey, however, was nowhere to be seen.

Judge MacAndrew took the bench and we began the proceedings. After we had completed the "good-morning-counselors-good-morning-Your-Honor" ritual, the judge asked Tinoo Barahi, "Have you arranged for Mr. Salameh to be in the courtroom this morning as I instructed?"

"Mr. Salameh is visiting his brother in Michigan," Barahi answered. "I am told that his brother is quite ill and is not expected to live much longer." I had no idea if the brother was ill, or even if he existed, but I did know that Salameh was visiting garden centers in northern New Jersey, not a sick brother in Michigan.

The judge's facial expression suggested he wasn't buying Barahi's explanation. Unfortunately, as a practical matter, there wasn't much he could do at this point. So, he did about the only thing he could do. "Very well," he said. "In that case, we'll put the Salameh matter aside for the moment and begin by addressing the first motion filed, the plaintiff's motion and the defendants' cross motion, each seeking summary judgment on the second count of the complaint."

Since Stacey was nowhere to be seen, I had no choice but to risk the judge's ire by asking for a continuance. Barahi saved me the trouble by committing what turned out to be a tactical blunder. "I would like to address the first count of the complaint first."

"No, Mr. Barahi," the judge said. "We'll deal with the motions in the order in which they were filed."

"I must object to that."

"You can object all you want," Judge MacAndrew said in a tone of voice that made it clear he was somewhat less than happy with how the hearing was starting, "but that's the way we're going to proceed."

"That is unfair to my client," Barahi insisted.

"Mr. Barahi," the judge said, "I fail to see how hearing testimony on the motion for summary judgment that you yourself filed could possibly be unfair to your client."

"The first count of the complaint alleges that Mr. O'Brian's clients falsely accused CIRR of being connected to terrorism," my adversary explained. "Once I show that no such connection exists, my client can then explain why the defendants have defamed Islam, which is the subject of the second count of my complaint. But if I do not first show that CIRR is not connected to terrorism in any way, Your Honor might be prejudiced against my client's testimony regarding the defendants' slanderous comments about Islam. Allowing my witness, the imam at the mosque, to testify first will also establish him as an expert on Islam."

There may have been a scintilla of logic to Barahi's clumsily worded argument, but his use of "prejudiced" destroyed any chance he might have had to convince Judge MacAndrew. So I decided to lend a helping hand. I stood up, motioned to get the judge's attention and said, "Your Honor, what my adversary is suggesting might expedite things. The witness I planned to call in connection with the second count hasn't arrived yet. If Mr. Barahi is ready to proceed on the first count, I have no objection to handling that first."

"Are you ready to proceed?" the judge asked Barahi.

"I am ready."

"Very well," Judge MacAndrew said. "Mr. O'Brian, you may proceed with your argument."

"No, I wish to call my witness," Barahi said.

"No, Mr. Barahi," the judge instructed. "Mr. O'Brian filed the motion for summary judgment on the first count, so he goes first. I want to hear oral argument from the attorneys, not testimony from a witness."

Tinoo Barahi wasn't about to give in. "But Your Honor has just agreed that I would first have an opportunity to prove that CIRR is not connected to terrorism in any way. And to do that, you must allow Imam Mustapha to testify."

Judges don't like to be told what they "must" do, especially not by attorneys who don't know what they're talking about. The judge had a few choice words for my adversary. He was considerably less strident than Judge Latisha Washington, but the message was essentially the same, namely that attorneys don't tell Superior Court judges how to run their courtroom.

While Barahi was undergoing this tutorial on courtroom procedures, I surveyed the public gallery. I found Emerson Lambert, Proctor's attorney, seated in the third row, and Ezra Bramfield several rows behind Lambert. Stacey, however, was nowhere to be seen. I managed to make eye contact with Bramfield. A sideways nod and a shrug of his shoulders told me that my prime witness – my only witness now that Dr. Stern was unavailable – wasn't likely to make an appearance, and that her boss didn't know where she was.

Barahi unwittingly provided a solution to my problem. When the judge finished what passed for a tongue lashing in his courtroom, Barahi did something completely unexpected. He apologized to the judge, and made it sound sincere. He concluded his apology with an explanation. "When Your Honor combined the two hearings into one, I assumed, incorrectly as it turns out, that you would want to take testimony with respect to both counts of the complaint. I arranged for Imam Mustapha to be with us today to provide that testimony."

That was the opening I needed. "Your Honor," I said, "if I may, I'd like to offer a suggestion that I think will expedite this matter." Offering to expedite the proceedings is guaranteed to get the attention of any jurist, and Judge MacAndrew was no exception. He nodded for me to continue. "Since Mr. Mustapha is in the courtroom and ready to testify, I would propose allowing him to testify about all aspects of the case. Hopefully, I can elicit sufficient testimony on cross-examination that I won't need to call another witness."

The judge was delighted with the prospect of being able to resolve the case by taking testimony from just one witness. Barahi was somewhat taken aback by my proposal, but there was nothing he could do but call Mohammed Mustapha to the stand.

After being sworn in (without a bible), Mustapha identified himself as the imam of the Troy Forge mosque and the president of the Council for Islamic Religious Respect. I knew that wasn't correct. He was president of the New Jersey chapter of CIRR, not the national organization, but I didn't object. His misstatement would come in handy during cross-examination.

Mustapha spent the first hour explaining that CIRR was a civil rights organization established to ensure Muslims received the same treatment as followers of other religions. "There is much prejudice against the Muslims," he said at one point, "because people do not understand Islam." He took great pride in listing all of the "outreach" programs that his organization was involved in, most of which had little or nothing to do with civil rights. He also named over a dozen politicians who supported his organization. That testimony, apparently presented to legitimize CIRR, brought to mind "our friends in high places" mentioned in the Muslim Brotherhood memo that had been introduced into evidence in federal court in Texas.

As the morning progressed, Barahi asked fewer and fewer questions, allowing Mustapha to give what amounted to an uninterrupted lecture about the glories of Islam, just as Dr. Stern had predicted. I knew from my reading that his testimony was somewhat less than accurate, but I sat back and let him talk. Judge MacAndrew glanced in my direction several times, apparently anticipating – or perhaps, inviting – an objection, but I was quite content to allow the imam to ramble on. In my experience, witnesses like Mohammed Mustapha, if given enough time, will eventually become their own worst enemy. Rather than object, I simply noted all of his misstatements, exaggerations, and outright lies on a legal pad.

Shortly before noon, as Mustapha was explaining, perhaps in too much detail, the obligations a Muslim wife owes to her husband, the judge's poker face dropped away to reveal first bewilderment, followed by incredulity, and finally consternation. "I think I've heard enough," he said. "We'll recess for lunch, and when we continue, Mr. O'Brian will begin his cross-examination of the witness."

"I am not finished," Barahi said indignantly.

"Yes, you are," the judge informed him. "I've given you considerable latitude, but this testimony has nothing to do with the issues of the case." He looked directly at me as he added, "Frankly, I'm surprised Mr. O'Brian hasn't objected to much of this testimony."

I don't know why he was surprised. Mohammed Mustapha had provided me with ammunition for cross-examination ... and alienated Judge MacAndrew in the process.

46

"The television is reporting it was a bomb."

As soon as Judge MacAndrew left the bench I headed for the courthouse lobby where I caught up with Ezra Bramfield, the *Ledger's* managing editor. He was talking with a young man wearing a plaid jacket and sporting a haircut right out of the 1950s. He reminded me of the actor who played Jimmy Olsen on the old Superman television show I remembered from my youth. Bramfield introduced the kid as a *Ledger* reporter before dispatching him to grill one of the paper's courthouse contacts. When we were alone, I asked Ezra where Stacey was.

"She didn't say," Bramfield answered.

"Then, you have spoken to her?" It was phrased as a question, but it came out sounding more like an accusation.

"No, I *haven't* spoken to her," Bramfield replied. "She left a phone message saying the threats had escalated, so she decided to get away until the trial ended."

"Did she say where she was going?" I asked.

Bramfield shook his head. "Not really, just that she went to visit a friend from college."

I tried to think who that might be, but quickly realized Stacey had never talked about any friends from her college days.

In fact, come to think of it, I couldn't name any of her friends, from college or otherwise.

"Not having her testimony creates a problem," I said. "Instead of having a friendly witness to lay out my case, I have to get the testimony I need from a hostile witness. That's not easy, and it can be dangerous."

Bramfield patted me on the shoulder. "I guess we'll find out if you're as good as Stacey claims." Then he turned and walked away.

I crossed the street to the luncheonette where I eat whenever I have a case in Morristown, and had my usual tuna on rye, washed down with a cup of coffee. When I returned, the courthouse lobby was buzzing with conversations suggesting something was amiss. I found out what that was when I called the office from one of the payphones.

"Have you heard the news?" were the first words out of Carolyn's mouth.

"What news?"

"There was an explosion at the World Trade Center in Manhattan."

"A gas main leak?" That seemed the most obvious cause. Lower Manhattan is honeycombed with underground gas lines, water lines, sewer lines, electrical cables, subway tunnels, and who knows what else.

"The television is reporting it was a bomb," Carolyn said. "But nobody is sure of anything yet. It just happened a few minutes ago. I've tried to reach Scott and Avery on their cell phones, but my calls go directly to voicemail. They must still be in that seminar on law firm security."

"Keep trying to reach them," I said before hanging up and heading back to Judge MacAndrew's courtroom.

47

"The witness will answer the question."

I began my cross-examination of Mohammed Mustapha by asking him to explain his affiliation with the Council for Islamic Religious Respect. He repeated what he had said during direct examination, that he was the organization's president.

"Then who is Rashid Mohammed?" I asked.

My question caught the imam off guard, as I intended, and he became flustered. "No, no, no, you do not understand. I am the president of the Council for Islamic Religious Respect of New Jersey. Rashid Mohammed is the president of our national organization."

"So they're two entirely different organizations?"

"Yes and no," the witness said.

"Which is it?" I asked. "Yes or no?"

Tinoo Barahi objected at that point, telling the judge that I was badgering the witness. The judge waved Barahi back into his seat, signaling the objection was overruled.

"Allow me to explain," Mohammed Mustapha said. "The Council for Islamic Religious Respect is a nationwide organization with chapters all around the country. I am the president of the New Jersey chapter."

I was about to ask my next question when Mustapha saved me the trouble. "Although these are separate organizations, they are all related and share the same goals."

"So, your organization, the Council for Islamic Religious Respect of New Jersey, is seeking the same thing as the Council for Islamic Religious Respect?"

"Yes, that is correct, Mustapha said.

"And what, exactly, is your organization and its national counterpart seeking?"

"As I have already said," Mustapha explained, "we are a civil rights organization seeking to ensure the Muslims are not discriminated against."

Instead of challenging his characterization of CIRR, I asked, "Who is Muhammed Akrami?"

Tinoo Barahi objected. "This Muhammed Akrami, whoever he is, has nothing to do with this case. The question is irrelevant."

"On the contrary," I said as I walked back to the counsel table and retrieved four copies of the memorandum that I had received from Mr. Shapiro, the federal prosecutor in Texas. "Mr. Akrami has everything to do with this case."

I handed a copy of the memo to Barahi, and another to the court officer who delivered it to Judge MacAndrew. I was in the process of giving Mohammed Mustapha the third copy when Barahi shot to his feet, waving his copy in the air. "This document is not admissible."

"Grounds?" the judge asked, calling on Barahi to explain the basis for his objection.

I assumed Barahi would respond with "improper foundation," contending that I had failed to present sufficient facts to authenticate the document and establish its relevance. But, instead, my adversary launched into a convoluted argument that concluded with the accusation that I had created the document to slander CIRR and Islam.

Instead of responding to Barahi, Judge MacAndrew just looked at him for a long moment before turning his attention to me. "Mr. O'Brian, response?"

"This document has been certified as a true copy of an exhibit entered into evidence in federal court in Texas. That makes it self-authenticating under our Rules of Evidence."

The judge nodded, signaling that I was correct, but Barahi wasn't about to give up. "There is no proof whatsoever that the document is genuine. Mr. O'Brian or his client could have created it, along with that certification."

The judge responded with an exasperated sigh. "Mr. Barahi, let me remind you that I had instructed counsel that objections to proposed evidence were to be raised prior to this hearing." Barahi started to protest, but Judge MacAndrew held up his hand to silence him. "I called the court clerk in Texas and confirmed that the document is genuine." The judge turned toward me. "Proceed, Mr. O'Brian."

I handed the document to Mohammed Mustapha and pointed to the title on the first page. "Please read the title of this memorandum."

Mustapha hesitated for a moment before responding. "An explanatory memorandum on the strategic goals of the group in North America."

"And this a memorandum from Muhammed Akrami of the Muslim Brotherhood, correct?"

Tinoo Barahi was on his feet before the witness could answer. "Mr. O'Brian is leading the witness," he protested.

"Mr. Barahi," the judge said, "I suggest you review the Rules of Evidence before your next courtroom appearance. Leading questions are ordinarily prohibited on direct examination, but permissible on cross-examination."

Barahi wasn't about to let rules get in his way. "My client did not write this memo. My client did not send this memo. My client did not receive this memo. There is no reason why my client should be required to read any part of this memo in open court. It is inflammatory and prejudicial."

"Mr. Barahi," the judge said, "as I explained earlier today, this is a hearing, not a jury trial. I think you can rely on me to properly evaluate the evidence presented." It was delivered in a calm, patient tone of voice, but it was clear that Judge MacAndrew was becoming increasingly annoyed with Barahi.

The judge nodded for me to continue. I asked the question again. This time Mohammed Mustapha responded with, "Yes, this appears to have been written by someone named Muhammed Akrami, but I do not know the man."

"But you are familiar with the Muslim Brotherhood, aren't you?"

Mustapha looked toward Tinoo Barahi.

"The witness will answer the question," Judge MacAndrew said before Barahi could object.

"I am familiar with it, but I am not a member," Mustapha said. "I am a member of CIRR."

"Okay," I said, "let's talk about CIRR. Please turn to the second page of the memo you're holding." The witness did as I asked, as did the judge and Barahi. "Is CIRR listed as a recipient of this memo?"

Barahi was on his feet again. "There is no proof that anyone connected with CIRR ever received this document, much less read it."

"I didn't ask if anyone connected with CIRR read the memo," I said to the judge. "I simply asked if CIRR was listed as a recipient."

"The witness will answer the question," Judge MacAndrew said.

"Yes, the Council for Islamic Religious Respect is listed on this page," a clearly unhappy Mohammed Mustapha said.

"Please turn to page ten," I said. Mustapha did as I asked, and once again, both the judge and Barahi did likewise. "Please read the passage highlighted in yellow," I instructed.

Barahi was on his feet once again. "This is outrageous!" He was either visibly angry or doing a great job of appearing angry. "The imam is not responsible for these words. He did not write them. Requiring him to read them is highly prejudicial."

"Mr. Barahi," Judge MacAndrew said, "once again I must remind you that this is a hearing, not a jury trial. I assure you that you can rely on me to properly evaluate the evidence presented." The judge turned to the witness stand. "The witness will answer the question."

Mohammed Mustapha went from clearly unhappy to downright belligerent. "I did not write this. I will not read this."

Judge MacAndrew, one of New Jersey's most tolerant, even-tempered Superior Court judges, had apparently had enough. He leaned toward the witness stand and made eye contact with Mustapha for several seconds before telling him in a quiet, slow, deliberate voice, "The witness will read the passage highlighted in yellow."

Mustapha looked down at the document he was holding, and then back at the judge, who was still staring at him. Judge MacAndrew's normally quiet courtroom became completely silent as everyone waited to see how the staring contest would play out. After what seemed like several minutes, but which was really only a few seconds, Mustapha conceded defeat and began to read. "The Council for Islamic Religious Respect is assigned two tasks. The first is to popularize Islamaphobia as a term to stifle opposition to the group's agenda. The second is to establish, through its local affiliates, a nationwide network of mosques and Islamic Centers to facilitate the group's ultimate objective."

"And what is that ultimate objective" I asked.

"I do not know," Mohammed Mustapha replied. "I am not a member of this Muslim Brotherhood that wrote this memo or of any of the groups you claim received it. I am president of The Council for Islamic Religious Respect of New Jersey."

"Which, as you have testified, shares the same goals as the national organization, one of the recipients of this memo."

Barahi was on his feat yet again. "How can Imam Mustapha be expected to know the answer to that question? He did not write the memo. He did not send the memo. He is not..."

I interrupted my adversary in mid-sentence. "All he has to do is read the last page of the memo." I turned to face the bench. "With the Court's permission, I would ask that the witness read the last page of the memo, captioned *The Group's Objective*."

"The witness will read the last page of the memo," Judge MacAndrew instructed.

Mohammed Mustapha looked at Barahi and then back to me before complying with the judge's instruction. There was pure, unbridled hatred in his eyes as he read, "The process of settlement is a civilization jihadist process, with all that the word means. The Brothers must understand that their work in America is a kind of grand Jihad to eliminate and destroy Western civilization from within and to sabotage its miserable house by the hands of the believers so Allah's religion is made victorious over all other religions."

There was a collective gasp from the public gallery, followed by absolute silence.

"I'll see counsel in my chambers in ten minutes," the judge said as he gaveled the hearing to a close.

48

"Why do you suppose judges wear a robe in the courtroom?"

About half the people in the public gallery, apparently assuming the hearing would continue after a short recess, remained in their seats, guarding them from the standees, who eyed them like hungry cats stalking an unsuspecting mouse. The rest of the crowd left the courtroom, hurrying to restrooms or the luncheonette across the street.

I weaved through the restroom/luncheonette crowd to the bank of pay phones on the back wall of the lobby and called the office. "What's going on in New York?" I asked my secretary when she answered the phone. "Have you heard from Scott or Avery?"

"Not a word," Carolyn said, "and we're starting to get worried. Rick called their cell phones several times, but his calls go directly to voicemail." I could hear the tension in her voice. "According to the television reports, it was definitely a bomb. There's speculation it was in one of the vehicles parked in the underground garage, but nothing's certain at this point. The FBI has been called in." She paused to collect herself, and then changed topics. "How's the hearing going?"

"Stacey's a no-show, so I had to put on my case by cross-examining the mosque's imam."

"What happened to Stacey?" Carolyn asked.

"According to her boss, she got spooked by the hate mail and took off for parts unknown." It wasn't until months later that I discovered Stacey's departure had been triggered by something a bit more extreme than hate mail. The day before the hearing, she had awakened to find her living room furniture rearranged and her cat dead in the middle of the room.

Carolyn spent the next few minutes relaying messages from some of my other clients, including several from Eddie Rizzo. "He says he has information about Mohammed Salameh and needs to talk to you immediately. He left a cell phone number where you can reach him."

"If he calls back, tell him I'm in court and will call him when I get back to the office."

"He says it's urgent," Carolyn said.

"With Eddie Rizzo it's always urgent."

Had I known then what I know now, I would have called Eddie immediately. But instead, I hung up with Carolyn and headed for Judge MacAndrew's chambers.

Ezra Bramfield caught up with me as I threaded my way through the crowded lobby. "Nice job with that Muslim Brotherhood memo. What do you have planned next?"

"Oh, I'm thinking it might be fun to force the imam to play a little game of *what would Mohammed do?*" That elicited a raised eyebrow from Bramfield. "A good way to illustrate Islam's so-called prophet wasn't exactly a saint," I explained. "Remember, we have three statements we have to prove are factually correct to prevail on the second count of the complaint. One of them is that Mohammed could more accurately be described as a criminal than a prophet.

"In retrospect," Bramfield said, "that one may have been a bit incendiary."

"A few months ago I would have agreed, but I've come to realize that it's probably much closer to the truth than anyone wants to admit. I've found dozens of passages from the Qur'an and the hadiths that demonstrate Mohammed was a liar, a thief, a murderer, and a pedophile. If you thought Mohammed Mustapha was pissed when he was forced to read that Muslim Brotherhood memo, wait until I make him read these little gems."

We walked in silence down the corridor leading to Judge MacAndrew's chambers. "Heard anything more from Stacey?" I asked as I opened the door to the outer office. Bramfield sighed. "Not a word."

The judge's secretary looked up from her desk as I entered the room. "He's waiting for you," she said, nodding toward the door to the judge's private office. "Mr. Barahi is already there." The way she said it led me to believe Tinoo Barahi wasn't on her list of favorite attorneys. Of course, I probably hadn't made the list either.

I entered the room to find Judge MacAndrew sitting at his desk, pouring tea from a small blue pot into a matching cup. Barahi was seated across from him, studying the diplomas and other documents hanging on the wall behind the judge's desk. "Have a seat, Mr. O'Brian," the judge said, pointing to the empty chair next to Barahi. He continued to silently prepare his tea the same way he had the morning I had been there to examine Bob Proctor's tax returns. The heaping teaspoon of sugar, carefully leveled with the blade of a knife, was added to the cup and slowly stirred. As the stirring transitioned from clockwise to counterclockwise, the judge asked, "Why do you suppose judges wear a robe in the courtroom?"

Assuming the question was rhetorical, I said nothing, waiting for Duncan MacAndrew to reveal some great jurisprudential secret. My adversary, apparently thinking an answer was required, said, "I don't know" in a tone of voice that made it clear he not only didn't know, but didn't care.

The judge stopped stirring and looked at Barahi before returning his attention to the tea. "I think it's because robes add to the solemnity and seriousness of the proceedings. Our legal system only works if people take it seriously. When people stop taking proceedings seriously, the system loses credibility." He took a sip of tea and carefully replaced the cup on the saucer before continuing. "I'm not about to let attorneys turn what should be a serious proceeding into a three ring circus. And based on what's happened so far, I have a feeling things could get out of control pretty quickly. So instead of continuing with the hearing, I'm going to decide these motions on the papers. I'll expect briefs from both of you in two weeks."

I was about to protest, but then thought better of it. The judge's decision seemed final. And besides, a well-written brief could prove more convincing than oral arguments to a scholarly jurist like Duncan MacAndrew.

As it turned out, that brief never got written.

49

"Didn't you talk to Stacey?"

When I returned to the office from the courthouse in Morristown, I found everyone watching television in the conference room. Every fifteen minutes Rick would mute the sound and call Scott and Avery on their cell phones. He never got an answer.

Shortly after four o'clock we got the news we had been expecting, but hoping would never come. After attending the seminar about law firm security, Scott and Avery had returned to their car, parked in the underground garage of the World Trade Center, just moments before a bomb in a nearby vehicle exploded. They had both died instantly.

The following morning, Rick and I met at the office and had a conversation that lasted over an hour. "The law firm of Santorini, Woodson, Glickman and O'Brian is no more," Rick said to begin our meeting. There was profound sadness in his voice. I waited, assuming he was about to tell me he was retiring from the practice of law. But he surprised me. "I guess from now on, it's the law firm of O'Brian and Santorini."

"You mean the law firm of Santorini and O'Brian," I countered.

"No, you've earned top billing," Rick said. "Your litigation skills are what makes the money. At this point in my career, I'm happy to be your second chair, if you'll have me."

"You're still the senior partner," I insisted. We spent several minutes discussing the appropriate firm name. I put an end to the discussion by telling Rick, "Okay, we'll do it your way if you'll answer a question for me." I wasn't sure how to broach the subject of Rick's mental lapses, but it's something that had to be resolved before I could commit to a partnership with him, regardless of what it was called.

He saved me the trouble of asking that difficult question. "No, I don't have Alzheimer's, and no, I'm not getting senile." He looked me in the eye and smiled. "I assume that's the question you wanted to ask. At least, that's the question I would have asked if our roles had been reversed." He went on to explain that his mental lapses had been caused by the interaction of three different drugs, each prescribed by a different doctor.

Rick explained that the medication snafu was finally solved thanks to Elaine, the firm's receptionist, who insisted Rick get a second opinion from another doctor. In the course of the explanation, Rick disclosed that he and Elaine had been living together for several years. When I expressed surprise at that revelation, Rick responded with a shrug of the shoulders. "I assumed everyone in the firm knew." Carolyn later confirmed that, in fact, everyone in the firm did know. Everyone but me, that is.

The following week we attended to the seemingly endless list of tasks needed to downsize the firm, from advertising for tenants to take over part of our office space to ordering new stationery. On Tuesday, while Rick was at the bank getting the forms needed to open new accounts, I arranged for a sign company to change the name on the door to our office suite. Rick returned to find "Santorini & O'Brian, Attorneys at Law" in gold letters on the door. "They did it backwards," he said when he saw their handiwork.

"No, they did it correctly," I assured him. He smiled, shook his head, patted me on the shoulder and retreated to his office.

Late that afternoon, Carolyn entered my office holding a stack of papers. "You'll never guess what just came over the fax."

"A letter from the president asking me to join his cabinet?"

"Wrong."

"A letter from the Vatican asking me to be Pope?"

"Wrong again."

"Okay, I give up."

"Something even less likely than a letter from the president or the Vatican," Carolyn said as she put the papers in my hand, and then stood back to watch my reaction while I read them."

"The cabinet post would have been more likely," I said when I finished reading.

"Amen to that," Carolyn said on her way out of the room.

I picked up the phone and called Ezra Bramfield at the *Ledger*. His secretary told me he was in a conference and would call me back. "Interrupt him," I told her. "This is important."

"I'm busy, O'Brian," was the first thing Bramfield said when he came on the line.

"Too busy to hear good news?" I asked.

"What good news?"

"Tinoo Barahi just faxed over a copy of a motion to dismiss."

"What, exactly, does that mean?" Bramfield asked.

"It means CIRR is no longer suing Stacey and the *Ledger*. And my gut tells me Bob Proctor's case is also going to be dismissed. Bottom line: you win and they lose."

I thought there was a slim chance Bramfield would say something like "good job" or "congratulations." Instead, he said, "Are you kidding? We paid your firm a small fortune to try this case, and they end up walking away from it?"

"It's what Dr. Stern calls lawfare, using the law to wage war. CIRR is notorious for using it to silence critics."

"There's something just plain wrong with a legal system that allows this sort of nonsense. Isn't there some way you can make them reimburse us for all the money we shelled out?"

"I can try," I said, "but it's a long shot. In some countries, the loser ends up paying the winner's legal expenses. But in our system, each party usually pays his own expenses." I let Bramfield mutter and fume for a few moments before adding, "But I'll tell you what; if I can't get CIRR to reimburse you, I'll consider your account paid in full as of right now."

"What's the catch?" Bramfield wanted to know.

"Promise me that when Stacey returns from wherever she went, you'll have her pursue this mosque story. There's no way the fairgrounds property got magically rezoned without some sort of backroom shenanigans, and people have a right to know what happened."

There was an awkward silence.

"Ezra, are you still there?" I finally asked, thinking perhaps we had been disconnected.

"Brendan, didn't you talk to Stacey?"

"I called her cell phone more times than I can count, but my calls keep going to voicemail," I answered.

"She never called back?" I heard something in Bramfield's voice I had never heard before. He sounded apologetic. There was another awkward silence, this one longer than the first. "Brendan, Stacey resigned from the *Ledger*. She's moving somewhere out west." He added, "sorry" before I could ask for details. Then he hung up.

I was still holding the phone and staring into space when Carolyn appeared at my office door. "Eddie Rizzo is on line two. He says he has to talk to you right away. He says it's about Mohammed Salameh."

"Tell him I'll call him back."

"He say's it's important."

"Tell him I'll call him back," I repeated, perhaps a bit too forcefully.

Carolyn retreated to the outer office, and I called Stacey's cell phone once again. Instead of hearing Stacey inviting me to leave a message with the promise to return my call, I got a mechanical voice informing me the number I had called was no longer in service.

I never spoke to Stacey again.

50

"I got my revenge"

I had just settled into my favorite chair by the fireplace, with a tuna sandwich and a glass of Jameson, when the phone rang.

"I called your office this afternoon to tell you my guys found Salameh, but your secretary said you were busy." It was Eddie the Skunk. Before I could come up with a plausible excuse for not calling him back, he asked, "You seen the news?"

"No," I said. "I just got home and haven't even turned on the television. Why? What's going on?"

"They had a story about that bombing in New York. Showed film from a bank camera of the vehicle with the bomb as it was going into the garage."

"Okay," I said somewhat tentatively, wondering not only where Eddie was going with this, but how he had managed to get my unlisted home phone number.

"It was a white Ford van with rust on the back, a roof rack, a busted tail light, and a painted over company name on the side. Sound familiar?"

That got my attention. "Sounds like the van that hit you in Jersey City," I said. "Guess we know why Omar Obduhali couldn't make it available for inspection. Salameh must have been hard at work turning it into a bomb on wheels." I assumed it also explained Salameh's fertilizer purchases, as well as CIRR's decision to drop the case against Stacey and the *Ledger*. "Yup," came the very satisfied reply. "Different plates, but same van. When I didn't hear from you, I had someone who owes me a favor call the Feds and tell 'em where they could find Salameh. I'll probably never get a dime from that bastard, but I got my revenge."

Epilogue

Cleanup and repair of the World Trade Center began even before Scott and Avery had been laid to rest. It was a five hundred million dollar undertaking, involving the removal of 6,000 tons of debris.

A few weeks after the Trade Center re-opened, a task force from the Justice Department's Public Integrity Section arrived in Troy Forge. Commonly referred to as PIN (rather than PIS for obvious reasons), the Section was created in 1976 in the wake of the Watergate scandal to prosecute criminal abuses of the public trust by elected and appointed government officials.

What the PIN task force uncovered astounded even the most cynical of the town's citizenry. Bob Proctor, or whatever his real name was, had embezzled over three million dollars from the Town of Troy Forge with the help of a small army of town employees.

The building inspector, the chief of police, the fire marshal, and eleven members of the police department were charged with a laundry list of crimes. A PIN spokesman vowed that the Department of Justice will prosecute Bob Proctor for the murders of Machias Phelps and Cecilia Marcus ... if they ever find him.

A Note from the Author

The events, characters and organizations in the novel you've just read are all products of my overactive imagination. Any similarity to actual events, organizations or persons, living or dead, is purely coincidental, with the following exceptions:

All the cases and court rules mentioned are real, including *NY Times v. Sullivan*, the leading case on the law of libel involving public figures. However, the application of laws and rules in the story may not necessarily reflect how they would be applied in real life.

The research sources O'Brian consults to learn about Islam are not only real, but considered authoritative by Muslims.

The 1993 bombing of the World Trade Center is obviously all too real. Six people died in that tragic event, which has been overshadowed by the even more tragic event of September 11, 2001.

The social security numbering system described in chapter 42 is an accurate depiction of how numbers were assigned at the time the story takes place. In 2011, the Social Security Administration "randomized" social security numbers to eliminate the geographical significance of the first three digits. According to the SSA, this was done "to help protect the integrity of the SSN" and to "extend the longevity of the nine-digit SSN nationwide."

The Muslim Brotherhood is a very real organization. Its goal is to see Islam spread throughout the world, replacing other religions and political systems. The memo from the Brotherhood referred to in the story is based on an actual memo that was introduced into evidence in federal court in Texas. In fact, the passage read aloud by the witness at the end of chapter 47 is taken almost verbatim from that memo.

Lastly, the character who had an auto accident with Eddie the Skunk shares a name with one of the perpetrators of the 1993 bombing of the World Trade Center. However, everything about that character, aside from the name, is fictitious.

Readers seeking accurate information about Islam are urged to consult the writings of bona fide experts like Robert Spencer, whose meticulously researched and well-written books are available on Amazon.

-- J.W. Kerwin

Contact the author at: kerwinbook@icloud.com

Made in the USA
Lexington, KY
25 October 2016